"I wish I could have you alone for a moment. . . ."

Startled by the tortured look in his eyes, Felicia took a step backward. She had never seen a man who looked more confused and unhappy.

"I couldn't help myself, not after seeing you last evening with Ormsby kneeling at your feet. . . . I wanted to kill him then and there for daring to touch you. . . . I wanted to take you in my arms and kiss you—protect you from such as he. . . . I wanted . . . Miss Simmons—no, Felicia! Will you marry me?"

"Have you gone mad?"

Also by Barbara Hazard
Published by Fawcett Books

MONDAY'S CHILD

TUESDAY'S CHILD

Barbara Hazard

FAWCETT CREST • NEW YORK

A Fawcett Crest Book
Published by Ballantine Books
Copyright © 1993 by BW Hazard, Ltd.

Library of Congress Catalog Card Number: 93-90533

ISBN 0-449-22208-X

Manufactured in the United States of America

First Edition: December 1993

"Tuesday's Child is full of Grace"

grace: elegance or beauty of . . .
manner . . . action. A
pleasing or attractive quality
or endowment.

One

"WHAT ON EARTH is that unholy racket? Timms? Timms? Devil take it, where is the man?"

"You called, sir?"

"Find out who is making that din, and get them to stop it at once! It's barely dawn!"

"I regret I must contradict you, sir. It's eleven in the morning. However, I shall attend to it immediately."

The manservant bowed himself away, and Bartholomew Whitaker subsided on his pillows, wondering if he would be able to get back to sleep even if the noise he could hear on the stairs outside his rooms, and on the floor above, should stop. He frowned when he realized he probably would not, and he sat up cautiously, holding his head. A bad mistake, broaching that last bottle of wine, he thought, and giving in to Duke's insistence on another rubber of piquet when it was so late.

Remembering that he had won that rubber handily brought a grim smile of satisfaction to his long face as he padded to his dressing room. A loud thud directly overhead made him wince again and shake his fist at the ceiling.

The rooms above his on the third floor had been vacant when he arrived in London for the Season, and although he knew it was futile to hope they might remain so in such a fashionable part of town as Upper Brook Street, hope he had. Now he could

1

only pray that whoever had taken those rooms would be your quiet sort, not given to noisy striding about in the morning hours.

Another load of furniture or baggage was being carried up the stairs. Whitaker could hear the porters cursing as they maneuvered the bend in those stairs. Well, he told himself as he splashed his face with cold water and cleaned his teeth, best he resign himself to the day, order breakfast, and have Timms shave him.

He left the house well over an hour later. By that time quiet prevailed, but he was not appeased, and he gave the windows above his a ferocious frown. No one was there to witness his displeasure, and he laughed at himself a little before he strode off in the direction of Park Lane and the sanctuary of his club. At least there he could be assured an almost funereal hush.

He did not see the new occupant of the house that let rooms to noble gentlemen until late that afternoon when he was returning from a stroll through Hyde Park with some friends. Then, as he was about to mount the steps, another man turned toward them at the same time.

As Bartholomew Whitaker stared at this stranger, his brows rose. Why, the man was as dark as a blackamoor, in spite of his auburn hair that was liberally streaked with gold. And his hands were as dark as his face! The Indies, West or East, Whitaker told himself as he reached the door.

"Good afternoon," he said as he sounded the knocker. "I take it you're our new tenant? I'm Bartholomew Whitaker. My rooms are directly below yours, as I discovered this morning to my sorrow."

To his surprise, the man grinned at him, a lazy grin that showed strong white teeth in that deeply tanned face.

"I know who you are. But how depressing to re-

2

alize you haven't a clue who *I* am," the stranger replied, still smiling. As Whitaker frowned in thought, he went on, "Of course we were only boys at the time, for it was a good many years ago. But how lowering when I recognized you immediately. Alas, how soon we are forgotten!"

As Mr. Kenton, the owner of the house, opened the door and bowed them in, Whitaker asked, "Dunsford? Eton? Cambridge?"

"We were at Eton together, but I'll tease you no more. I'm Christopher Wilde. Sir Christopher, now."

"Chris Wilde! 'Pon my soul!" Whitaker exclaimed, grabbing his hand and shaking it. "Why, I've not seen you for a dozen years, my dear fellow!"

"Thirteen, to be exact," Wilde replied coolly. "I left England without bothering with university, if you remember."

"I do indeed. There was some talk about it. Why ever did you do it?"

"Come up and have tea and I'll tell you," Wilde said, leading the way to the stairs.

"No, you must come to my rooms. You're not settled in yet," Whitaker protested.

"I'd better be, or Bowers will hear about it. My man," he added. "Been with me for years. By now he's sure to have organized the place, acquired help, ordered food. Very dependable man, Bowers."

The two climbed to the top floor, where Wilde knocked once and opened the door. As he stepped in and called for his manservant, Bartholomew Whitaker studied him. Yes, faintly he could see the boy Christopher Wilde had been, now that he had been given his name, but surely he could not be blamed for not recognizing him! He had changed so, grown taller, broader. His shoulders stretched the rather outdated coat he wore, and those tanned hands looked capable of holding much more than a pair of gloves or even a set of reins. As Wilde turned toward him again to indicate a pair of chairs set near the fireplace, Whitaker was startled by his gray eyes. In his tanned face they seemed so light as to be almost silvery, and they were set in whites so clear, it was obvious the man had no weakness for strong drink. His face, too, with its solid jaw and straight nose, those heavy chestnut eyebrows, and the strong planes of his cheekbones, made him look formidable and very unlike the seventeen year old he remembered.

"Tea or wine?" Wilde asked as his servant appeared for his orders.

"Either," Whitaker replied, studying the man with interest. Surely he was not your ordinary servant! Although only of average height, he had a powerful muscular build and piercing gaze. He was ugly, too, and even more formidable than his master.

"Hock then, Bowers. I trust all is now secure?"

"All right and tight, guv. We've a cook, two maids, and a footman."

Wilde nodded and waved a hand, and his most unconventional servant went away.

"Of course I can't fault you for not remembering me," he said to his guest as they settled down in their chairs. "I believe I have changed, and besides, since I am two years older than you, we were not in the same form."

"But why did you forsake Cambridge? Oxford? You were a brilliant scholar, always being held up as an example to the rest of the school," Whitaker said, curious.

His host shrugged his broad shoulders. "I couldn't see the sense of reading any more Greek and Latin. I was eager to get on with life, if you understand what I mean."

4

Whitaker nodded. "I do. And how did you 'get on with it?' "

"I went out to India, first as a clerk with the Company, later branching out on my own. I'd probably be there still, except I had word that my father had died. That was over a year ago, and since I had come into the title, I knew I had to return home. I wasn't all that reluctant to do so. Since I had never taken home leave, I hadn't seen England for a long time. Do you know, I'd forgotten how damp it is here, how often it rains? And how seldom the sun shines?"

"Well, best you stay out of it when it does," Whitaker advised him. "You look like an Indian yourself, indeed you do."

"So that's why everyone stared at me today!" Wilde said with a wry grimace. "I thought it was merely my outdated clothes.

"But tell me, Bart, what have you been doing with yourself? Did you go to university? Take your degree? And what have you been up to since?"

"Yes, yes, and not much. I manage the old family place at Dunsford, of course, visit my friends, enjoy the Season. All the usual gentlemanly pursuits. My condolences on your father's death. I believe your elder brother predeceased him?"

"Yes, he died in a carriage accident shortly before my father's demise, and much, I am sure, to my father's regret. William was his fair-haired boy, while I was always a problem. We did not get along at all, and he wasn't a bit pleased when I decided to join the Company, for it went against all his plans for me. And how he hated having his will crossed! But I'd no intention of bowing to that will, nor any liking for the life of a country gentleman. Not at that time, anyway. Now, well, I'll have to see. Wildewold is mine now. That might make a difference."

5

"I forget. Have you other family? Other brothers? Sisters?"

"My mother, of course. And an elder sister. Nell's married now, lives in some out-of-the-way place in Northumberland. She appears to have devoted her life to fertility, since she's given me eight nieces and nephews over the years."

"Perhaps there's not much else to do in Northumberland?" Whitaker remarked as the manservant brought in a large beaten brass tray with hock and glasses on it. As he served them, Whitaker studied the room he was in. It seemed strange to him, exotic. Perhaps it was all those brilliantly colored silk pillows, the large statue of a trumpeting elephant, or the intricately carved, dark wood furniture? Or the faint aroma of burning incense? The crystal goblet he was handed was very fine and the hock, when he sipped it, excellent. Still, Wilde's appearance was exotic, too. His rooms suited him. And his servant was downright odd. To Whitaker's eyes, this Bowers looked like a thug, not a gentleman's gentleman. But at least he was English, he told himself. He didn't fancy living under the same roof with some dagger-waving foreigner.

After the servant had left the room, and without bowing either, Whitaker noted, Christopher Wilde said, "I can see Bowers intrigues you. It's true he's not your ordinary servant, but I'd have no other man beside me or, more importantly, watching my back! And I don't care to cut a swath in Society, you know, so I don't mind what the high and mighty might think."

"But you're a baronet now, one of them," his guest reminded him.

Wilde shrugged. "I'm stuck with the title for life—forced to accept it. Nor will I do anything to shame my name. But after the way I've lived for over a dozen years, I'll not start posturing about

6

waving lace-trimmed handkerchiefs, painting my face, or wearing perfumes and patches."

Whitaker laughed. "No one paints anymore! Well, only a few elderly gentlemen to hide their lifelong propensity for strong drink. But I can understand what you mean. Having gone your own way for so many years, you could have no liking for fusty rules. By the way, I'm most anxious to hear about your adventures in India."

"Come and dine, then," Wilde invited. "We'll see how this new cook of mine does."

Whitaker frowned. "I can't," he said. "I'm promised to m'cousin this evening. But say! Why don't you come along? It's true you don't know Jaspar Howland, Earl Castleton. How could you? He's only twenty-three. But he won't mind. And to tell truth, it would be a kindness. The boy's been sunk in depression for months. Gets tedious, you know."

"A woman?" Wilde asked, his brows raised.

"A lovely older woman who wouldn't have a thing to do with him. Thank the Lord for that! Most unsuitable. She married a farmer from her home village, which surprised me a bit, for she was a dowager viscountess and one of the most beautiful women I've ever seen."

"Your cousin might not appreciate an unexpected, uninvited guest," Wilde said.

Whitaker waved a careless hand as he rose. "Be easy, sir. He won't care. We don't stand on ceremony, Jaspar and I. I'll send him a message so he'll know you're coming. I believe there'll be a few others in the party, all men, so there's no need to dress."

"That's a good thing, for I've nothing suitable," Wilde said as he escorted his guest to the door. "I've ordered the usual today from Weston, but it will be a while before I'm fit for the ton."

"Seven-thirty, then? Castleton House is in Portman Square. We can easily walk there," Bartholomew Whitaker said.

"I look forward to it," his host said, smiling a little.

As Whitaker went down the stairs, he wondered at that smile. It had seemed so pleasant, so open, yet he had the feeling that the man was complicated, deep, and his smile had been merely a courtesy. And, he admitted, he would not like to be the one who made him frown. Wilde looked a determined sort, capable and firm, even hard. Whitaker wondered what he had been doing since he had left the Company, to turn him into such an enigma? The Christopher Wilde he remembered had been an easygoing lad, as full of foolish pranks as anyone, with a devilish smile and a real talent for cricket. And, he recalled, an excellent singing voice. He admitted he had looked up to him as a boy, admired him and tried to emulate him. And here he was again, changed beyond recognition. How strange life was!

Later, as the two were admitted to Castleton House, they heard male voices coming from a nearby salon and then a burst of raucous laughter.

"Appears Jaspar has assembled a number of his cronies," Whitaker said as the butler took their hats and gloves. "Good! Might cheer him up, and you, dear chap, are sure to pique his interest. He's been talking of traveling lately. I'm not sure it wouldn't be the best thing in the world for him, getting out of the country for a while. If only there wasn't so much unrest in the world now!"

"Yes, traveling can be dangerous," Wilde murmured, as the butler announced them in measured tones.

He saw a young man separate himself from a group and come toward them, a polite smile of welcome on his handsome face. But he also saw that his dark blue eyes were full of unhappiness, and that smile disappeared as quickly as it had come. Strange, that, he thought. All this woe because of a *woman*? The boy must be a weakling!

"Jaspar, give me leave to introduce an old friend of mine, Sir Christopher Wilde. We were at Eton together, and he's just returned home from the East Indies."

"Delighted to meet you, sir," Howland said as they shook hands.

"I must thank you for including me, m'lord," Wilde said. "I would not have imposed, if Bart had not insisted."

"Nonsense! You're his friend, so it follows you must be my friend as well. Come and meet the others. Ah, this is Marmaduke Ainsworth, Alan Feathers, Lord Priestly, Sir Joshua Severance. Sir Christopher Wilde, chaps."

"I say!" Mr. Feathers exclaimed. "Where on earth have you been, sir, to acquire such a ghastly complexion? Oh, my, I do beg your pardon!"

"In India, where the sun is very bright," Wilde said, hiding his amusement at the slight little man's confusion. "But I had forgotten that in England a gentleman is known by the whiteness of his hands, his face, for of course, gentlemen do no work. What a problem! I am—yet I am not."

"You were gone long, then?" Lord Priestly inquired. "For some years, perhaps?"

"Thirteen," Wilde admitted.

"Fascinating! I look forward to hearing of your adventures, sir. But do not begin just yet, if you please.

"I say, Jaspar, what are you saving the sherry for? I'll have another glass, and fetch one for our new acquaintance as well. Bart, old son, you're on your own unless Jaspar bustles about."

He went over to the decanter that was set on a table against the wall so the guests could help themselves, and as the others began to question the newest member of the group, Bartholomew Whitaker watched carefully.

He saw Chris was easy with them, even forthcoming in his answers, but he thought he could detect a slight impatience, even a hint of superiority in his manner, and it annoyed him somehow. These were friends of his, good fellows all. True, they had not sailed to a faraway land, lived dangerously there, but they were none of them cowards or worthless fops. Even Alan Feathers, for all his affected ways, was not of that class.

He was to see Wilde's impatience a number of times that evening. Once at dinner, during the second course of salmon and trout surrounded by smelts and accompanied by a selection of vegetables and a salad, when the guests began to discuss the latest wager.

"I've heard tell Lockwood is determined to drive his curricle, blindfolded no less, to Brighton," Sir Joshua said. "And that he expects to best anyone's time in doing so. Wouldn't care to be his groom, would you? Poor chap!"

Duke Ainsworth agreed. "Gettin' good odds, though. Man's such an idiot, may well pull it off. No sense of danger, y'know, so therefore, no fear."

"I've put a monkey on him myself," Alan Feathers confided. "He's to drive his new team. Havering's breakdowns."

"Well, at least he's not pledged to run around the ledges of the boxes at all the theaters," the earl remarked. "I heard a rumor he was considering that."

"Hard luck on the pit if he fell. He's such a heavy chap, he might have taken out a dozen innocent playgoers," Lord Priestly contributed. "But didn't Colonel Dan McKinnon already do that once?"

"Yes, it was one of his most famous jests," Bart Whitaker said.

"I've always liked the story about McKinnon and the lady who demanded he return the lock of her hair that she had given him before their passion cooled," Sir Joshua said. Turning to Christopher Wilde, he added, "I doubt you've heard that one, sir! It seems he sent the lady a large box filled with hair of all shades and colors and told her she must pick hers out since he couldn't remember what it looked like. Isn't that superb?"

At that moment, Bart Whitaker chanced to look across the table to where Christopher Wilde was seated. He appeared to be attending politely, but once again there was that little hint of impatience. Of course, Bart told himself as he forked up another mouthful of trout, such doings were completely foreign to Chris, even childish now. No wonder he sneered a little.

"I say, Wilde, were you ever on a tiger hunt in India?" Sir Joshua asked

"Yes, once. The Maharajah of Rampool invited me. A tiger had been savaging one of his villages, stealing livestock, even children. He presented me with the skin and the head later."

"How excitin'!" Duke exclaimed. "Fired the fatal shot, did ye?"

Wilde nodded as he wiped his mouth with his napkin. His eyes were far away as he remembered that day. The oppressive heat, the thick jungle they had stalked the tiger through, the eerie sense of imminent danger he had felt as he whirled just in time to see the beast crouched above him ready to pounce. He had fired almost as a reflex, without even aiming carefully, and he had had to leap out of the way as the tiger crashed down through the rich vegetation to land at his feet, shot through the heart. How lucky he had been! And the feast that had been prepared later at the Maharajah's vast white palace, even, he remembered, the young girl his grateful host had sent him to amuse him during the night. Young though she might have been, she had been old in the ways of love.

"It was exciting," he remarked now, aware everyone was waiting for him to expand the story. "Frightening, too. I thought my heart must stop, it was hammering so quickly in my breast. And you would not believe how I shook later! Delayed reaction, I suppose. But tigers are not predictable animals, especially when they are angry at being hunted. I was lucky he didn't get me. I could easily have been his next meal.

"But there are any number of dangers in that country. Cobras and other deadly snakes, for example. In my household I had a man whose only responsibility was to kill the snakes that came into the grounds. Wouldn't have been safe to walk about otherwise."

"Is it very hot there?" Feathers asked, his eyes wide.

"Unbearable at certain times of the year. The wealthy go to the hills then, where they can get some relief. Those in the coastal cities merely swelter. And it's impossible to stay dry, no matter how often you bathe and change your clothes. Eventually, you just give up and drip."

Feathers shuddered delicately. "I shouldn't care for that," he said.

"Were you only in India?" Bart Whitaker asked, wondering at the way Wilde's eyes narrowed and his face grew cold at the question.

"No," he said at last. "I sailed to China a few times. On business."

"Trading?" Whitaker persisted.

12

"Yes. Trade with China can be very profitable, if you grease enough palms with cumshaw of course."

The others demanded to know what cumshaw might be, and Wilde explained the system of bribery so prevalent in China; how mistrusted, even hated the English were by people of a much older civilization.

"Can it be you've come home as rich as a nabob?" Bart Whitaker asked next, his voice lazy. Once again he noticed how Wilde's eyes narrowed, even though he listened politely. "I've heard many a tale about the fortunes that can be made in the East."

"Let us say I am well enough before with the world and leave it at that, shall we?" Wilde said. Some of the others shifted in their chairs at his icy tone. Almost it seemed to be warning Bart that he had better go no further with this line of questioning.

"No doubt you'll find England tame after all your adventures," the earl remarked. "*I* certainly should."

Christopher Wilde nodded. "No doubt I shall, m'lord, although it is sure to be restful. At the moment it is a novelty to me. My estate in Devon seemed pleasant when I was there recently. But I shall have to see how I go on. I told Bart I ran away as a boy to escape the life. Perhaps I shall do so again."

"Back to India, you mean?" the earl asked as he signaled the butler to pour more wine before the next course was served.

"No, I shall never return there," Wilde said, his voice even. "I might try my luck in the other Indies next time. Although piracy can be so—so final if you get caught at it. Even with a letter of marque. And growing sugar cane doesn't sound all that exciting either, does it? Might just as well stay home and concentrate on mangles and peaches and pigs.

"But enough of me, sirs! Tell me, if you would be so kind, of our new Prince Regent. Is it true the king is badly ill?"

Conversation became more general then, and Bartholomew Whitaker sensed his long-lost friend was relieved. He suspected there were things Chris did not want to speak of, besides his possible fortune, and he wondered what they might be and why. Perhaps he had been involved in some nefarious doings while he had been abroad. Perhaps things he could even be prosecuted for, now he was home. But he suspected he would never know. The man was close, in spite of his easy conversation, and he sensed there was a side of him that would remain a closed book, no matter how intimate a friend. He kept his own counsel—enigmatic, contained.

Later, drinking port after the last course had been removed, he saw how Chris parried certain questions or returned a vague answer. He wondered if he were the only one to notice. Of course, the others had drunk deep by now and probably were not aware of it. Still, when they rose from the table at last, Mr. Ainsworth came to his side for a moment.

"Strange fellow, your Chris Wilde," he said quietly. "Knows more than he's tellin'. Keeps a deal buttoned up, I'd say."

Whitaker nodded, watching soberly as Chris left the room arm in arm with Sir Joshua Severance. "Yes, he's a stranger to me now," he agreed. "Still, I remember the boy he once was. A fine chap, one of the best. Perhaps he'll open up a bit after he's been home for a while. And you must admit he tells a good story."

"That he does," Duke said. "A very good—*story*. Wonder how much truth there is to them?"

Much later, when they strolled back to Upper

Brook Street, Bart invited Wilde to ride the following morning but was refused.

"I've some business in the city tomorrow," Wilde said. "I expect it will keep me busy all day. Besides, I've got to get to Tattersall's for a good horse before I can accept your offer. The slug I rode from Devon would disgrace us both. Perhaps another time?"

In spite of his easy words, Bart felt rebuked, and he stiffened a little. However, when they parted outside his rooms, Christopher Wilde's smile was warm, his handshake firm. "Thanks for taking me along tonight," he said. "I found it very interesting. And I like your cousin, Jaspar, silly ass that he is to let a woman upset him this way. Ah well, the throes of first love, eh? You must be patient. Some other charmer will no doubt appear before long and save him from continued melancholy."

"But then I'll have to be on my guard again," Bart complained, as diverted as Christopher Wilde had hoped he would be. "I don't know which is worse, his depression or his penchant for unsuitable connections."

"Such a problem, women, aren't they?" Wilde chuckled before he turned and ran lightly up the stairs.

Two

A SOMBER COUNCIL met around the big deal table in the basement kitchen of Seventeen Upper Brook Street the following afternoon at two. The master of the house, Mr. Reginald Simmons, always took a nap after his luncheon, so his valet, Livingston, who had been with him for over twenty years, was able to make one of the group. He sat, as was his right as upper servant, at the head of the table. Flanking him was Lucie Watts, Miss Simmons's so-called maid, and Mrs. Doherty, the elderly Irish cook. Seated next to this woman was a former sailor, Joe Griffen. He had been sorely wounded at sea in the Battle of Trafalgar, and his face was puckered with scars so dreadful that children cringed away from him and cried. Since he had lost his left leg to a cannonball as well and wore a wooden peg as a replacement, he was a fearsome sight even to those grown-ups who came upon him unexpectedly. Facing him across the table, a little girl sat quietly, her eyes darting from one face to another, although she contributed not a word to the heated conversation that was taking place.

"An' I say we got ter speak ter Miss Felicia, an' soon!" Lucie Watts exclaimed, her voice shrill. "End up in the streets, we will, an' her as well, the way she's goin' on!"

"It's true she's a deal too free with her money," Joe Griffen contributed.

"She's a saint, she is, an' I'll not hear a word agin her!" the cook exclaimed, pounding the table for emphasis.

"No one, I believe, is *saying* a word against her, Mrs. Doherty," the valet said in his soft, well-bred voice. " 'Tis only that we all know how things are placed here, how little money there is. And I agree that somehow we must impress on Miss Felicia that things cannot go on as they have been."

"It pains me so ter see 'er goin' out ter teach music every day," Lucie Watts mumbled, shaking her brassy blond head in regret. "But when I tells 'er it ain't fittin' fer one o' 'er station, she jess laughs at me and sez we need the money. But wot, I asks ye, does that money go fer? Not fer 'er own use and only a little more fer 'er Pa. No, she spends it feeding those dirty little beggars!"

"An' there's more of 'em showing up at the back every single day," Mrs. Doherty complained. "Don't she know we can't feed all the poor in Lunnon?"

"She's too good-hearted, that's all," Griffen said. "But saint or no, it's got ter stop."

"And here's Mr. Simmons saying he thought he fancied breast of pheasant for his dinner," Mr. Livingston said. He sighed heavily and threw out his hands before he continued, "And where does he think we can get that delicacy in the spring, except at a ruinous cost?"

"Pr'haps I could do something with a bit o' chicken, sir?" Mrs. Doherty volunteered. "Put it under a game sauce, like? He might not notice."

"I do assure you he would notice, madam," the valet said primly.

"He'll probably have forgotten all about it by then," Lucie Watts said. "Ye know 'ow 'e is."

The others nodded. Mr. Reginald Simmons was not a well man, in mind or body. Indeed, his valet knew that ever since his wife's death three years previous, his absentmindedness had become a serious derangement. But thank heavens he had kept his sweet nature and was no danger to anyone, including himself. And he was sick as well with a mysterious ailment the doctor had been unable to cure, an ailment that caused him to suffer excruciating headaches on occasion.

"Well, best I get busy," the old cook said as she hoisted her heavy frame out of her chair. "There's the bread to see to for tomorrow an' supper to make as well. Though it won't be much. We'll have to make do with soup and rusks tonight. There's only enough chicken for the master an' Miss Felicia, o' course."

Everyone in the kitchen began to hope their mistress would be paid what was owed her today. Mrs. Alfred Garrison was behind in her payments for her daughter's piano and singing lessons. Way behind. And reminded of that fact by a pale Miss Simmons on her last visit to the house in Henrietta Place, Mrs. Garrison had only shrugged and said she had no money by her. She had promised to see to it today. If she did not, Joe Griffen told himself gloomily, they might all have to resort to begging—or stealing. And if they were caught, it meant at the least deportation and at the worst, hanging.

As if she had read his mind, the child across from him spoke for the first time. "I could—I could dress in me boy's clothes an' sneak out ter see wot I could swipe," she volunteered in a rough little voice.

"No, ye don't!" Lucie Watts told her, frowning fiercely. Her face, raddled by the injurious use of heavy paint during her years in the theater, was pitted and scarred. "Ye know wot Miss Felicia told ye!"

The child nodded, bowing her head. "Aye," she whispered. "I ken it well. But—but wot are we ter do else?"

"I suggest we wait and see what the mistress brings home. If she has been paid by that horrid cit's wife, there'll be no problem, not for a while, anyway. And I promise you, I'll have a little chat with her soon about throwing her money away on beggar children," Mr. Livingston said firmly. "Best I be getting back to the master now. You know how upset he gets if he wakes and I'm not there. Miss Watts, surely you have some chores to do? And Joe, Mr. Simmons needs more coal. See to it please. You, Jacqueline, can dust the front salon. But be careful not to break anything!"

He left the room before anyone could disagree with this program, but the child stuck her tongue out at his retreating back. She was a pale little mite, looking far younger than her twelve years, and she was the newest member of the establishment. Brought home starving by Miss Felicia only a month before, she had been dressed in ragged boy's clothes, and she had claimed her name was Jack. Her disguise had only lasted until she had been given a bath forcibly by a determined Lucie Watts, and when questioned about it, she had admitted it had been safer for her to pretend to be a boy. Miss Felicia had shaken her head sadly and given the scrawny little child a hug.

It had taken quite a while for the others to accept this newest member to their ranks, and they were in danger of not doing so at all when Miss Simmons noticed how coldly they were behaving to the child and accused them all of playing Molly, Bar the Door.

"For surely," she had said in her gentle voice, "you are not generally so cruel. It must be just that having found a haven here yourselves, you want no one else to invade it. But that is horrid, and I'll not have it!"

Still, Mr. Livingston had had a serious talk with

19

her, and he had finally obtained her promise that she would saddle the household with no more waifs. The ones who appeared at the back door for a bite of bread or cheese, a mug of hot soup, didn't count to her, although the valet would have liked to banish them as well. But knowing there was only so much he could accomplish, he had accepted this small concession with good grace.

The object of all her household's thoughts was even then standing in Mrs. Alfred Garrison's overly fussy sitting room, waiting to be paid the money owed her. Mrs. Garrison did not look best pleased, and she slammed one of her desk drawers so hard, Felicia Simmons winced.

"How it has come to pass that I am dunned in my own house, I do not understand," she said sharply, as she riffled through a stack of bills and letters. "It is not at all genteel, and you a lady, too! Or so you told me! I begin to doubt that, after today!" she added spitefully, her protuberant pale blue eyes glaring at the hapless music teacher.

"I do beg your pardon, ma'am, but you are in arrears for twelve lessons," Miss Simmons told her. "I should be sorry to have to give up teaching Miss Sybil, but give it up I must unless I am paid for my labor."

"Hmmph!" Mrs. Garrison said as she held out a slim sheaf of bills.

Miss Simmons took it with composure and counted it slowly. When she looked in astonishment at the fat, overdressed mistress of the house, that lady had the grace to redden.

"I cannot pay you all at once," she admitted. "Take that on account, and be grateful for it!"

"I am indeed, ma'am," Miss Simmons made herself say as she tucked the bills away in her reticule, although inwardly she was seething at the way she was being treated. "But next week, shall we say, you will give me the remainder?"

She waited until Mrs. Garrison gave a grudging nod before she curtsied and went away.

Walking home to Upper Brook Street, Felicia Simmons grimaced to herself. How horrid it was to have to beg for what was rightfully hers, she thought as she waited for a hackney cab to pass before she crossed the street. And even more horrid to have to have anything to do with such people as the Garrisons! If little Sybil had not been so sweet and agreeable and talented, she would have stopped going there long ago.

But no, she admitted, as she hurried across the busy thoroughfare, that's not the truth and I know it. We need money too badly at home for me to entertain any such extravagant dreams as telling Mrs. Garrison exactly what I think of her and making a grand exit to sweep the dust of the city's splendid townhouse from her shoes forever. Ha! For Mrs. Garrison paid her—when she paid her at all— a princely sum to teach her youngest daughter. And Felicia knew that she bragged to her cronies about the grand society lady she employed, for she had overheard her doing so. Her other pupils were nowhere near as well-to-do as Mrs. Garrison, more's the pity.

It had taken only a few months after her mother's death when she was eighteen for Felicia Simmons to realize that what little money there was, was not going to go far in keeping the household, unless she could augment it herself. And as much as she had regretted the necessity of advertising her talents, she had not hesitated to do so, for she knew there were others in London who were in much worse straits than the Simmons's menagerie. She saw them every time she walked out. The disabled soldiers and sailors, discarded by an ungrate-

ful nation now and left to beg; the elderly crones
sitting in gutters wrapped in rags mumbling to
themselves as they drank cheap gin to keep out the
cold; and most heartbreaking of all, the children.
Chimney sweeps' boys, all soot and burned legs and
hacking coughs; little flower and vegetable girls
calling their wares in shrill piping voices as they
strove to sell their last bedraggled bunch of cress
or violets. It made one's heart ache to see them!
And so she had tried to help, although she knew
the mite she was able to contribute to their sustenance made little difference in the end. Oh, how she
wished she had money! she told herself. Lots of
money! She would build orphanages if she had,
clean places with lots of healthy food. And she
would see to the children's schooling, have them
taught trades so they need never beg again.

It was her fondest dream, not, she told herself as
she turned into Upper Brook Street, that there was
the slightest likelihood of it ever coming to pass.

She looked at the front door of her home with a
critical eye as she approached it. Yes, the doorway
looked well with its glossy black paint, its immac-
ulate marble steps and wrought iron palings, although the brass knocker could stand a polish.
You'd never know that poverty lurked inside that
door, and that was important to Miss Felicia Simmons. A proper front must be maintained, for she
and her father were, after all, quality.

But sometimes, generally when she was very
tired, she wearied of the subterfuge, even wished
they might sell this house and take a smaller one
in a meaner part of town. The money from the sale
of it would be so welcome! But she also knew that
it would kill her father if she tried to remove him
from the house he had brought his bride to twenty-
four years ago.

Where had all the money gone? Felicia wondered

as she stepped inside and closed the door behind her. She had heard her mother murmur of bad investments, gambling debts, loans that had never been repaid. For as well as being impractical, Reginald Simmons had been a generous man who had often reached into his pocket to help others. And look where it had landed them. As poor as the poorest church mice! Ah well, Felicia thought as she took off her bonnet and gloves and smoothed her hair in the hall mirror, I still love him after all, poor Da. So confused he is now, so sad. And so often in pain as well.

As she went into the library, she reminded herself she must use some of Mrs. Garrison's partial payment to buy laudanum. Livingston had told her that her father's supply was getting low. If only it were not so expensive! But at least now they had enough money for food. She rang the bell for Lucie Watts. She and Joe could go out and buy enough to see them through the next few days. And she herself would not have to sell yet another Dresden figurine or any more of the silver. Not this week, anyway.

Very early the next morning, Felicia Simmons went out to polish the brass door knocker and wash the marble steps. She peeked around the door first to see if she would be observed. As she had hoped, Upper Brook Street slumbered on in genteel silence. The occasional milkman calling his wares or a footman walking m'lady's pug did not bother her. They were sure to think her just a servant in her faded old house gown and apron.

Of course, she told herself as she set to work with the brass polish and a rag, she could have asked Lucie to do the work later, or even Jacqueline. No, not Jacqueline, she thought with a little smile. The child couldn't even reach the knocker, her growth was so stunted. And she herself enjoyed doing it. It was so pleasant to be alone in the early morning hours when the air was fresher than at any other time of day.

Across the street, at Number Eighteen, Christopher Wilde stared down from his third floor front windows at the maid working so industriously. He had begun to pay attention to that house the afternoon before when he had chanced to see a scarred peg-legged man and a brassy-haired, raddle-faced female walk away from it. He could tell they had been arguing from the way the blond woman had tossed her head and shook her fist at the man. The two had intrigued him, for they were not the kind of people he associated with Upper Brook Street. Then there had been the pale little girl he had seen at the front windows of the first floor, staring out into the street so smugly. He wondered who lived there. Perhaps Bart Whitaker would know.

At last, the door knocker polished to a fare-thee-well, the maid nodded and went down on her knees to scrub the steps. She was certainly worth her wages, Chris Wilde thought. When she was finished, she tossed the dirty water into the gutter and leaned back against the palings, waiting for the steps to dry before she went back inside. He saw her lift her face, eyes closed, to the sun, smiling as she did so. She seemed so happy that Wilde was startled. He knew servants had a hard life of constant toil. But perhaps the girl was in love? That would account for her smile and her contented air. She had a neat waist under her faded gown, intriguing curves, and her ash blond hair shone with cleanliness. He thought her chosen groom or footman a lucky man, whoever he was.

As the door of the house next to hers opened and a most superior butler appeared, the maid gathered up her bucket and scrub brush and scurried inside.

It was almost as if she didn't want the butler to see her there, and surely that was singular, was it not?

Christopher Wilde was so fascinated, he watched the house carefully whenever he was at home for the next few days. Finally, coming back from a ride in Hyde Park's Rotten Row late one morning, he saw the maid again. His eyes narrowed as he observed her in her neat gown and bonnet. How different she looked now! he thought in some astonishment. Quite the proper young lady, in fact. And as he watched, she walked down the street, stopping once to chat with an elderly dame who lived a few doors away and who had been about to step up into her carriage.

She could not be a servant then, he told himself as he dismounted and gave his horse into the groom's keeping. But if that were the case, why had she been scrubbing the steps and polishing the knocker? And where was the maid who should be attending her?

"I say, Bart, do you know who lives in that house directly across the way?" he asked his companion as they entered their own house.

"I believe a Reginald Simmons and his daughter," Bart told him as they climbed the stairs. "I think the man's ill. Certainly no one ever sees him. Why do you ask?"

"No special reason. I was only wondering, for some of the inhabitants of that house are very peculiar people. There's a horribly scarred man with a peg leg who rolls like a sailor when he walks, a coarse looking blond woman, even a small child. And then there's that young lady. . . . "

As his voice died away, Bart smiled to himself. Could it be that the contained, ice-cold Mr. Wilde was succumbing to an attraction for one of the opposite sex? He himself had never noticed the girl he spoke of, and he told himself he would be on the lookout for her. She must be beautiful to catch Wilde's eye, for he had never even blinked when introduced by his new friends to some of society's loveliest ladies.

After he had changed from riding clothes, Christopher Wilde waited for his luncheon to be served before he must return to the city for yet another meeting with his man of business. There was still a great deal to settle—his investments, the final details of the sale of his ships in India, improvements he wanted to undertake at Wildewold. The day was warm and, for a miracle, sunny, and he opened the front windows. As he did so, he saw a proper gentleman's gentleman also opening the windows wide across the way at Number Seventeen, and he leaned forward, his eyes intent. The valet, for so he assumed he must be, swept the draperies aside and stepped out of sight. No one appeared at the windows, but in a moment, the sweet sound of bells from all of London's myriad churches began to chime the twelve strokes of noon.

From the city to Camden Town, from Cheapside to Cadogan Square they rang, a cacophony of bells, not at all in unison. Their melodious notes sounded, one after the other above the impressive mansions of the wealthy and the wretched tenements of the poor, and rose toward heaven as surely as their makers must have intended. When the last echoes died away, the valet stepped forward again to close the windows and the draperies.

Wilde sat back in his chair, rubbing his chin with one big tanned hand.

"What's to do, guv?" Bowers asked as he came in with a tray of food. "You look thoughtful-like."

"It's that house across the street," Wilde said. "I admit I'm intrigued by the people who live there. See what you can find out about them, will you?"

Bowers stared at him sharply for a moment before he nodded. Queer do, that, Mr. Chris's curiosity, he thought. But then, he'd been in many a queer do with Wilde over the years.

"Good as done, guv. Oh, are you eating in tonight? The cook wants to know if there's anything special you fancy."

"No, not tonight. I'm promised to Duke Ainsworth. He's taking me to some soiree his mother is giving. Seems there's a female cousin of his up from the country who must be presented this Season, or some such. Bah," he added with a grimace. "How senseless all this is! It's almost enough to send me back to India as fast as I can go."

"Nah, it won't do that," Bowers said, his ugly face twisted in a grin. "We shouldn't go back there ever again, guv, and you knows it. Still, there's plenty of other places in the world we haven't seen, if you're starting to get restless-like."

His master sighed as he cut a piece of ham and smeared it with mustard. "So there is. But I'm afraid I'm tied here, at least for now. I'm thinking, however, that as soon as my business is done, I'll go down to Devon. I've no patience with all the airs and graces I have to deal with here in town. And the endless parties and social engagements, the theater, the gambling, visits to the jeweler, the tailor, the bootmaker! No one does anything but amuse themselves at worthless things and spend money, yet they claim they are always busy. Fools!"

Ted Bowers shook his head as he took the tray away later. It was too bad Chris Wilde had had to come home, he told himself. Or perhaps it was too bad he had ever left England in the first place, for if he had stayed here, he would not now be so disappointed in the way of things, so scornful of the society he had been forced, by his father's death, to join. Still, Bowers reminded himself, if Wilde had never traveled, he wouldn't be the man he was today, and that was something anyway.

He had a word with the cook before he took himself down the back stairs for a chat with Mrs. Kenton, wife of the owner of the house. Maude Kenton was a font of knowledge about London, especially Upper Brook Street, for she had come here to work when just a young girl. Her future husband had been the butler of the house then, and when their master died and left them the property as a reward for their loyalty to him, they had begun to rent out the rooms and make a very good livelihood from it.

Bowers had discovered that Mrs. Kenton was a garrulous soul, always ready for a bit of gossip. If anyone knew anything about the inhabitants of Number Seventeen, it would be she, and by evening, he'd have some answers for Chris Wilde.

He found her seated in her parlor, her sewing on her lap, and he had her talking about the house across the street in only a matter of minutes.

"My, yes, the stories I could tell you about that place," she said, her round little eyes snapping. "A Mr. Reginald Simmons bought it twenty-four years ago for his bride. Such a nice young couple they were—so much in love!" She sighed. "How things have changed, that's for sure. Mrs. Simmons is dead now, and they say her husband had never been the same man since. Lives secluded, y'know. And I've heard tell he suffers from terrible headaches and has lost all touch with the world. So sad!

"But times were when the house was full of people coming and going—all gentry, o' course. As good as a show it was, to watch the carriages pull up, all those lovely ladies and handsome gentlemen going in for dinner, or a musical evening or cards. Now there's no one there but the master and his only child, Felicia. Poor young lady! Tch, tch."

"Why do you say so, ma'am?" Bowers asked respectfully.

"I've a notion—mind, it's only a notion—that the family has come down in the world. A long way down. No parties are given anymore, no one ever visits, and Miss Simmons doesn't attend any of the ton affairs. Which is her right, y'know, for she's a second cousin of the last Earl of Leeds, and there's nobility on her mother's side as well. And why wouldn't she do so, unless she doesn't have the money for grand clothes? Mr. Simmons was a warm man, as the saying goes, and a generous one, but I recall our late master saying once that he had the devil's own luck with his investments and suchlike. And he was always giving his blunt away to anyone with a hard luck story."

"But surely they must have paid him back," Bowers argued, more to keep her talking than from any real interest in her story.

"I've heard tell he can't remember who owes him what, his mind's so far gone. And, o' course, his debtors, convenient-like, have forgotten, too. That Lucie Watts over there did let it slip once when I met her on the street. 'Course she never said another word, and my! she did look that upset that she'd talked so free, I can't tell you! But Miss Watts, as she calls herself, is no better than she should be. She was in the *theater* and, I'm sure, much more besides. You know actors. No morals at all. Lots o' good being one o' the muslin set did for her, though. Hmmph!

"But Miss Simmons goes out every day, although I don't know where. I'd give a deal to find out! Always dressed the same, too. Such a plain old bonnet, such a severe gown. And there's those in the street who don't approve her servants, if that's who they are. I must say neither me nor Mr. K. do either."

She sniffed, and Bowers leaned forward in his chair a little. Now he was getting someplace!

"How so?" he asked, as casually as he could.

"Well, there's Mr. Livingston, Mr. Simmons's valet. Nothing wrong with him, or with the old cook. I've known Mrs. Doherty for years, and except she's Irish, and therefore foreign, she's a good woman. But then there's that scarred, peg-legged old sailor. Scare you out of a year's growth, he would, if you were to come on him unexpected. And the common Lucie Watts. What do those two do over there in a gentleman's house?

"And now there's a new one. Come a month ago, she did. Skinny little girl, too small to be much help even as a scullery maid, to my mind. But where did she come from? And why is she there, I ask you?"

Unable to tell her, Bowers only shook his head.

"And that's not all. Mrs. Stevens, next door but one, told me her mistress is some upset at the ragged children she's seen sneaking in the back way. Don't do a thing for the tone of the street, if you get my meaning. This is a genteel neighborhood, not for the likes of those little ragamuffins. Why, every butler from top to bottom both sides chased them away whenever they dared to come and beg here in the past. But now they don't beg. They only run straight to Number Seventeen. Mrs. Stevens told me she wouldn't be surprised if that old sailor and Lucie Watts wasn't running some kind of child thieves' ring from the house. Imagine!"

Bowers let her ramble on for another few minutes before he took his leave. Mrs. Kenton had nothing else to add to her tale of the strange people across the street, but at least he had something to tell Chris Wilde. And, if necessary, he might be able to strike up an acquaintance with the maimed sailor and find out more. He decided he'd wait for the right moment, admitting that now he was as intrigued as his master was at the unusual doings across the way. Sure didn't seem like the behavior of any gentry he had ever known!

Three

A FEW DAYS later, Felicia Simmons broke her solemn promise to her father's valet, although she refused to be sorry for it. She had been coming home from a music lesson late one afternoon when she saw a little black boy sitting on the curb and crying. Her heart was touched by his sobs, the way he clenched his fists and rubbed his eyes, how his fat shoulders shook with his grief.

"Here, now, what's the matter?" she asked, stooping to touch his shoulder.

He jerked away, turning quickly, his whole face consumed by fright. Felicia wondered what horrors he had known in his young life that a gentle touch could bring such terror to his eyes.

"I'll not harm you," she said, smiling at him. "Tell me, why do you cry? Are you hurt?"

The little boy stared at her for a moment, two fat tears sliding down his cheeks. Then he shook his head. "Not lessen ya mean in me breadbasket," he said in a piping little voice. "That hurts, it do, fer there's nuffin in it."

"Oh, dear, that's too bad," she said as she dug into her reticule for her handkerchief. As she drew it out, she saw the boy's face fall, and she wondered why as she wiped his tears away. "Now, you must not cry anymore," she said. "Just you come along home with me, and I'll see that you are fed. It's only a little way."

"Iz ya gwine make me ya page boy, ma'am?" he asked eagerly. "Ah wuz one oncit, and Ah be good at it, too! An' Ah looks real fine dressed up in a fancy satin suit."

Felicia Simmons smiled at the very idea. "No," she said. "I've no need for a page boy." Seeing his crestfallen face, she added, "Not that I'm sure you wouldn't be an excellent one, mind! Is that what you've been doing? Why aren't you one anymore?"

"Ma'lady sent me away," he said, taking hold of her hand as if he were afraid she might disappear. "She said it wuz 'cause Ah got too big."

"You don't look very big to me," Felicia said, wondering how old he was. Eight, maybe? Nine? But she admitted she had very little knowledge of black page boys, although she had heard they were all the rage now. To her the practice seemed the worst kind of affectation, besides being a form of slavery. And she had never even considered what happened to those little boys as they grew to manhood.

"Ah iz big fer mah age," her companion confided. "An' Ah wuz sorry Ah grew outta mah livery. But it weren't mah fault, dat! But—but Ah never thinks she'd just turn me out with only a few coins. She tole me Ah wuz never ter come back neither, ever agin."

Horrified at such callousness, Felicia squeezed his hand in reassurance. "What did you do?" she asked, not at all sure she really wanted to know.

"Oh, Ah begged some. Stole, too," he added, almost in a whisper. His black eyes sneaked a peek at her face as to gauge her reaction to that confession. Thinking he saw a little reproof there, he added quickly, "Ah had ter, missus! Some mean boys stole all mah money. They wuz bigger dan me, an' Ah couldn't fight so many. So Ah hadda steal, when Ah couldn't beg enough."

"But where have you been sleeping?" Felicia asked, remembering the cold winter London had just endured.

He shrugged. "Here 'n there," he said evasively. "Iz we almost there, missus? Ah'm powerful tard!"

"Just up the street here," she said as the unlikely pair of them turned into Upper Brook. "You can have a hot meal and sleep at my house tonight. And I'll think about what we can do for you."

White teeth so prominent in his black face beamed in a grin that wrung her heart, and it was then that she decided that, Livingston or no, she could not let this child go back to his precarious life on the streets. For if she did, she knew he would not survive long. There was too much prejudice against blacks in London.

But perhaps she could discover his late mistress's name, go and tax her with her lack of humanity, shame her into seeing to his care. "Where did your lady live?" she asked with this in mind.

"A big square, it were, with a park in da middle. Don't know da name."

"And what was her name?" Felicia persisted.

He thought for a moment, his face screwed up with effort. "Doan know dat neither. Ah only called 'er Ma'lady. But her husband an' her Mama, dey called 'er Anne."

Which doesn't help me at all, Anne being such a common name, Felicia realized as they reached the door of Number Seventeen.

"Here we are," she said as she went up the steps and opened the door. "Oh, what's your name?"

"*She* called me Sambo, but it ain't mah name! Ah hates dat name!"

"I don't blame you. Do you remember your mother? Your father? What did they call you?"

He shrugged again. "Doan know. Caint remember. Dey went away a long time ago when Ah wuz jess a baby."

"Well, then you can pick out your own name— any one you like. You think about it while you're eating, and when you decide, let me know."

Attracted by the voices in the hall, Jacqueline had come to the top of the stairs that led down to the kitchen. Her eyes widened when she saw Miss Felicia's companion, and she scowled. "Who's *he*?" she demanded. "Wot's he doin' here then?"

"He's having supper, and then he's going to sleep here tonight," Miss Simmons told her as she removed her bonnet. "I want you to be especially nice to him, Jacqueline. He's been having a very bad time. Now, you show him the way to the kitchen and tell Mrs. Doherty to feed him. I'll be there shortly, after I've seen my father."

Jacqueline stared at the little boy as Miss Felicia went up the stairs. Nice ter him, indeed! she thought. An' he didn't look hungry to *her*.

"Where's dis kitchen?" he asked. "Ah'm starvin'!"

"No, you ain't!" she said, tossing her head. "You're fat!"

"Ain't fat, neither. Ah iz *big*! It's diff'rent," he retorted. "An iffen ya don't take me to da kitchen, Ah'll tell da lady ya wuz mean ta me, see iffen Ah don't!"

Jacqueline turned, seething. She had hated this little boy on sight, and she knew the others wouldn't like him either. And hadn't Miss Felicia promised Livingston she'd bring home no more waifs? Yet now here was this black boy who was not only cheeky but looked as if he'd eat them out of house and home.

After Jacqueline explained the situation in the kitchen, Mrs. Doherty merely rolled her eyes and told the boy to wash if he wanted food. He sniffed the aroma from a pot of stew simmering over the coals, eyed the big loaves of bread cooling on the table, and gave her a beatific smile.

"What did Miss Felicia say about him, Jackie?" Mrs. Doherty asked as the boy splashed water into a basin and began to scrub his face and hands.

"Said he was ter eat and sleep here, least fer tonight," she admitted, frowning. "Where's Lucie and Joe then?"

"Gone out for a walk like they do sometimes. But never mind them. Miss Felicia didn't say he was going to stay, did she? For good?"

Jacqueline shook her head. "Bet he does, though," she said, sulking. "She's got that look. You know the one."

Mrs. Doherty sighed and shook her head. Indeed she did know that look. She filled a bowl with stew and cut a thick slice of bread. There was only enough butter for the master's and Miss Felicia's dinner, but from what she had seen of the little black boy, he could well do without it. And she'd save what milk was left for little Jackie. Wanted fattening up, that one, but no matter how well she ate, she never seemed to gain a pound or grow an inch.

As the boy hurried to the table, his eyes shining, Mrs. Doherty wondered what Mr. Livingston was going to say about this newest arrival, and she hoped he would be firm when he spoke of him to Miss Felicia. A saint she was, but then, saints weren't exactly *practical*, now were they?

Upstairs, Felicia Simmons tapped softly on her father's door. She often visited him in the late afternoon, for it seemed his most lucid time.

As she entered the room, she saw he was sitting wrapped up in a shawl before the fire, staring vacantly into it and humming tunelessly.

"Here I am, Da!" she said brightly as she bent to kiss him.

He grasped her hand for a moment, staring at her as if he had never seen her before, and Felicia's heart sank.

"The master is having one of his bad turns, ma'am," Livingston whispered behind her. "Very sad he's been all day, mumbling about the past but not making much sense of it, although I did catch a name or two."

Felicia nodded as she sank to a hassock near her father's feet and rested her head on his knee.

"It's Felicia, Da," she said, trying to smile up at him. "I'm sorry you aren't feeling well."

"Well, well, well, well," he mumbled. "Well . . ."

"Shall I tell you what I saw on my walk this afternoon?" she interrupted, for sometimes he got hold of a word and didn't seem able to let go of it. "It was lovely, so summery! And the rain has held off, too. I saw a bird in Green Park I'd never seen before. It was brown and gold and had such a sweet song."

"Song, song, song, song," her father repeated.

Half a frustrating hour later, Felicia rose and kissed his white cheek. He did not seem to notice, and she went to the door, followed by the faithful valet.

"He may be better tomorrow, Miss Felicia," Livingston said, trying to ease the sorrow he saw in her blue eyes. "You know he seldom has two bad days together."

"I hope so," she said. "But when he is in bed and asleep, I must see you, for I have broken my promise to you. But I had to do it! The poor little boy!"

Mr. Livingston bowed, his face serene, although inside he was filled with despair. Another waif to house, feed, clothe? What was he to do with his mistress and her kind heart?

Down in the kitchen, Lucie Watts and Joe Griffen, who had returned from their walk only minutes ago, sat at the deal table and stared at the little black boy. His bowl was empty, indeed, it looked like it had been licked clean, and there wasn't a crumb of bread left.

The boy looked longingly at Mrs. Doherty, but when that good woman ignored him, he pushed the dish away, sighing in regret that there was to be no more.

Joe glared at him, and Lucie didn't look best pleased, either.

"Wot's yer name, then?" Jacqueline asked from where she sat on a stool in the corner. "Ye got a name, don't ye?" she added when he hesitated.

"Missus say Ah kin pick out a new one," the boy told her. "Trouble iz, caint think o' one Ah likes."

"How about 'Unwanted?' " Joe growled.

The boy's expression was bland. "Doan lak dat name," he said. "Mebbe Ah'll call mahself George, after de king."

Joe snorted, but the royal name he had chosen in his thin, piping voice made Mrs. Doherty chuckle, and even Lucie's lips curled in a smile for a brief moment.

"George is a very good name," Mrs. Doherty said. "But so is Tom or Bill or Harry."

"Ah laks George," the child said, pouting. "Ah *be* George. And Missus sez Ah could choose."

"All right, George, then, time you started earning your keep," Joe told him sternly. "Take that hod down to the cellar for more coal."

The little boy looked stunned, and then he drew himself up and said in a haughty voice, "Ah don't fetch no coals! *Ah* iz a page!"

"Not in this house, you ain't," Lucie Watts told him coldly. "Ye'll do wot yer told, or ye'll be out on the street before the cat has time to lick 'er ear!"

George looked around, but when he saw only hard, unsympathetic faces, he scowled and got to his feet. "It be too heavy fer me," he whined as he picked up the hod.

"Then you can make a lot of trips," Joe ordered. "Avast now, an' be off with ye!"

As soon as the child had disappeared, dragging the hod behind him, Joe began to curse. "Aye, we might have known," he concluded bitterly. "Wot's Miss Felicia thinking of? Wot use is *he* goin' ter be, except to eat three squares a day?"

Lucie shook her head. "He's got a sly look ter him, don't ye agree? Might be plannin' ter rob Miss Felicia blind, fer all we know."

They heard their mistress coming down the back stairs then, and they fell silent. She was still in the kitchen when George reappeared, lugging a half-empty hod and panting heavily. He dropped it with a crash, and Felicia rounded on the others and berated them for setting the child such a difficult chore. As she did so, the newly named George stayed behind her skirts, a smug smile of satisfaction on his face. It was then that Jacqueline told herself she would not rest until she had seen him banished.

Felicia Simmons did not sleep well that night. She knew she was upset that her father had lost his tenuous hold on reality again, and she was also disturbed by the servants' reaction to the little boy she had brought home. One and all, they had taken her to task for it. And, she knew, they were probably right. She didn't have the money to care for another soul. But the child had been so sad, so helpless, how could she just pass him by pretending she didn't see? It went against everything she had been taught by her parents and the church.

When she rose the next morning, she had a slight

headache, and her eyes were heavy. She spent the day doing housework and teaching Jacqueline her lessons. The little girl had rebelled at lessons at first, but now she could read Felicia's first primer, and she had grown interested. And, as Felicia had discovered to her great delight, she had a lovely, true contralto.

At last, Felicia changed her clothes, and, taking up the battered satchel that held her music and lesson plans, set off for Henrietta Place and her weekly lesson with Miss Sybil Garrison. And as she instructed the little girl, first on the piano, and then in singing, she prayed Mrs. Garrison would pay her in full today.

But although the lady agreed to receive her later, she wore a truculent look that boded no good for any immediate payment. Felicia's heart sank. Still, she held her ground, standing in the center of the fussy room, for of course Mrs. Garrison had not asked her to be seated.

"Well, what is it you want now?" that woman asked, her voice harsh.

"I believe it was agreed that you would pay me the remainder of my fee today, ma'am?" Felicia tried to say evenly. "Counting last week and today, you owe me for eight lessons."

"What?" Mrs. Garrison cried, starting up a little from where she had been lounging on the sofa. "How dare you! To think you would try such a trick on me! I never!"

"I—I beg your pardon, ma'am?" Felicia asked, bewildered. "What trick?"

"You know very well I gave you the entire amount last week!" her employer said in her loud, common voice. "And yet here you are, as bold as brass, dunning me for money you know has been paid. Well! That certainly opens my eyes to the kind of woman you are, for all your die-away airs of gentility. You, Miss Simmons, are discharged!"

Felicia felt as if she were in the middle of a bad dream. When she only stood there, her face turning pale, Mrs. Garrison went on, "I tremble to imagine what terrible damage you might have done to my darling Sybil's character, these weeks you have been teaching her. To think I allowed you to be alone with her! One can only pray she has not been corrupted beyond redemption.

"Well, what are you waiting for? Leave me at once! If you do not, I'll have the butler throw you out!"

She picked up the bell beside her, and Felicia found her voice at last. "But it's not true!" she cried. "You know it isn't true! You only gave me half last week, and you promised to pay me the rest today!"

Mrs. Garrison rang the bell, hard.

"If you persist in this scheme to bilk me, my girl, I'll have the law on you," she said, her fat face florid with indignation and both her chins wobbling. "Ah, there you are, Manley! Show this—this person out. And by my order, she is never to be admitted here again. For any reason!"

Felicia felt the butler's hand on her arm, and realizing there was nothing she could do in the face of such outright lies, she let him lead her away. When they reached the sitting room door, she murmured, "One moment, if you please."

Obediently, the butler paused, and she turned to face her triumphant former employer. It was very quiet in the room when she said, "You, madam, are even more dishonest than you are common."

Her words were twice as effective for the genteel way she spoke. "And you are a liar as well," she went on. "I am glad I do not have to deal with such as you again. I pity your daughter sincerely, to have a mother like you."

As Mrs. Garrison pushed herself to her feet, sputtering and gasping, Felicia wheeled and walked away. As she went out the front door, head held high, the butler whispered, "I believe you, lass. That one's nothing but a terror. An' as common as dirt!"

Felicia could only nod, and it was all she could do, her knees were trembling so, to begin the walk home. And as she went, she felt a despair she had never known before. Losing Mrs. Garrison's custom was a desperate blow, for without the money she earned there, her household would fall on hard times again.

For a moment she toyed with the idea of approaching Mr. Alfred Garrison and pleading her case. But only a little reflection told her that would do no good at all. It was her word against his wife's. She had no proof. And of course, he was bound to side with his wife, not a strange music teacher.

But what am I to do? How can we go on? she asked herself silently as she trudged slowly down the street. There must be something else she could turn her hand to earn money, although right now she was so heartsore and depressed, she could not think of anything. And not the least of her worries was what everyone was going to eat tonight.

She had almost reached her home again when the handle of her satchel broke. The case fell to the ground, disgorging the music sheets inside, her notes and lesson plans. For a moment, Felicia could only stare down at it in despair. Then as the breeze began to scatter everything, she knelt to gather it up and cram it back into the broken satchel again. She felt her eyes fill with tears as she did so, for surely this put the final seal on an already dreadful day.

She looked up as a man knelt beside her to help collect her scattered belongings.

"Thank you," Felicia whispered through a throat clogged with tears. "You are very kind."

She felt a little uneasy, close to this big, tanned stranger. His unsmiling face looked so stern, so hard, that she marveled he had even come to her assistance.

"Allow me to carry it for you," he said. "I know you live two houses beyond, and broken as the case is, it would be awkward for you."

Still startled, Felicia could only nod. As they walked toward her house, the stranger said, "I do beg your pardon, ma'am. I am Sir Christopher Wilde. I live across the street at Number Eighteen."

Felicia stole another glance at him. His tanned face was still serious and cool, and he had none of the glinting look of a beau hot in pursuit. She began to feel more at ease.

"Across the street?" she echoed.

"Yes, I have taken rooms at Mr. Kenton's," Christopher Wilde told her, wondering why she had tears in her eyes and looked so sad and undone. But even as he spoke, he saw those blue eyes light up and a little smile curve her lips, and he thought that smile turned a merely pretty face into a pure delight to behold.

"But of course," she murmured, as if to herself. "How perfect! Now why didn't I think of that?"

He frowned. "But why should you?" he asked, bewildered. "You have a perfectly good house of your own. You don't need rooms!"

She blushed and lowered her lashes. "I admit I was thinking of something else, sir. I do beg your pardon," she said.

He paused to cup her elbow and help her up the steps of her perfectly good house. After she had

43

turned the key and opened the door, he handed her her battered satchel and bowed.

"You know, you have not told me your name," he said, a little amused. "I realize this is hardly a formal introduction, but since we are neighbors, perhaps . . . ?"

"I am Felicia Simmons," she admitted, trying to balance the heavy case and extend her hand to him at the same time. The satchel began to escape her grasp, and Sir Christopher was quick to restore it to safety. As he pressed it close to her, both his hands touched her waist.

"Thank you again," she said, trying desperately to appear dignified and cool. "It is very good of you to bother."

He made an impatient gesture. "Not at all, ma'am. Give you good afternoon."

Felicia nodded and stepped into the house, wondering why her breathing was so uneven. But then she forgot the good Samaritan that Sir Christopher had been as she considered again the wonderful scheme he had so inadvertently presented her.

Lodgers! It was the perfect solution! Oh, not many, of course. There wasn't room for many, and she did not think the household could take care of a large crowd. But perhaps an elderly couple come to town to see the sights for the Season? Or a small family? No young children, though, she thought as she set the useless satchel down on the hall table, frowning a little. And no animals. They would upset Da.

Without even bothering to remove her bonnet and gloves, she walked through the ground floor rooms. The drawing room was a splendid size, she thought, and not at all shabby since it got so little use. And the twin parlors that faced each other across the hall beyond could be turned into bedrooms. The small morning room would make a cozy retreat, for it overlooked the strip of garden behind the house. And everyone here could use the back entrance while the lodgers were in residence.

She wondered if she could retain the library, however. Her piano was there, and she would miss it. But she would do without it gladly, if she had to.

Now, she thought, how does one go about this? I suppose I shall have to ask Livingston, he's sure to know. And I'll have to get the name of a good house agent, see about carters to move the furniture. They'll have to do that quietly, so as not to disturb Da. How fortunate he never left his room! Why, he wouldn't even have to know there were strangers in the house, if she were careful about who she rented to. And neither would the neighbors, if she only took one couple. Surely everyone would think she had friends visiting from the country. She must be sure to impress on the agent that only gentry would be welcome here.

Across the street, Christopher Wilde sat at his front windows staring at the house opposite and wondering about the girl he had just met.

So, she was a musician, Miss Felicia Simmons? Perhaps even a teacher? Yes, that must be it, for he had been quick to note the lesson plans she had as he had collected her papers. And that would gibe with what Bowers had told him, that the family had fallen on hard times. It was of course unfortunate that that was so, but he felt a grudging admiration for the gently bred girl who, by her own determination and talent, was doing what she could to ease the situation.

He wished he might get to know her better, although he realized there was small chance of that. Miss Simmons did not attend ton parties. And since she did not, the most he could hope for was a bowing acquaintance when they chanced to meet on the street.

He was surprised to find he regretted that more than he could say, even hoped she might regret it, too. But although he was not a conceited man, even he would have been amazed at how quickly he had been forgotten by the young lady across the way, as she made plans to acquire a windfall of money by opening her house to lodgers.

Four

A SHORT TWO weeks later, all was in train, and
Felicia waited anxiously for her new lodgers to arrive from their home in Oxfordshire. They were to
be a Mrs. and Miss Perkins, who, the agent had
assured her, were gentry to the core.

It had not been easy to prepare for them, any of
it, Felicia reflected, but she had done it. First, of
course, she had had to overcome Livingston's horror that she would demean herself and her father
in such a way. And not all of her assurances that
no one, especially her beloved Da, would ever know,
had changed his revulsion for the scheme.

"For, Miss Felicia, and if I may be so bold as to
say so, it doesn't *matter* who knows," he had said,
his lined face pale with suppressed emotion. "It's
bad enough it will be done."

And neither Joe Griffen nor Lucie Watts had approved either. How they had argued and objected,
tried to get her to change her mind! Felicia was
amused at how careful they were to guard her reputation, they, who had none of their own.

Jacqueline had pouted and sulked, sure she would
see even less of her adored Miss Simmons than
usual, and Mrs. Doherty had complained about the
extra work, the hot water, early morning chocolate,
and tea trays that would have to be carried upstairs—the bells that would have to be answered.

"No, indeed, you must not be concerned about

that, Mrs. Doherty," Felicia had promised her. "The lodgers will bring their own servants of course. And we are going to have the dining room and pantry fitted out as a kitchen and larder. The agent tells me it will not be difficult to do at all."

Only George had been enthusiastic about the plan, but since his approval seemed to result from the knowledge he would now get regular hearty meals, no one paid any attention to him. Not even when he said, in his piping little voice, "Mebbe dem ladies will need a page!"

Felicia had summoned a Mr. Chauncy Filmore, a house agent who dealt only with the gentry. Mr. Filmore had been delighted with the rooms and her plans for them, for Upper Brook Street was a most desirable location, and they were sure to be snapped up at once. In fact, he told her, he could even assure her that he would be able to let them to two ladies as soon as she could ready them. When he mentioned the amount of rent she could charge for the Season, Felicia had had all she could do not to grab his hands and swing him into a wild, triumphant jig of delight. Not that she had done so, of course, for Mr. Filmore, a tall, reedy man with a long thin nose, looked altogether too prudish for any such thing.

She had had to appeal to her father's man of business for some advance money to outfit the rooms, but that hard-pressed gentleman had been so delighted with her scheme to make money she had had no trouble in doing so.

All the rooms had been cleaned thoroughly, carters had brought down beds and armoirs and dressing tables, comfortable chairs and accessories, and had carried upstairs in return the furniture that would not be necessary. A full load of coal had been delivered, candles ordered, and Felicia had even bought fresh flowers for all the rooms to welcome her new paying guests. Indeed, sometimes she had trouble remembering they were strangers, it was all so very like readying the house for the visit of family or beloved friends.

Still, on the appointed day, she did feel a little qualm as she walked through the rooms, checking to make sure all was in order. Yes, the bedrooms had lamps on the tables next to the beds, soft rugs and pretty draperies, and coal was laid ready for a fire in the grates. Her mother's elegant needlepoint adorned the chairs in the drawing room, the furniture there shone with polish, and the brass and silver sparkled.

Felicia hoped the ladies from Oxfordshire would approve, hoped as she never had for anything in her life that they would be pleasant people, easy to get along with, friendly and, above all, quiet. For so far, at least, all knowledge of what was happening on the ground floor of his house had been kept from Reginald Simmons. Pray it continued to be so, Felicia thought, as she stared out into the street.

As she watched, she saw Sir Christopher Wilde leave his house across the way. He was accompanied by another man who was tall and loose limbed, with a pleasant long face. The two mounted their hacks and set off for Hyde Park, and for a moment, Felicia wished she might be one of the throng there, parading in the bright spring sunlight. Then she laughed at herself. Such things were not for her, not anymore, and she had given up thinking of them long ago. Whatever was the matter with her that she should do so now?

The Perkins arrived at five that afternoon. Felicia was at the front door to welcome them, and if she felt reassured by Mrs. Perkins's lovely smile and gentle demeanor, she took an instant antipathy to her daughter, Miss Cecily Perkins. The girl, who was a beauty of the first water with her black curls and dark eyes, could not have been more than eighteen. She greeted Felicia with a curt nod, her gaze going over her from head to toe as if to assess her figure and the quality of her gown. It was obvious she found her wanting, for she sniffed and turned away to give an order to the maid.

Felicia noted she had a rather loud, high voice and prayed her father would not hear her as she ushered the ladies into the drawing room and closed the doors behind them. The ladies' maid and a footman were already unloading the coach of what appeared to be a mountain of baggage.

"What a charming room," Mrs. Perkins said, smiling at her new landlady. "I am sure we will be very comfortable here, won't we, darling Cecily?"

Darling Cecily did not look impressed. She had picked up one of the silver candlesticks displayed on a table and turned it over to check the hallmark, before she replaced it carelessly.

"It is very old fashioned, Mama, not at all the crack," she pouted, gliding over to the mirror over the mantel to check her dark ringlets. "I had hoped it would be more elegant and impressive, for how we are to entertain in such *dowdy* surroundings, I do not know."

Felicia stiffened, and Mrs. Perkins looked distressed. "Now, now, my dear, that is unkind," she said in a placating voice. "And I do assure you, this room is vastly superior to the usual rented quarters I have seen in years past. We were very lucky to get it. Fresh flowers, too! I thank you, Miss Simmons. So kind."

"If you would care to see the rest of the rooms, ma'am?" Felicia asked, ignoring Miss Perkins, who had disposed herself in a chair and was perusing today's *Morning Post* which Felicia had left for them.

Mrs. Perkins was loud in her praise for the bedrooms, the small morning room, the new kitchen.

Her daughter, who had joined them by that time, fortunately had no more comments, except to commandeer the larger bedroom for her own. When Felicia would have left them, she asked about the room on the other side of the hall at the front of the house, whose door was firmly closed.

"That is the library, Miss Perkins," Felicia told her. "It is not included in the rental, as I believe we agreed? My piano is placed there, and Mr. Filmore assured me there was no need for me to give it up."

"Heavens! Are we to be annoyed by amateur music at all hours of the day and night?" Miss Perkins demanded. "It simply won't do!"

"The piano cannot be heard when the doors are closed," Felicia made herself say. "Still, I will be glad to practice only at a mutually agreed time."

Cecily Perkins shrugged and ordered the maid to make tea. Since that woman was still bringing in bandboxes and portmanteaus and looked harried, Felicia was quick to offer to prepare a tea tray from her part of the house as a welcome.

Mrs. Perkins gave her a gentle smile of thanks, and Felicia curtsied and went away. But as she sped down the back stairs, she was seething. Miss Perkins might be gentry, but she was also very rude. Why, she had acted as if Felicia were some menial hired to do her bidding. But I suppose since her father is paying me to let her stay here, that is what I am, Felicia told herself sadly as she instructed Mrs. Doherty to prepare tea for the lodgers—just this once. For even though I know I am her equal socially, I am only her landlady. And it was obvious Miss Perkins saw no reason to treat underlings kindly. Any of them. Well, that was too bad, but no doubt she would see little of the girl.

When she delivered the tea tray, she was sure of it, for she heard Miss Perkins already making plans to visit the best modistes, informing such friends as she had in town of her arrival, and looking forward to her first large party in three days' time. Felicia was sure she was also scheming to procure that all important little ticket that would admit her to the sacred portals of Almacks, for it was obvious Miss Perkins had come husband hunting with a vengeance. Felicia wished her well at it. And perhaps if she fell in love, she might be more pleasant?

There were several complaints in the next few days. First, Miss Perkins said her mattress was so uncomfortable she found it impossible to sleep on it. Felicia had it exchanged with her own, although she could see no difference after she had spent a restful night on the rejected one. Then Miss Perkins expressed a distaste for the coverlet and draperies in her bedroom. She could not abide green. It made her bilious. She would prefer rose or pink.

Felicia was deaf to that complaint. She had no intention of discarding brand new hangings merely for a whim. Instead, she supplied a number of pink pillows and a dainty pink cloth for the bedside table. Miss Perkins sulked but was forced to capitulate.

The most terrible scene, however, came when the girl chanced to see Joe Griffen stumping past her window on his way to the street. Her screams brought Felicia hot-foot from her own rooms and longing to smother her with one of the new pillows.

For several minutes all was pandemonium, Miss Perkins demanding that her mama find other rooms; Mrs. Perkins trying desperately to soothe her hysterical daughter; and Felicia waiting for a chance to explain.

When she was allowed to do so at last, it made no difference.

"I find this completely unacceptable, and I don't care if he did fight with Nelson," Cecily Perkins complained. "He is just too horrible looking, even if he is, as I suspect, a relative of yours. Too upsetting, and I, so sensitive, too. He must leave, or we do! I shall expect him gone by this evening."

Felicia took a deep breath. She was almost tempted to inform Miss Perkins that she might begin packing. After all, she had the deposit for the rooms that they had paid, and she was sure Mr. Filmore could find her new tenants. But Mrs. Perkins apologized so prettily and begged her understanding of her daughter's nervous condition so humbly, that Felicia finally only nodded and said she would see to it that Joe did not use the back way unless the ladies were either out or in the drawing room.

In no time at all, the Perkins's maid Gladys, and footman Melvin, discovered Mrs. Doherty and the others, as well as the comfort and company of the big basement kitchen. And the cook heard many a bit of gossip about Miss Perkins to pass on to her mistress. The two servants from the country had been astounded by the unusual people at Number Seventeen and stunned by the army of starving little beggars who appeared so regularly for a handout. Admonished by Lucie and Joe, they had promised to keep all this from the ladies they served.

"Ter be sure, it would just set *that one* off again," Gladys said as she sat at the table sewing a new flounce on Miss Perkins's favorite afternoon gown. "Such a temper she has! And so hard to please! I've a mind to look about while I'm in town and see if I can't find another position. 'Course I will hate to leave her dear mother. What a saint that woman is!"

"Seems strange ter me, her daughter is such a

cross-patch then," Lucie said truculently. She had already heard Miss Perkins describe her as an ugly old wench who was unsuited to a gentleman's house and, since that time, had never hesitated to cast whatever stones she could find at her.

Gladys shook her head and sighed. "It's the girl's father's fault. Treats her like a royal princess and spoils her rotten, he does. An' nothin' she does displeases him, not even her worst temper tantrum. Fact is, he just laughs at her and says she's just like him, so hot to hand as she is. Ha!"

"Ha, indeed," Melvin contributed. He was a man of few words, one who was glad to let Gladys do the talking for the both of them.

The two spent many hours in the kitchen with the others, for the ladies Perkins were seldom at home except the one afternoon a week when they received visitors. Then it seemed the knocker was never still, for as unattractive as Cecily Perkins's personality might be to menials, her beauty drew a host of admirers. Felicia made sure the rest of the house was quiet those afternoons, and she never practiced the piano, lest Miss Perkins catch even a tinkle of a note and protest.

She herself still went out to give lessons to those pupils that remained to her, for she knew the Perkins would leave in July, and there was no guarantee that she would be able to rent the rooms for the rest of the summer, or even, perhaps, during the little season in the autumn.

Yes, things were easier now, but it behooved her to be as careful as she could with the money that was coming in, spending it frugally and saving as much as she could for the lean winter ahead.

She still sent Joe and Lucie foraging through the markets for the cheaper food and supplies available, refused to consider any new gowns for herself, and cut down and turned one of her old ones for

Jacqueline. Of course she had to pay a dentist bill of Lucie's, see to new shoes for George, and be sure Joe had the regular tots of rum that he had grown accustomed to in the Royal Navy. What little she spent for luxuries went for special treats of food for her father, a soft new shawl to wrap around his aching head, and fresh flowers for his room.

Still and all, and in spite of Miss Perkins's unpleasant presence, Felicia was content, happy with even the little bit of breathing space she had found for herself and her household.

Happy, that is, until she received a most unusual invitation in the post.

It came from her godmother, a lady Felicia had not heard from in some time. Lady Marjorie Bradford had left the country shortly before Felicia's mother died three years before, and she had remained in Jamaica ever since. It had seemed strange to Felicia, for she remembered the Lady Bradford as one of the world's flighty souls, one who adored gaiety, parties, and the ton and indulged herself in jewels and endless new gowns. Felicia could not imagine her being happy on a small distant island with so few of her kindred spirits around to amuse her. But stay there she had.

Yet now, according to the scribbled note that was included with the invitation, she and Lord Bradford had returned, taken up residence in their house in Berkeley Square for the Season, and were planning to celebrate the end of their exile with a gala ball on the third Saturday in May.

And, the lady had ended, they would look forward to having dear Felicia attend. Since her birthday occurred only days later, she was to consider the ball a special celebration of that occasion.

Felicia smiled a little sadly to herself. How like the Lady Bradford! Dashing off this careless note, when she had not even bothered to come and call, or even offer her condolences on her dear friend's death in person. Felicia wondered how long she had been back in London. A month? Two? And she wouldn't have been surprised if it hadn't been Lord Bradford who had reminded his wife of her goddaughter. For even though she had never forgotten Felicia's birthday, her gifts and letters were apt to arrive at any time of the year. Once, Felicia had even received one in March! Of course it had been accompanied by the most profuse apologies, but still. And the fact another caressing letter and lovely gift had come by the first of June that year did not excuse the lady's carelessness.

Fingering the heavy card with its gilt edge, Felicia put it to her cheek, deep in thought. She would have to write to Lady Bradford and excuse herself, of course. For even if she had wanted to attend such a fashionable party, she had nothing to wear and no money to purchase a new gown.

Lucie Watts came in then with a pile of freshly ironed chemises and petticoats. As she put them away, she saw the card and asked what it was.

Felicia smiled at her. "Only an invitation from my godmother to attend a ball she and her husband the viscount are giving. Of course I shall refuse."

"*Wot?* Refuse? Wotever fer?" Lucie demanded, hands on hips. "Why, 'ere ye've got a chance ter go an' 'ave a foine time fer a change, an' ye want ter *refuse*?"

"How can I go, Lucie?" Felicia asked patiently. "I've nothing to wear that's grand enough."

Seeing the indignation in the woman's eyes, she hurried on, "And no, I've no intention of spending a lot of money on a gown I can only wear once. And if I did start to move in ton circles, what would I wear next, for a breakfast, a tea, walks in the park, soirees? I—I don't want to talk about it. *Any* of it."

56

As Felicia turned away, Lucie opened her mouth and shut it thoughtfully.

When she went back down to the kitchen later, she was still thinking hard. And as she took her seat at the table and stared into space at the wall beyond, Joe Griffen looked at her askance.

"Wot's up then, Lucie?" he asked. "Lost yer tops'l or summat?"

"Nah, not that," Lucie said slowly. Then she told Joe and Mrs. Doherty what she had just learned. The cook shook her head, and Joe's scarred face grew even more horrible as he frowned.

"Don't seem right, do it?" Lucie concluded. "But I could tell from 'er voice, she don't want ter be bothered about it, fer she's determined she won't go, not even this once. Wish there was somethin' we could do!"

"Mebbe there is," Joe said, idly moving the salt trencher this way and that.

Lucie looked at him sharply. Joe didn't have a groat. None of them did. What was there *to* do?

"You remember the last time we wuz down ter the markets?" he asked. As Lucie nodded, he went on, "Plenty o' stalls sellin' ol' clothes there, weren't they?"

"Well, o' course, but Miss Felicia can't wear an old stained gown ter a fancy do with all the posh folks. Yer mind's goin' soft!"

"I remember there was a gown there must 'ave been made fer a lady built like a schooner. Yards an' yards o' fabric it 'ad, an' only a little o' it were stained. Mebbe we could find others like that, lot's o' 'em."

Lucie was leaning forward now, looking more interested. "Well, it's true I'm a good seamstress," she said slowly. "Many the stage costume I've made over the years. But I don't rightly know. . . . "

"Ye could furbish it uplike with new ribbons or

57

lace, mebbe even a pretty overskirt," Mrs. Doherty contributed. "We could save fer that out o' the housekeeping money Miss Felicia gives me."

Jacqueline and George came into the kitchen then. They had been out running an errand for the cook, and now Jacqueline gave her the twist of spice they had been sent to fetch.

The two settled down at the table, George sniffing the rich aroma of a pan of gingersnaps that Mrs. Doherty had just taken from the oven, his eyes hungry.

"But then there's shoes, no, satin sandals," Lucie went on. "An' a pretty reticule and gloves. Those would have ter be new. Oh, an' she'd need hats, too, fer later on."

"One thing at a time," Joe growled. "First we got ter get 'er ter this ball."

Lucie nodded. "I'll ask Gladys fer some fashion plates from the lady's journals Miss Perkins buys. They'd give me a good idea o' the new styles. An' I'm that sure Gladys would help me with the sewing. Feels sorry fer Miss Felicia, she does."

"Is Miss goin' ter a ball?" Jacqueline asked, eyes wide.

"Ah could be her page!" George contributed. "All Ah'd need iz a satin suit wit' lace on it, an' . . ."

Lucie ignored him. "She's goin' if we can convince her ter," she said. "Wouldn't it make a nice surprise fer 'er, if we wuz ter get everything ready before we showed it ter 'er?"

"You'll 'ave ter find a way ter keep 'er from answerin' that note then, sayin' she can't come," Joe reminded her.

Lucie frowned. "Aye, there's that," she said slowly. "Mebbe I'll jess have a word with Mr. Livingston; see wot 'e suggests."

The valet was duly approached, and he was as vehement as the rest that not only should Miss Felicia attend the ball but be dressed as finely as all the rest. When questioned as to how they could make that happen, he only smiled, and told the others to leave it all in his hands.

The next morning, before Felicia left on her teaching chores, he begged a moment of her time. She invited him into the library and closed the door behind them, sure she was to be lectured again for feeding the waifs. To her surprise, the valet told her he had heard about her invitation to the ball and, with all the eloquence he could bring to bear, begged her to attend.

"For even if it were to be only the one time, miss, surely you deserve the treat," he said, his kind old eyes intent on her frowning face. "I know you do not see the sense of it, but believe me, it is fitting. And since m'lord and Lady Bradford have been so kind as to include you, it would be rude to deny them.

"As for the money necessary, I have some laid by that I would be happy to give you—no, please. Do not say anything! I can see you are horrified by the idea, but, if I may be so bold as to say so, you and your father are all the family I have ever known. It would be an honor and a privilege for me to assist you, and I shall take it very hard if you refuse that assistance."

Felicia could hardly speak for the lump in her throat. "Whatever can I say?" she murmured, shaking her head. "You are too generous, Livingston. So in spite of my reluctance, I suppose I have no choice but to accept your kind offer, even if I will feel like Cinderella."

The valet coughed behind his fist. "I would remind you, ma'am, that you are related to nobility. Any reference to that old fairy tale about a scullery maid who became a princess is far from the mark in *your* case."

"Yes, I suppose it was an unfortunate simile, wasn't it? And you don't look anything like a fairy godmother, now do you?" Felicia teased.

To her surprise, Livingston colored up a little, and she went and gave him a hug. "Very well, I'll say no more. And I promise to write to my godmother and accept her kind invitation. But that must be the end of it, Livingston! I've no mind to try and enter the ton, nor attend their parties. It cannot be, not for me. Not anymore, and we both know it."

She went away then, and Livingston nodded to himself. We'll see about that, lass, he told himself, smiling in satisfaction. We'll see about that, indeed we will!

Five

Wʜᴇɴ Bᴀʀᴛʜᴏʟᴏᴍᴇw Wʜɪᴛᴀᴋᴇʀ saw the piece of perfection who tripped in and out of the house opposite with such regularity, he wondered how he could have been so blind. Surely his eyesight wasn't going, was it? he asked himself. But Christopher Wilde speedily disabused him of the notion that the young lady with her glossy black ringlets was the daughter of the house.

The two were having luncheon in Bart's rooms at the time, before they were pledged to join a riding expedition to Richmond.

"The lady I've seen has dark blond hair," Wilde told him. "And she's nowhere near as fashionable. Wonder who this one is?"

"Perhaps a relative or friend, come to town for the Season," Bart suggested idly. "I can assure you I'll be on the lookout for her at all the parties. Neat ankles, didn't you think?"

"You were looking at her ankles?" Wilde asked in pretended amazement, for the lady they had seen only moments before, entering a small carriage with an older woman, had been wearing a very low cut morning gown.

Bart laughed. "Finished, Chris? We don't want to be late to the meeting place," he said as he pushed his plate away. "Heard you're going to race Bell today. Should beat him easily. Man's a hamhanded rider. And he has no seat."

"We'll see," Wilde told him as he wiped his mouth and rose. "It's been a long time since I've done any horse racing. Ships were my means of transportation these past few years. Although I have ridden an elephant more than once."

"Don't think that expertise will help you today." Bart chuckled as they left the room and clattered down the stairs.

Once on the street, Wilde paused to check his horse's tack. As he did so, he saw Felicia Simmons step from her door and down the steps. He paused for a moment to watch her. She was still dressed in plain gray muslin and a severe bonnet, and she looked even more the Puritan now after the modish appearance of her friend or relative. He wondered she did not have some becoming gowns made—purchase a smart new hat.

"Is she the one you meant?" Bart asked, leaning down from his saddle.

He sounded so astounded that Chris Wilde hid a smile, even as he nodded.

"Very plain Jane. Not at all your style, dear boy," Bart told him, adding, "Or anyone else's for that matter."

"Oh, I've no interest in her romantically," Wilde said as he mounted and wheeled his horse. "Or in any other woman, come to think of it."

"I know," his companion said. "It's been re-marked, for even the Incomparables can't get you to flirt with them."

He studied Wilde out of the corner of his eye as he spoke and saw his indifferent shrug.

"Plenty of time to get riveted," Wilde said easily. "I'm only thirty. But from what I can see, there isn't a female in London who isn't on the hunt for a husband. Regular Dianas they are—merciless! I find the whole thing tedious."

"Well, watch what you're about then," Bart advised. "There are more ways to catch a man in parson's mousetrap than you or I could ever imagine."

"I'm not concerned," Wilde told him as they entered Park Lane and headed for the outskirts of the city. "I've a great deal to do here, and none of it involves getting a wife."

"Going to the Bradford affair?" Whitaker asked next. "Supposed to be the party of the Season. Of course, everyone will say that until it's over. Then the next one becomes *the* party."

He was surprised to see Chris frown. "I've received an invitation, but I'm tempted to refuse," he said, his voice gruff. "I find such evenings boring beyond belief. So crowded they are, so stuffy and uncomfortable. All that bowing and smirking and dancing! To say nothing of avoiding the Dianas and their even more determined Mums.

"Still, I suppose I have to attend. Lord Bradford and my father were cronies. I'd never hear the end of it from my mother if I offended the old boy. But I'm not looking forward to it one bit."

Later that same afternoon, when Felicia Simmons came home, she found Lucie Watts in her room, poring over a number of fashion plates.

"Look 'ere, Miss Felicia," she said, waving one of them at her. "Ain't that prime?"

Felicia studied the print. The artist had drawn an impossibly tall and haughty-looking female with very long legs. To say the gown she was wearing was elaborate would be to understate the case, for in addition to several lace flounces at the hem, caught up with satin ribbons, the gown featured a half skirt of net, hundreds of tiny tucks, and a very low neckline.

"No, not that one, Lucie," she said firmly. "I should be overwhelmed in it, it's so fussy."

Lucie sighed in regret for a moment before she

studied the slim figure of her mistress. "Aye, ye might at that," she admitted. "But there's another one 'ere I fancy. . . . "

An hour later, Felicia had decided that a simple gown almost completely unadorned would be both modest and becoming. Now, she thought, if I can only keep Lucie from overtrimming it.

"Me 'n Joe'll go ter the market termorrow. She wot's ter be had," Lucie said. "Any special color you'd like, Miss Felicia?"

"Anything but gray," Felicia said hastily, and then amended that to add, "But nothing too loud or—or blatant, Lucie. I think a soft color would be best. I don't want to call attention to myself."

Lucie stifled another sigh and nodded. She herself would have chosen scarlet. She'd had a gown of it years ago that had made her look a proper treat! But if Miss Felicia wanted pastel, a pastel she should have. And with the money they would save making over an old gown, she would have plenty left for sandals and trimmings. And kid gloves, she reminded herself as she went away to confer with Gladys.

The Perkins's maid had entered into the scheme with a will. Such a nice young lady, Miss Simmons was! Didn't seem fair she'd never had any fun! And, she told Lucie, she had several yards of lovely lace laid by that she would contribute.

"Miss Cecily bought it, then took a dislike to it and gave it to me," Gladys confided. "We can decorate the sleeves and the bodice with it. It's a cream color. Look perfect, it would, on pale blue."

Lucie said pale blue sounded namby-pamby to her, and it took Gladys quite a while to convince her it would be all the thing, if she could find a gown of that color.

When she returned from the market stalls the next day, Lucie had not only the blue but also a

soft yellow satin that was only spotted a little by
candle wax and what looked like port wine. Somehow Lucie wasn't a bit surprised when Miss Felicia
chose the blue.

Still, she set to work with a will. It was a nice
fabric, she thought as she smoothed the soft silk.
Maybe some cherry ribbons would smarten it up?

She worked at first on the big kitchen table. Jacqueline helped by holding the fabric steady and col-
lecting the scraps that Lucie cut away. Afternoons,
when the Perkins ladies went out, Gladys came to
help, and in short order the two had fashioned a
simple sheath confined under the bosom by a dark
blue velvet ribbon and with tiny puffed sleeves. Everyone admired the lace as they sewed it at the
round neckline.

When Felicia tried on the gown for a fitting, she
was amazed at what Lucie had accomplished. And
taking a small sample of the fabric, she went out the
next day to purchase sandals to match and long white
kid gloves. She frowned when she saw how expensive
they were, and she still had to get a stole, stockings—
even a reticule. It seemed so frivolous to waste Livingston's money on such things! Still, the others were
so excited, it was hard not to catch their enthusiasm.
Even, she began to look forward to the ball.

The blue gown complete, Lucie began to make
over the yellow satin. She had always liked to sew,
and when everyone complimented her on her work,
she said with pride that she could have been an
excellent modiste if she hadn't been lured to theater life instead.

Livingston told her she should also make some
morning gowns, a walking dress or two. Informed
of this, Felicia would have thrown up her hands
and had none of it, but Mr. Livingston was adamant. At last she agreed to the additional gowns,
but she refused to shop for hats. "I shall never wear

them," she said firmly. "It would be a waste of money."

Lucie would have argued the point, but Livingston caught her eye just then and shook his head a little and she subsided. Time enough later, he told her, after Miss Felicia had gone away.

"After Miss is launched and rigged," Joe added wisely.

The day of the ball, Lucie washed and curled Felicia's ash blond hair. As she did so, she went over the preparations again. No, she hadn't forgotten anything. The gown hung ready in the armoir, the matching sandals beneath it. There was a pretty beaded reticule, kid gloves, a stole. Miss Felicia even had her mother's pearl necklet to wear as well. She'd look just grand, Lucie told her as she heated the curling iron over the fire.

Suddenly she gasped. "But however will ye get there?" she asked. "Never thought o' that! Ye can't jess walk! Ye'll need a carriage!"

Felicia stopped admiring her curls in her hand mirror. "I shan't need anything of the kind," she said. "Why, it's only a step to Berkeley Square."

"Ye can't walk, an' that's that!" Lucie told her. "I may not know much about wot's proper an' all, but that I do know. I'll jess step down an' 'ave a word with Mr. Livingston."

When she returned, she assured her mistress that a hackney would be at the door at nine sharp. "Joe's gone out ter get a good one. There's no denying 'twould be better to have yer own carriage, but there! Best we can do."

When Felicia was dressed and ready at last, she went down to the kitchen to show everyone as she had promised them. For a moment, there was only an awed silence.

"You look beautiful, Miss," Livingston said at last, his old eyes misty.

Felicia laughed a little self-consciously. That she does, Lucie thought fondly. Ah, I used to be young like that, pretty, too, with skin as soft as a ripe peach and bright blue eyes. Long ago. Very long ago. She had such a lump in her throat, she had to swallow hard. To her surprise, Joe took her hand in his under the table and squeezed it hard, almost as if he knew what she was thinking—and regretting.

"Ah wish Ah wuz goin' as yer page," George said disconsolately as a tear ran down his fat cheek. "Ah could o' worn a suit o' dat yallow satin. Boy, I'd look grand in dat! 'Tain't fittin' you goin' 'lone, Missus, when you-all look so special."

"Thank you anyway, George," Felicia told him, resisting the urge to hug him. He would have hugged her back, and small though he was, George was very strong. And she did not intend to arrive at the ball in a crushed gown.

When she stepped into the cab, she thought again of Cinderella, and she smiled to herself. With its leather seat and odors of snuff and tobacco, it was so unlike a transformed pumpkin.

Berkeley Square was crowded with fashionable carriages making their slow way to the Bradford town house on the east side. A red carpet had been laid on the steps, and footmen lined it to assist the guests from their vehicles. Felicia felt a little uneasy as she left her cab, for she sensed others were staring at her and whispering about her humble mode of transportation. Holding her head high, she joined those entering the house.

A maid relieved her of her stole, and Felicia made her way up the wide winding staircase. Her heart was pounding so in her breast now, she had to take several deep breaths to steady herself. The house looked impressive, filled with flowers and all the elite of society. When the butler announced her in sonorous tones, she made herself move forward.

With a little shriek of recognition, Lady Bradford came from where she had been greeting her guests to throw her arms around Felicia and kiss her. "My *dearest* child! How *wonderful* to see you at last!" she exclaimed in her quick, breathless voice. "And how *pretty* you look," she added, smiling and nodding. "Montmorency, *do* come here and renew your acquaintance with my goddaughter."

Felicia curtsied to the tall, austere-looking gentleman, whose twinkling eyes belied his stern appearance. "Delighted, Miss Simmons," he said. "I do remember you from years ago when you were a child. How nicely you have grown up."

"Thank you, m'lord," Felicia said, smiling.

Lady Bradford tugged her hand. "*Do* come along, dear! I want you to *meet* people. Some of them knew your mother. I understand you have been living close since Mary's death? So *sad* that! And your father has been ill?"

"Yes, he hasn't been well for some time," Felicia told her as they walked toward a group of older ladies.

"Most unfortunate," Lady Bradford said in an absentminded way. "Lillian, here's Mary Simmons's daughter. Felicia, the Duchess of Kyle. She's my *goddaughter*. Oh, not you, Lillian! I know for a fact I am three years younger than you. It would be *impossible*!

"You must be *sure* to introduce Felicia to your daughters, and of *course*, to your sons," Lady Bradford instructed the lady. "She's yet to meet Society. Indeed, tonight is *really* her come-out, isn't it, dear child?

"Oh, there is Montmorency waving. How *bothersome*! But I must *dash*, for I quite forgot in the delight of seeing you again, Felicia, that I had abandoned my own receiving line. Do have a *wonderful* time, now!"

Whirling, she hurried away, her elaborate gown of deep rose satin swaying as she went.

"Dear Marjorie," the duchess said wryly. "I had hoped that age and her self-imposed exile in Jamaica might have finally reformed her, but as you see, Miss Simmons, she is still the same scatterwit she was at seventeen."

"Her stay in Jamaica was self-imposed?" Felicia asked curiously.

"Indeed. She told me she was seasick from the moment she stepped on board ship in London, and after a series of violent storms on the passage, she told the viscount she would never set sail again. She'd be in Jamaica yet, as much as she disliked it, except her husband had to return and said if he must go alone, he would. That settled it for Marjorie. She can't manage without Monty."

Felicia smiled as the duchess beckoned to a tall young lady nearby. After that, Felicia was introduced to a number of people. Some of the gentlemen signed her dance card, and one of the young ladies begged her to call.

She found herself relaxing, beginning to enjoy herself. From what she had observed, her home-made secondhand gown was indistinguishable from other, more modish ensembles, and her largest worry, that she would look dowdy, disappeared. Her eyes began to shine with pleasure, and she found several occasions to laugh. How glad she was she had come, she told herself. She wouldn't have missed this for the world!

Then, as she turned to answer a question the duchess's son was asking, she came face-to-face with Miss Cecily Perkins. The two stared at each other for a moment, Felicia in dismay, Miss Perkins in complete astonishment.

"Well!" she exclaimed in her high, loud voice. "Can I believe my *eyes*? Our *landlady* is here? At

69

the *Bradford ball*? And, if I'm not mistaken, Mama," she added to the lady at her side, "she is wearing the lace I gave to my maid when I discovered it would not do. The nerve of it! *My* lace, on the *landlady's* gown! I never!"

From where he had been conversing with a group of gentlemen, Christopher Wilde heard her comments, and when he turned quickly, he saw Bart's dark beauty from Number Seventeen staring at Miss Felicia Simmons. He also noted that girl's sudden pallor, the way she looked down at her tightly clasped hands. As he hurried to her side, a buzz of conjecture began.

"My dear Miss Simmons," he said with a glowing smile as he bowed and took her hands in his. Squeezing them in warning, he added, "What a pleasure to see you this evening."

Bending closer, as if to whisper a secret, he went on, "Smile! Laugh a little if you can. And stand tall!"

Felicia forced herself to do just that, even though she could still hear Cecily Perkins telling anyone who would listen about the rooms they had taken in Upper Brook Street, and the incongruity of coming face-to-face with the woman who had rented them.

"I do trust you have some dances left, ma'am," Wilde added, taking up the little card with its attached pencil that dangled from her wrist. "Ah, how fortunate for me! This dance is free, and I do believe the supper dance as well. You will permit me?"

Without waiting for her nod, he calmly wrote his name down before he offered her his arm. "Shall we stroll about?" he asked. "Such a crush of people, is there not? I have discovered, you know, that the more people, the more successful the party. Now I, myself, would invite fewer, so there would be less chance of anyone being crushed to death or stifled for lack of air. Don't you agree?"

They had gone some distance away from the excited, indignant Miss Perkins and those who listened to her so avidly, and knowing m'lord spoke at random to give her time to recover her poise, made Felicia say softly, "Thank you, You—you are very kind, sir."

"I dislike petty back-biting," he told her shortly. "Now, if you would be so good, ma'am, try to look a little more at ease. At the moment, you give the appearance of one being led out to the gallows. That's better," he added encouragingly as she tried a tentative smile. "Ignore her—try to forget her.

"Ah, Bart, I'd like you to meet a neighbor of ours, Miss Felicia Simmons. She lives across the street at Number Seventeen."

"Delighted, Miss Simmons," Whitaker said easily as he bowed. "I find it hard to understand why we have never come to meet before, for I have taken rooms at the Kenton's for years."

The three stood chatting for a while. Other of Christopher Wilde's new friends came up, and when Felicia's attention was claimed by the attentive Mr. Whitaker, Christopher had a quiet word with them. By the time the music began again, Felicia's little dance card was filled.

Still, even as she minded her steps, smiled and conversed, her heart was heavy. She should not have come. It had all been a horrible mistake. For what had she to do with the ton anymore, a woman who took lodgers and taught the piano to earn her bread? She should have known better, should have ignored Mr. Livingston's entreaties—should have realized that even one night among the elite would be most unwise. For look what had happened. Her reputation was ruined, and her father's as well. Pray he never learned of it! And no doubt Lady

Bradford would be aghast to be embarrassed like this. She wished she could die.

She saw Christopher Wilde speaking to her godmother, and she wondered what they could be saying. It was just as well for her peace of mind she did not know, for he was asking if he might call on the lady tomorrow, to discuss a matter of great importance. Marjorie Bradford's blue eyes were wide.

"But of *course* you may, sir," she said pertly, smiling up at his rugged, handsome face. "It will be like a breath of Jamaica for me, your visit."

At his querying look, she explained, "Your *tan*, sir. I have not seen its like in months! Shall we say three o'clock in the afternoon? I shall make sure we are *completely* alone then."

Christopher Wilde saw her eyes grow sad for a moment before she shrugged and laughed. As she turned to leave him, she said over her shoulder, "How *many* times I have said those same words before over the years. And how *sad* that I say them now and mean something entirely different. Life is *unfair*, that we must *age*, sir."

Sir Christopher made himself smile a little, even though he thought the lady a complete bubblehead. Of course she was aging. Everyone did. But still, he hoped she would be able to help, for he had learned from Miss Simmons that their hostess was her godmother. Then he wondered why he was going to so much trouble. True, the girl looked very pretty tonight in her soft blue gown, with her hair dressed in curls. But he had been immune to feminine beauty for a number of years, and he had no intention of succumbing to a pretty face now. Still, it was true what he had told her. He did dislike seeing people abused. And Miss Simmons had looked so lost, so uncomfortable, he had found he could do nothing but hurry to her aid. As for Bart's proud beauty, he wished he could have her alone for a few minutes, to give her at the very least the tongue-lashing she deserved for her arrogance and spite.

By the time he came to claim Felicia for the supper dance later, she was very tired. Tired of smiling when she had never felt less like doing so, tired of pretending she did not notice the whispers, hear the muffled laughter as she passed by. Tired of making conversation about things of which she knew nothing.

No, she had not attended Lady F—'s masquerade. No, nor Lord G—'s salon, either. She had not ridden to Richmond, seen the exhibit at the National Gallery, gone to Mrs. M—'s ridotto. Nor had she been invited to the Duke of Embersly's lavish party that people were still talking about. Imagine, inviting eight hundred people, serving a supper of fourteen courses, having not one or two, but three orchestras playing for dancing. And so crowded had been the rooms, a dozen ladies had swooned. Even an elderly gentleman has done so, and he had had to be carried out into the street before he could be revived. The ultimate crush, dear lady, I do assure you, her partner had told her. Felicia smiled, but she was not sorry to have missed that!

If it had not been for the kindness of Sir Christopher, she knew she would have tried to slip away, out a side door for home, and never mind her hackney was not called for till one. But she had to stay, at least until after the supper dance. She couldn't be rude to the gentleman who had come to her rescue, leave him partnerless without a word or a quiet thank you for his timely intervention. She knew that intervention had done little to help the situation, but at least he had tried. And she did owe him a great deal for that.

Six

"YOU HAVE DONE very well," Christopher Wilde told Felicia as he seated her at a table for two some time later.

"You've been watching me?" she asked, surprised.

He nodded as he beckoned to a footman to serve them. "But of course," he said. Felicia noted his voice was almost expressionless and his rugged face, serious.

"But why?" she persisted.

He shrugged. "As I told you, I dislike cruelty. There was no need for the lady, if one can even call her that, to say what she did. It was done with malice. Would you agree with that assessment? I would not like to malign her, if what happened was only an inadvertent slip caused by astonishment."

In spite of herself, Felicia had to smile at his acerbic tones. "No, I do not think you are wrong," she said as the footman put plates of delicacies before them. "She has disliked me from first meeting, although I have no idea why."

Sir Christopher waited until the footman had poured them both a glass of champagne and withdrawn before he said, "Is it true, then? You are letting rooms?"

Felicia put down her fork, her appetite gone. Not even the salmon or the lobster patties could tempt her now. Feeling miserable, she nodded.

Calmly, Wilde picked up her fork and closed her fingers around it. "Eat your supper, Miss Simmons," he ordered. "These infernal affairs go on for hours, and you will need your strength, since I understand your dance card is filled?"

He waited, staring at her until she took a tiny bite. Only then did he begin to eat his own supper. "I shall not inquire as to the reasons you did so, ma'am, so be good enough to take that terrified expression from your face.

"However, I do think it important for you to be seen here, there, and everywhere from now on. Otherwise, people will talk even more. And talking is what the ton does best."

Felicia shook her head. "Oh, no, I couldn't do that," she said quickly. "I—I don't even want to. And indeed, I cannot agree with you, sir. Surely it would be best for me to disappear quietly, return to my former life without further ado. Only then may I salvage what remains of a suddenly tattered reputation. Not that I can ever do that, as well I know."

Busy with a mouthful of lobster, Wilde saw the stubborn set of her jaw, her determined eyes, and knowing that defeat stared him in the face if he tried to change her mind, he made no attempt to do so. Time enough for that later, he thought, remembering his appointment with Lady Bradford on the morrow.

"I see," he said so meekly she gave him a suspicious glance. "Do try the new peas, ma'am. They are outstanding."

Felicia began to eat her supper with more appetite then, although she still felt heartsore. It is a relief that Sir Christopher accepts what I say as truth, she told herself as she sipped the dry, bubbly wine. The ton will never acknowledge me now, in spite of his efforts tonight. Well, I don't care if they do, but I am sorry for Da and most especially for Godmother. Now she will be held up to ridicule, too, after tonight's disaster. It is too bad.

"Were you enjoying the ball before that virulent girl insulted you?" Wilde asked next, interrupting her revery.

"Yes, to my surprise I was," Felicia told him, wondering why she was so at ease with him, and unable to dissemble. Perhaps it was because his unusual gray eyes, so intent on her face, demanded the truth?

"Ordinarily, I do not move in these rarified circles, you see. And I would not have done so tonight if Livingston—all the others—had not insisted on it. I should not have listened to them! But still, it was interesting to observe the ton that my mother had told me so much about, and which, up to tonight, I had never seen for myself."

"You did not make your—I believe it is called—your come-out?" he asked.

Felicia shook her head as the footman poured more wine. "No, I was just about to when my mother fell ill. Then, after her death, I was in mourning of course for a year. And after that, well . . . it was impossible for me to do so."

Her blue eyes dared him to ask more, but he only nodded, as if he understood completely. What an easy man he was to be with, she thought. And how comforting to know he was looking after her still. She felt so safe with him, so protected. He was so big, so strong, so—invincible somehow.

She looked around the crowded supper room as the footmen cleared their plates away and brought them some pastries and comfits. The room held a gay throng, all laughing and conversing over their suppers. The hum of their conversation was a cheerful background to her own intimate conversation with the baronet. Suddenly, her gaze caught that of Cecily Perkins, and she stiffened. The girl was staring at her, looking disdainful, and although Felicia longed to look away, somehow she could not. She saw Miss Perkins lean closer to her partner and begin speaking, her eyes still intent on Felicia's face, and she paled.

"You must not give her the satisfaction of knowing she has upset you," Christopher Wilde said, after he had turned slightly to see who she was looking at. "What a vicious person she is! But I see she has snagged Bart Whitaker and the Earl of Castleton as supper partners. They will not only keep her occupied but defuse her gossip about you as well."

"How can they? She only speaks the truth," Felicia said bitterly.

Wilde selected a pastry for her before he said, "Well, that may be so, but I do assure you, better she regales them than others who would be as eager for scandal as she is herself. Bart's an old friend of mine from my Eton days. He knows my feelings in this matter. The earl is his cousin. I do not think Miss Perkins, even as beauteous as she is, would have secured them as companions else. And I think we have dwelt on this topic long enough.

"Now, allow me to regale you with tales of India while we finish our repast. For some reason, the ladies are thrilled by my carefully edited accounts."

Felicia thought they were probably more thrilled by the man himself, but she did not say so. And sometime later, so exciting were his stories, she had even forgotten her own problems completely when he said, "Now, Miss Simmons, if you are quite through, allow me to take you back to the ballroom. No doubt your next partner is already searching for you."

"I must beg to be excused, sir," Felicia said, misery washing over her as she was reminded of her dilemma. "I prefer to go home."

"That you will not do," he told her as he drew back her chair and offered his arm. "Smile, damn it! I am not a conceited man, but even I must take offense at your woebegone face. Everyone will think I have been a most unsatisfactory partner, or even worse, that I have been boring. That would never do. Kindly remember my reputation, ma'am.

"As for leaving the ball, it is not to be considered. To retreat would give Miss Shrew the victory. Instead, it is important that you continue to appear to be having a wonderful time."

Suddenly he stopped walking, to ask, "How did you intend to get home, ma'am? You have a carriage?"

Once again, Felicia was forced to be honest. "No. There is a hackney called for me at one," she said, wishing she were a better liar, or he, a less persistent man.

He shook his head in exasperation. "A hackney cab? No, no, you cannot leave here in a *hackney cab*! I shall take you up in my own carriage. No, do not attempt to dissuade me, if you please, ma'am. There will be no impropriety. I'll ask Duke Ainsworth and his female cousin to join us. Your reputation will be quite safe."

Felicia could only nod, although she wondered he took such pains when that reputation was no more.

It was very late when she went down the winding stairs to collect her stole. Sir Christopher had gone away to fetch his friend and this Miss Pierce, and Felicia waited alone in the hall, trying not to hear the whispers about her as people came down the stairs and saw her standing there.

She was pretending to be studying a painting on the wall when she heard Mrs. Perkins's gentle voice behind her and was forced to turn. The older woman seemed very distressed, although her daughter, who stood behind her tapping her foot and looking anywhere but at Felicia, was still disdainful.

"My dear Miss Simmons, I must apologize for Cecily's untimely outburst," she said in a sorrowing but dignified voice. "And Cecily is very sorry for it, too, aren't you, dearest?"

In the one fleeting glance Felicia had taken, she had not thought that Cecily looked at all sorry. "Thank you, it is kind of you, Mrs. Perkins," she said evenly.

"Won't you allow us to take you home with us?" the woman persisted.

"I am afraid that won't be possible. I already have an escort. Sir Christopher Wilde is taking me up."

Mrs. Perkins put a deterring hand on her arm. "My dear," she confided, "you shouldn't go with him alone, indeed you should not. It is not at all the thing! You do not have a mother to advise you, but I beg you will allow me to take her place. You see, there has been so much talk already, that . . ."

"Miss Simmons?" the baronet's deep voice inquired. "Are you ready? Here's Mr. Ainsworth and Miss Pierce, you see."

"Certainly, sir," Felicia said, taking his arm before she swept past the indignant beauty who glared at her now, without favoring her with so much as a glance. "Give you good night, Mrs. Perkins."

The four went out to where m'lord's carriage awaited them. Miss Drusilla Pierce was a plain little thing, very shy, and in spite of her own unhappiness, Felicia found herself trying to make her feel more at ease. It appeared Sir Christopher terrified her, for she darted nervous little glances his way every time she spoke. It was left to Mr. Ainsworth who talked in his abbreviated fashion of the gossip he had heard that evening to carry the day, for Sir

Christopher was strangely silent. By the time they reached Number Seventeen Upper Brook Street, Felicia was glad to see Miss Pierce smile at her, but when her cousin suggested the two join him for a walk in the park at the fashionable hour of five, and Miss Pierce was quick to add her entreaties, Felicia denied them.

"I do thank you, and your cousin, sir, for I would have enjoyed it, but it's not possible," she said, thinking in relief of the music lesson she was giving at that hour. "Unfortunately, I have another appointment."

"Some other time, then," Ainsworth persisted. " 'Silla needs a friend. Feeling very much out of things here in town, don't y'know? Be a kindness, 'deed it would."

Felicia managed to escape before a firm appointment could be made. Sir Christopher took her up the steps and waited until Lucie Watts answered his knock. The maid looked astounded when she saw her mistress's escort, but she managed a fairly respectable curtsy.

"Thank you again, sir," Felicia said, giving him her hand.

He held it between his big ones for a moment, staring down at her in the light of the flambeau that had been left for her, to see her safely home.

"You refine on it too much, ma'am," he told her at last. "Believe me, it was my pleasure."

Abruptly he let her go and turned to rejoin his friends. Felicia stepped into the hall and closed the door behind her. When Lucy would have begun to question her, she pointed to the Perkins's door and hurried up the stairs. They would be home soon, and she had no desire to see the girl again this night. Or ever, she thought as she went to her own room, the faithful Lucie close behind. Then she began to wonder what she could possibly say to the maid, who was sure to demand a minute account of the evening so she could regale the others with it in the morning. Felicia realized that as tired as she was, it would be a long time before she could seek her bed and the solace of tears, for she owed at least that much to all of them, so anxious had they been that she have a wonderful time. And then she said a small prayer of thanks that Lucie, unlike Sir Christopher Wilde, would be so easy to deceive, for of course she could not tell her the truth. No, never that.

At three the following afternoon, Sir Christopher was admitted once again to the Bradford town house. All signs of the gala evening before had disappeared by that time, and no one would ever have suspected from the ordered rooms, the silence and lack of clutter, that some two hundred guests had disported themselves there only hours before. Wilde thought rather cynically of the army of servants who had worked through the night to make that possible.

The viscountess received him in a small salon on the ground floor. It was a feminine room, decorated in dainty shades of blue, and Wilde felt very large and ungainly as he took his seat on a chair that he hoped was sturdier than it appeared on its little gilt legs.

"I must admit I am intrigued," Marjorie Bradford said after the butler had served them wine and bowed himself away. "Not that I have *ever* refused a handsome man's request for a meeting, you understand. And I do assure you, there have been many of *those* over the years!

"But why did *you* ask to see me, sir? I declare, I have been wondering about it ever since I woke."

"It concerns your goddaughter.... " Wilde began, only to be interrupted by the impulsive and garrulous Lady Bradford.

"Felicia?" she asked, her china blue eyes wide. "You *met* her then? I was so *delighted* to see her having such a lovely time last evening, dancing every dance, so *well* received by all, and most especially the gentlemen. *Poor* poppet! Her mother's death—her father's illness—no come-out. She has not had an *easy* life."

"Nor is she to have one now," Wilde managed to interject, to stem the lady's flow of chatter. At her questioning glance, he went on, "She was insulted last evening by a very ill-bred young miss named Cecily Perkins. Miss Perkins and her mother are up from the country for the Season, and . . ."

"Yes, I am aware, for I sent Leila Perkins the invitation. She is a lovely woman. I knew her well when we were girls. But you were saying her daughter *insulted* Felicia? How could that be? I find it difficult to imagine, for I do not see how they even came to be *acquainted*. Felicia has lived secluded since her mother's death. And you don't insult *strangers!*"

"Oh, they are acquainted all right," Wilde told her grimly. "You see, the Perkins rented rooms from Miss Simmons for the Season."

Lady Bradford's mouth formed a perfect O of astonishment. "They rented rooms?" she echoed, sounding amazed. "From *Felicia*? Oh, no, no, sir, you *must* be mistaken! My goddaughter would never do anything so awful as *rent rooms!*"

She sounded as horrified at the idea as she would have been to learn that her goddaughter had taken to the stage as an opera dancer or joined the muslin set, and Sir Christopher was forced to hide a grin.

"I do assure you I am not, ma'am," he said, firmly repressing the quiver of amusement he felt. "And

I have rooms myself, right across the street from Miss Simmons's home in Upper Brook Street.

"I take it you do not know her situation well?" he added.

As the viscountess shook her head, too stunned to speak, for which he was exceedingly grateful, he went on, "She appears to be struggling to hold her household together. She does so mostly by her own efforts, from what I can gather. She also gives music lessons and . . ."

"*Music* lessons?" Marjorie Bradford whispered. "Is there no *end* to the unsuitable activities she engages in? Oh dear, where *are* my salts? My vinaigrette? Never mind, I'll just have another glass of wine for a composer, if you would be so *kind* as to pour it for me, sir. Oh dear, *oh dear!*"

"I believe she teaches in order to eat, ma'am, not because she enjoys it," Wilde said as he rose to obey her. "From what I have been able to unearth, the family has fallen on hard times. Her father is ill and his investments in disarray. Surely what Miss Simmons has done, and all by herself, too, is admirable, is it not?"

Lady Bradford didn't look as if she thought any such thing, and he would have continued, except he heard a knock on the door and Lord Bradford came in. The viscount's brows rose slightly when he saw his wife's visitor, and Christopher Wilde was quick to bow.

"Oh, Montmorency, how *glad* I am to see you!" his wife exclaimed. "Here is Sir Christopher Wilde come to see me and tell me the most *appalling* news of . . ."

"Wilde? Not Harry Wilde's son!" her husband interrupted. Coming closer, he peered up into the rugged face of his wife's guest. "You must be the younger one who went out to India with the Company, are you not, sir? I knew your father well. Sad business, his death. I was sorry to miss the funeral.

"Well, well, so you've inherited the title, have you? I must say you don't look a bit like Harry."

"I am said to take after my mother's side, sir," Wilde told him.

"Indeed. Still, there is a look of Harry about you," Lord Bradford mused. "It's the eyes, I think, the set of your jaw. Stubborn man, Harry. Determined to get his own way. But I expect you know that well, don't you? You were his son, after all. And it appears to me, you've much the same traits as my old friend."

The two smiled at each other as they shook hands. Wilde was delighted the man had come in. He appeared much the more astute of the pair, and he himself had been making heavy weather of it with Lady Bradford.

"Montmorency, *do* stop blathering on and *on* about this Harry!" that lady demanded, her voice stern. "Sir Christopher has the most *awful* news! I *tremble* to think what you will make of it. I, myself, am so *shocked* I cannot credit it even now. For surely . . ."

"What news?" Lord Bradford demanded as he took a seat and waved Wilde back to his own.

Marjorie Bradford looked pleadingly at her visitor, and he began to explain, telling Lord Bradford just what he had his wife. Throughout the telling, the viscount looked first amazed, then perturbed, and finally thoughtful. His wife occupied herself by gulping her wine and then twisting her handkerchief in nervous fingers.

"Hard to believe," m'lord said when Wilde fell silent at last. "Of course, I did not know Reginald Simmons well, but from all accounts I've heard, he was a well-liked man. And his wife was a darling. Quite the dear friend of Marjorie's she was, which accounts for her naming my wife godmother, you know. But Simmons! Oh, I knew he was in financial difficulty some time ago, with debt and bad loans, but I had no idea things had come to such a pass."

"I've heard he is still owed a considerable amount of money," Wilde told them. "I wonder if it would be possible to discover the names of his debtors? Perhaps they could be made to, er, *realize* that their obligations, however ancient they might be, must be repaid at last? It would help the family so."

Lord Bradford studied his stubborn jaw, those determined eyes for a moment before he nodded. "Yes, I see what you're driving at, sir. But how could we find out who they are? No one who owes him money is about to come forward now. It would not put them in a good light, forgetting an honorable commitment when it is common knowledge their benefactor has been ill for years."

"They must be forced to do so," Wilde said grimly.

Lord Bradford was suddenly glad he was not one of Reginald Simmons's debtors. Wilde was very unlike your usual sprig of fashion on the town. Indeed, he looked like he could handle a problem of any magnitude, competently and firmly.

"But—but what good will *that* do?" Lady Bradford wailed. "After what was brought to light last evening, Felicia's reputation is ruined anyway. The whole *family's* reputation is ruined!"

"Perhaps if you would be so good as to take her up, ma'am?" Wilde said. "Let everyone see that you do not intend to desert her in her troubles. . . . "

The viscountess looked very doubtful of such a course of action and loath to comply, and he added, "For surely, with your impeccable credentials, your high standing in Society, others might be induced to follow your lead."

"No need to empty the butter boat over her, my

boy," Lord Bradford said wryly. "You're right, though." He gave his wife a nod that looked very much an order to Christopher Wilde. "We shall both do so. And I assure you I'll do what I can to discover Simmons's debtors. Perhaps if I were to call on him? Ask him outright? I understand his mind wanders these days, but he must have some lucid moments. . . . "

"Oh dear, oh *dear*! *Mental* illness as well!" Lady Bradford moaned from behind her handkerchief.

"I must warn you, ma'am, that Miss Simmons has every intention of disappearing from polite society, if she can," Wilde told her. "You will have to be very firm with her. Insist."

"She will be," the lady's fond husband said, his voice hard. "Poor little girl. Lodgers, piano lessons! If I had only known. . . . "

Sir Christopher rose then and bowed. "I have taken up too much of your time, ma'am, sir," he said. "But be sure I shall be doing whatever I can to help as well. I've alerted all my acquaintances in town of the situation, which is why Miss Simmons was never without a partner last evening. And they can ask their parents if they remember any men who borrowed money from Miss Simmons's father. Chivalry is not dead. No, indeed.

"Perhaps I might call here in a week or so, so we could compare notes?"

After Lord Bradford agreed, shook his hand again, and thanked him, Sir Christopher went away.

For a moment, there was only silence in the blue salon. Then Lady Bradford said, "*Whatever* were you thinking of, my dear? I don't see how *anything* we might do could make this right! And will we not be tarred with the same brush if we go to Felicia's assistance? It is not that I do not *care* for the girl, indeed, I will always love her, no matter what she has done, but ... but who would *marry* her now? In this case ..."

"In this case, you will take her here, there, and everywhere. And I suggest you go shopping early tomorrow morning for her birthday gift. Something to wear, I think. Something fashionable and very expensive," her husband told her sternly. "But you will know what would be most appropriate.

"And right now you will send a note to your goddaughter, inviting her to drive with us in the park tomorrow afternoon. Do not take 'no' for an answer. And Marjorie," he added as he rose to leave, "you will behave to her as if you have heard nothing of what she has been doing. For in truth she is blameless. She only did what she was forced to do, to survive and care for her father. Her actions can't tarnish her in the eyes of anyone but a few old sticklers, too proud and hidebound to accept the situation. We will not regard them."

Pausing by the door, he said, "Still, I have to wonder why Harry Wilde's boy is so interested in Felicia, so concerned for her, don't you? Even with his remark about chivalry, I find it very singular. Unless, of course, your worries that Felicia will never find a husband are very far from the mark."

Lord Bradford saw his wife's distraught face brighten a little, noticed the way she put her head to one side and looked beyond him, her customary habit whenever she took the trouble to think, and smiling to himself, he went away to allow her the solitude she needed in order to do so.

Seven

FELICIA FOUND HER godmother's note waiting for her when she returned from her teaching chores that same afternoon. When she saw the scribbled handwriting, she frowned a little. Had Lady Bradford heard the gossip? Was she writing to cut the connection? She herself wouldn't be at all surprised if that were the case.

Frowning still, she rubbed her forehead. She had had the headache all day, for she had not slept well in spite of the late hour she had gone to bed. And today had been so horrible she could hardly wait for it to be over.

First, Cecily Perkins had screamed at her maid so loudly that Reginald Simmons had heard her and become alarmed, sure that thieves and rapists had invaded the premises. It had taken all of Felicia's and Livingston's skill to calm him and assure him it was only a noisy Billingsgate wench selling fish and she would soon be gone.

And then, when blessed silence had prevailed again, Felicia had gone down to the kitchen to discover Gladys in tears, turned off without a reference. She was being soothed by both Lucie and Mrs. Doherty, while the Perkins's footman stood by with a frown on his generally good-natured face.

"It's not that I mind leaving her employ a bit, Miss," Gladys said when she stopped crying at last. "An' I know Mrs. Perkins will give me a character, for she whispered she would. But—but the things Miss Cecily called me! The things she said!"

"But why would she turn you off?" Felicia asked.

"It was all 'cause of the lace," Gladys admitted. As Felicia looked distressed, she hastened to add, "Now don't you regard that, Miss! She *gave* me the lace, an' it was mine to do with as I chose. I guess it was just the shock of seeing it on your gown that made her so angry. That, and realizing I'd been helping you. She couldn't abide *that*, the nasty thing!

"I'll have to find a new position. The only problem is she told me to pack my things and leave today. An'—an' I don't rightly know where to go. I've never been to London before, an' I don't have much money."

"You're not to worry about that," Felicia told her. "Of course you will stay with us while you look; we'll be happy to have you, after all you've done for me. Lucie, you show Gladys where she will sleep."

Gladys got up from the table all in a rush, to curtsy deeply. "Oh, Miss, that's good of ye, 'deed it is!" she said. "An' I promise to help about the house-like for my keep."

"We'll see," Felicia told her, a little embarrassed by her fervor.

Then at noon there had been those three floral tributes delivered for her. She had been admiring them in the hall when Miss Perkins and her mother left their rooms, and Cecily Perkins's eyes had narrowed at the lavish bouquet from Sir Christopher, the nosegay of rosebuds from Bartholomew Whitaker, and the huge sheaf of gladiola from Marmaduke Ainsworth. Felicia thought her sniff as she swept out the front door mocked both her and the flowers, and she paled at the insult. If she had but known it, Miss Perkins was incensed. She had only had one small posy of violets that morning, from a very poor young man whom she cared nothing at all about, and she was jealous.

And now, to set the final seal on the miserable day, here was this note from Lady Bradford. Felicia sighed as she opened it and smoothed the sheet. As she read, her eyes widened and she began to shake her head. Instead of a stiff, indignant missive, full of fury at being hoaxed, here was a loving invitation!

Oh, no, she thought, I can't! I simply can't drive in the park with them. If only she had another lesson at five tomorrow, but unfortunately, she did not. Still, she would have to think of some excuse, for it was obvious Lady Bradford could not have heard the gossip. But when she did . . . !

Frowning in thought, she went up to her room. An hour later she had what she considered an excellent reply ready to deliver. In it, she thanked her godmother profusely for the wonderful party and her kind invitation, but told her that her father was so unwell, she did not like to leave him for even an hour.

Livingston agreed to deliver the note for her, and Felicia went to keep her father company in his absence. The only bright spot in the day, as far as she was concerned, was that his mind was not wandering, and they talked quite sensibly of the past. The past was the only thing of interest to Reginald Simmons now.

When the valet returned some time later, he had another note to hand, and Felicia avoided his gaze as she opened it with a heavy heart.

"My dear child, do not be *absurd*," Lady Bradford began in her breathless way. "The servant who delivered your note assures me *he* will be happy to sit with your father while you are out driving. That being the case, I will not *allow* you to refuse. Montmorency and I will take you up at five. Be ready, now!"

"Livingston, how *could* you?" Felicia cried. "You knew I did not care to go, and . . ."

"That I didn't, Miss," the valet said, looking carefully past her shoulder. "How could I when you never said so? And it seems to me to be very ungenteel of you to be refusing the viscountess, when she is only being kind. And after you had such a wonderful time at her ball, as you told us all you did."

When Felicia shook her head and went away, Livingston permitted himself a little smile. Seeing his master was occupied reading one of his favorite books, he took the opportunity to slip down to the kitchen to inform the others of the treat in store for their mistress.

"Wot a good thing ye got turned off, Glad," Lucie Watts said. "I don't know as if I could o' finished the new carriage dress in time by myself. But if we both work hard, it'll be done. Couldn't bear it, I couldn't, if Miss Felicia had to go out in that old gray muslin o' 'ers."

"Has she a hat?" Gladys asked, opening her sewing box as Lucie ran to get the dress so they could begin immediately.

"Now that's a problem, that is," Lucie said, frowning. "She's only got the one. Mayhap we could do something with ribbons? Some tulle? But I don't rightly know if I've time ter get ter the market stalls. Ah well, we'll have ter see how it goes this evening. Might just be able ter do it, if we work fast!"

"She's so pretty, no one's goin' ter be lookin' at 'er *'at*," Joe volunteered as Mrs. Doherty brought more working candles to the table. Both Gladys and

Lucie withered him with a glance for his ignorance, and he subsided.

At the far end of the table, George sat listening beside Jacqueline, his round dark eyes intent. Then he leaned toward her and whispered behind his pudgy little hand. Jacqueline, who had looked scornful at first, grew thoughtful as he whispered, and when he was done, gave him a curt nod. The dislike she had for George was still there, but still, she had to admit it was more fun now that there was someone nearer her own age in residence. At least George was someone to talk to. The adults in the household so often seemed to forget she was even there. But George always sought her out and sat beside her, or told her jokes or things he had seen on the streets. If she hadn't resented him for coming in the first place, Jacqueline told herself she might even have learned to like him.

Felicia was sure she was going to spend another sleepless night, but to her surprise, she dropped off to sleep as soon as she closed her eyes, and when she woke the next morning, she was much refreshed. She lay quietly for a long time, trying to think what she was to do, and at last, she nodded to herself, threw back the covers, and went to the dressing room to wash.

There was no help for it, she told herself as she cleaned her teeth. She would have to confess everything to Lady Bradford. Pray she would not be too late! For surely, a full penitent confession coming from her own lips would be preferable to a gossip's nasty, distorted account. To that end, she intended to walk to Berkeley Square quite an hour before the appointed time to beg a private interview with the lady. And if the viscountess did not care to take her up in her carriage later, that would be no surprise, Felicia thought bitterly as she shrugged into her chemise and an old gown and did her hair up in its customary chignon.

She would spend the morning with Jacqueline and George, working on their lessons and hearing Jacqueline sing. Later she would clean the library. Oh yes, she would keep herself very busy so she didn't have time to think of the unpleasantness the afternoon was sure to bring.

When Lucie arrived with her morning chocolate, looking a little heavy-eyed, she also carried a new gown, and nothing would do but for Felicia to try it on for a fitting there and then. And when she tried to protest, Lucie wouldn't listen to her.

"Thinkin' o' wearin' that old muslin fer yer drive in the park, wuz ye?" she demanded, holding out the gown and shaking it for emphasis. "O' all things! An' ye, wot's been gettin' flowers an' notes ever since the ball—well! Come on now, try on the dress, do! Me an' Glad has been workin' ever so 'ard on it, so it'd be ready. An' I intend ter put a new trim on yer 'at as well."

Felicia shrugged. What was the use, she asked herself as she slipped into the gown. She must have told entirely too good a story about her evening at the ball, for everyone, from Livingston right down to Lucie, thought she was about to be taken up by Society with a vengeance. What a shame for them, with their great expectations, when that would never come to pass.

Still, she had to admit the carriage dress was impressive. Made of a deep green fabric, it sported gold buttons and a saucy black braid, and it fit her slim form to perfection.

"Now I'll be busy with the 'at, but Glad will do yer 'air in curls this afternoon, Miss," Lucie told her as she bundled up the gown and prepared to leave. "Ye jess ring fer 'er when ye want ter get dressed. That good with an iron she is! I can't 'old a candle ter 'er!"

Felicia looked up at the ceiling for a moment after the maid ran away, then smiled a little in resignation. But perhaps the new gown would give her courage when she confronted Lady Marjorie Bradford?

By four o'clock, she was walking toward Berkeley Square, accompanied by a sedate Gladys who had insisted on coming along. Gladys looked the complete and proper lady's maid in her black dress and shawl. And although she had said it would have been better for Miss to have a footman in attendance, she would have to do the trick. For as willing as Melvin was to oblige, it wouldn't do him a bit of good if Miss Cecily saw him. Likely to be turned off, too, he would.

To Felicia's surprise, she did attract a number of admiring glances, but that, she told herself as Gladys fixed the gentlemen with a baleful glance, was only because of her new gown, her becoming hairdo, and the tulle and ribbons that now adorned her plain old hat.

She was admitted to Lady Bradford's boudoir, where she found that lady deep in her toilette.

"Dear child!" Marjorie Bradford chided as she entered the room and curtsied. "Didn't I make it *clear* we would pick you up in Upper Brook Street? How *remiss* of me, when there was no need for you to *trudge* all the way over here. But how *smart* you look! Is that a new gown? And, Finnegan, do observe Miss Simmons's *marvelous* complexion. I am trying very hard not to *hate* you for it, dearest. Finnegan discovered another gray hair this morning, and I *swear* I have a new wrinkle every day. Tch, tch!"

Felicia realized she would not have a chance to tell her godmother anything until the maid fussing around her had finished, declared herself satisfied, and gone away, so she nodded as she took a seat out of the way.

"Well, your gown is very becoming. And I have a surprise for you as well, for your *birthday*. But we will get to that later. Tell me, did you enjoy the ball? And how many bouquets did you receive afterward, and *who* were they from?"

Felicia was forced to chat of the party and her tributes. It seemed an endless time before the maid curtsied and left them.

As the door closed behind her, Felicia took a deep breath. "Ma'am?" she said to Lady Bradford's back, where she was posing before the pier glass admiring her ensemble and adjusting her hat. "I—I have something I must tell you before we go out. . . . "

"Oh, no, no, we don't have time for *that*!" her godmother said gaily. "Montmorency becomes so *angry* if I keep the horses standing. We must go and join him *at once*!"

"Please, ma'am," Felicia begged, her eyes pleading. "It will only take a moment, I promise you."

As the viscountess reluctantly sat down across from her, Felicia began to tell her the true state of affairs, quickly, before she could lose her courage. She thought the lady looked suitably horrified by the tale, and she did not wonder she never even interrupted it. No doubt she was speechless with horror, she thought bleakly.

"So you see, it really will not do for you to take me driving today, ma'am," she concluded. "Everyone in Society must know my situation now, and no doubt they are all laughing at me, scorning me, too. And I could not bear to bring you into my problems, dear ma'am! Indeed, I should never have accepted your kind invitation to the ball, for just see where it has brought me."

Marjorie Bradford might have had a flighty, shallow soul, but she was kind for all that, and when she saw the misery deep in Felicia's blue eyes, she rose at once to hug her. "Oh, my dearest child, never *say* so!" she protested. "I am sure it is nowhere *near* as bad as you think. For didn't you tell me you received flowers from not one but *three* gentlemen the following day? And surely *they* must have heard the gossip! I only wonder I did not. But perhaps my friends put as little credence in it as I do. But it is *not* a disaster, my dear Felicia. Of course you *must* get rid of the Perkins *at once*; tell them to find rooms elsewhere. It would not do at *all* to continue renting the rooms. My, no!"

Felicia swallowed a hasty refusal. She had not mentioned how desperate she was for money, how these past few weeks of a regular income had lessened the heavy burden she struggled under. She could not let the Perkins leave. For even if she did, she would be forced to set the agent to finding her other lodgers. But Lady Bradford had no idea what a pass she had come to in the three years since her mother's death. No idea of her father's illness, his inability to help her, or the poverty she lived in now. And she was just proud enough to keep that information to herself. The lady might have offered her money if she knew, and Felicia would never be able to accept. As her goddaughter, the occasional gift was unexceptional, but she was not a relative of Marjorie Bradford—or her husband.

"Now then, we really must *dash*, dear," the viscountess said, urging her to the door. "Montmorency will be wondering where we are, and fretting, too, no doubt. Although," she added as they started down the stairs arm in arm, "he should be used to it by now. I don't think I have ever been on time for *anything*. Why, I was almost an hour late to our *wedding*!"

Felicia forced herself to smile as she curtsied to

the dignified Lord Bradford, who was indeed waiting patiently for them in the hall.

"How lovely you look, Felicia," he said. "And a drive is just the thing to put some roses in your cheeks. I pride myself on my team, y'know. Prime goers! But you'll see.

"Marjorie, do stop fussing over your hat," he ordered his wife as she stood before a large mirror. "You look as perfect as you always do."

The lady beamed her pleasure as she allowed her husband to help her down the steps to where a shiny black landau waited. The coachman and groom wore the Bradford livery of forest green and gold, and Felicia saw the upholstery of the landau was striped in the same colors. How grand, she thought as she climbed to her seat beside her godmother. Lord Bradford took the seat facing back and gave his coachman the order to start.

Felicia had not driven in the park since she had been a little girl, and today it seemed very crowded to her with all manner of smart carriages, numerous riders, and throngs of strollers. She concentrated on keeping a bright smile pinned to her face, sitting as tall and straight as she could manage it all the while. But still she wondered how many people had seen her and were once again telling each other of her plight. And how unworthy she was of the Lady Bradford's patronage.

"Oh, *there's* the Duchess of Kyle! Do pull *up*, Henry!" that lady ordered the coachman. "Lillian, my dear, how *nice* to see you! And your pretty daughters as well. You *do* remember Felicia Simmons, do you not?"

Felicia steeled herself for a distant nod, or, even worse, no acknowledgment at all. To her great surprise, the duchess smiled at her, her daughters as well. "I am so glad to come upon you this way, Miss Simmons," she said in her dry way. "I have been meaning to ask you to favor us by attending a small party I am giving for Sylvia on June fourteenth. Nothing elaborate—just dinner and a dance for some of the younger set."

Lady Bradford clapped her hands. "How *splendid*! Of course you will be *delighted* to go, won't you Felicia?"

With several pair of eyes staring at her so intently, Felicia could do nothing but agree. After a few more minutes, Lord Bradford reminded the ladies of the teams, and farewells were said. And as the carriages drove off in opposite directions, Marjorie Bradford winked at her husband, taking care Felicia did not see. Her calls on her friends were already beginning to bear fruit.

By the time they had made a complete circuit of the park, Felicia had another invitation to a tea, from a lady who had known her mother. Then she saw Sir Christopher Wilde wave to them from where he was walking with another gentleman, and she wondered what was to happen next. She was feeling rather bemused, for it seemed to her, no matter how carefully she observed people, that there were no reservations in their eyes, their manner, or their conversation. But surely the gossip had gone around by this time. Surely they could not all be so accepting! She felt as if she were in a dream.

"Sir *Christopher*!" Lady Bradford exclaimed. "What a *nice* young man you were to send me flowers after the ball!"

The tall, still-tanned gentleman waved away her compliment. "Allow me to introduce Jaspar Howland, Earl Castleton, ma'am, sir. Lord and Lady Bradford, m'lord. I believe you have already met Miss Simmons?"

The earl was soon deep in a conversation with Lady Bradford, who it appeared had once known a distant relative of his. They were watched by an amused Lord Bradford while Felicia found herself staring down into Sir Christopher's silvery gray eyes, and wondering why she shivered a little as she did so.

"Nice day for a drive, isn't it?" he asked abruptly. "I trust you might also be persuaded to walk someday soon with Duke Ainsworth and his cousin Drusilla? She does so admire you. And, as Duke said, it would be a kindness, for she's the shyest little thing I think I've ever seen."

"She is terrified of you," Felicia said before she thought.

His auburn brows rose. "Terrified? Of me? Are you sure? But why? It seems a very strong emotion when I don't think I've exchanged more than a few words with the girl. Innocuous ones at that. And I did dance with her once at the soiree Duke's mother gave to introduce her to Society. Had to. Duke insisted. And yet I *terrify* her? Surely you are mistaken."

"No, I'm not. As I myself have discovered, you have a rather *forceful* personality, sir," Felicia said, stung to honesty.

He grinned at her then, and Felicia thought he looked a great deal more approachable, even younger and handsomer, as he did so. But perhaps he had not favored Miss Pierce with that grin?

"How fortunate you don't appear to have any fears of me, ma'am," he said next. "That would never do, for I intend to spend a great deal of time in your company."

He waited, but when Felicia could think of nothing acceptable to reply to such an arrogant statement, he only smiled more broadly.

"Delighted to have seen you again, m'lady, m'lord," he said as he turned to rescue the hapless Earl Castleton. Lady Bradford seemed intent on inquiring for his entire family tree. "Miss Simmons, give you good-day."

Felicia nodded, but she did not smile. Sir Christopher seemed much more lighthearted this afternoon, and she wondered why. And she wondered why Lady Bradford seemed so complacent and smug. She would have been absolutely astounded to discover their reasons, never having a clue that Sir Christopher was pleased her godmother was obeying her husband with such a vengeance, while Lady Bradford was playing matchmaker.

When Lord Bradford would have ordered the coachman to drive her home to Upper Brook Street later, Felicia begged him to give her a moment of his time alone first. And although he suddenly looked as foreboding as only he could, he agreed to it.

"Yes, *do* come back with us to the Square, dear child," Lady Bradford said. "For you know, I *quite* forgot to give you your birthday gifts. Such a *featherhead* I am sometimes! We'll send you home in the carriage later."

While she went upstairs to remove her hat and fetch the gifts she had mentioned, Felicia told the viscount what she had told his wife. She *must* be dreaming, she thought, when that gentleman made so little of her tale. Only, he told her, she must act as if nothing was out of the ordinary.

"You see, Felicia, people do dislike spite in another. And this Miss Perkins, although I understand she is a beauty of no small degree, has behaved viciously to you. But if you ignore her, act the lady you are, the gossip will soon disappear.

"Aren't I right, Marjorie?" he added, as the viscountess came in followed by her maid bearing several large parcels.

"I didn't hear a *word* you said, Montmorency, but you are *always* right," that lady told him with a smile. "Sometimes I wish you were not quite so *infallible*, but there! No one can have *everything*."

Before he could ask about that questionable remark, she told the maid to put the packages down on a table, then excused her.

"Do open them at *once*, Felicia," she commanded, as she took a seat beside her husband. "Oh, I *do* hope you will be pleased with my choices!"

Obediently, Felicia pulled the ribbon from the first box. It held a stunning ball gown of gold brocade. The other boxes contained two other gowns, pairs of gloves, even reticules.

"But—but this is far too much," she protested at last from where she sat surrounded by tissue paper and gifts. "Really, ma'am, everything is just beautiful, but I cannot accept such largesse, indeed, I can't!"

"But if you don't you will hurt my feelings *dreadfully*," the viscountess told her, looking doleful. "I had such *fun* shopping for you."

"My dear Felicia, you are like the daughter we never had," Lord Bradford continued. "You must allow us the pleasure of treating you as if you were ours indeed." He waited until she nodded, still looking perturbed, before he added, "And to seal the bargain, here is a special gift, just from me to you."

He handed her a small blue velvet box, as his wife inquired with some excitement what it might be. "For you never told *me*, Montmorency, that you were going to do something, *too*! It is not like you to be so *secretive*! Why, I can't recall a time . . ."

As Felicia opened the box, the lady's high, breathless voice faded from her ears. Her eyes filled with tears as a pair of diamond ear bobs and a diamond pendant on a fine gold chain seemed to wink up at her from their bed of satin.

Suddenly those tears overflowed and ran down her cheeks unchecked.

"Now, now, my dear, you must not *cry!*" the viscountess exclaimed. "Oh, how lovely the jewels are! Just *perfect* for a young lady! But Montmorency has such *exquisite* taste. There now, do dry your eyes—you have a handkerchief?—and thank him *properly.*"

Felicia hastened to do as she was bade. When she looked up and saw Lord Bradford gravely regarding her, she made herself rise and go to him, to kiss his cheek and hug him. "Indeed, I do not know what to say, sir, except you are too good. Both of you are too good to me."

"Pishtosh!" her godmother said as she tossed her head. "This is just the beginning, dearest child. We shall go shopping *soon* to get you some *hats* as well. I saw one today that I thought you would look like an angel in, but hats, you know, must be tried on. . . ."

"Oh, no, ma'am, not another thing!" Felicia said. She sounded so distraught that Lord Bradford intervened before his impulsive wife could argue the point.

"Let me help you pack all this up, Felicia. One of the footmen will take it out to the carriage," he said briskly. "I am looking forward to having you dine with us soon, wearing my gift.

"Marjorie, where's the mate to this glove?"

A few minutes later, a bemused Felicia Simmons sat surrounded by parcels in the Bradford's smart landau, being conveyed home in solitary splendor. She clutched her reticule tightly to keep the new diamond set safe.

As she did so, she told herself over and over that this was not right! But she had not known any way to refuse the gifts without hurting their feelings. And they had been so kind, ignoring the awful news she had brought, and never censuring her at all, which she was sure they had every right to do.

As she stepped down before Number Seventeen on the groom's arm, Felicia told herself she would not be surprised to discover this whole afternoon was only a dream after all, although she couldn't help hoping, deep down inside, that if it were, she would never, ever wake up.

Eight

*F*ROM HIS WINDOWS across the way, Christopher Wilde saw Miss Simmons come home that afternoon, and he grinned when he observed the number of parcels the groom carried in the door for her. Lady Bradford was obviously doing her part with more than mere compliance to a husband's wishes, and nothing could be better, he thought as he went to his desk.

Now, he intended to write a note to Miss Felicia Simmons, inviting her to walk with him, and with Duke and the terrified Miss Pierce, on the morrow. And if she refused, he told himself, he would keep on asking until she had to accept. After all, she herself had told him how forceful he was, hadn't she? She would discover just how much in short order.

Ted Bowers took the note across the street for him and waited for the reply. Wilde knew his man had tried to strike up an acquaintance with the scarred sailor over there, but so far had had little success. The sailor did not frequent any pubs that Bowers could discover, and when he did leave the house, he was generally accompanied by the brassy blond woman. The most Bowers had been able to accomplish was a brief chat about the weather, and when he had tried to carry that further and had asked Griffen about the ships he had served on, he had won only a black scowl and an abrupt leave-taking. It seemed the former sailor was not the matey type.

With Miss Simmons's civil acceptance to savor, Sir Christopher went out to the theater that evening with a party of friends. The play was excellent and the acting superb, but even though he enjoyed it, Miss Simmons's face seemed to come to his mind more often than not. He hoped he could help her, even as he wondered why he bothered. He had never played the gallant knight to a woman before. It was most unlike him, this current concern.

Coming home alone later, he considered the day just past, over a nightcap before he went to bed.

He had spent his time making calls on his friends and their parents, to enlist their aid in his search for Reginald Simmons's debtors. He hadn't had any luck, but he told himself he would not be discouraged. It had all happened a long time ago. People needed time to search their memories.

He had had one victory, however. Bartholomew Whitaker had sent him to a crusty old great-uncle of his, and once that gentleman had had a second glass of port, his taciturnity had turned into a positive river of chatter about London in years past. He had known Reginald Simmons, too, and some of his friends, and Wilde had come away from his house with a list of names to investigate. He was so pleased with his success, he did not even mind the way his ears were still ringing from listening to a man with almost total recall, and a goodly number of years in his basket in which to reminisce.

Sir Christopher was a little concerned, however, about how he was to approach these people. He could call on them, of course, send in his card—hope they would receive him. But when they did, how was he to handle it? One could not ask a stranger point blank if he owed another man money!

He rose to pace the room. No, that wouldn't work, for they were sure, one and all, to deny it. Perhaps if he were to watch them carefully when he accused them, to see if they looked ashamed or conscious? Well, he would have to think of this further, he thought as he yawned and went to the window to check the weather.

It was a fine night, with only a little moonlight showing every now and then as the racing clouds overhead parted. Upper Brook Street was quiet, for it was very late. Then he saw something move across the way, and he bent closer to the pane. Was it a stray cat, perhaps?

The clouds relented then, and he was astounded to see two little figures moving away from Number Seventeen, so cautiously he was immediately suspicious. One of them looked up at the moon for a moment and scowled. Although she was dressed in boy's clothes tonight, he recognized the little girl he had seen staring out into the street. Her companion was shorter and difficult to make out, even in the moonlight. Suddenly Wilde grinned. Of course! He had seen a little black boy there as well, lately. But where were such young children going at this time of night?

As they started down the street, he made up his mind to follow them. And to be on the safe side, he thrust a dagger into his belt and checked to make sure his pistol was primed and loaded.

The children led him on a merry chase through town, soon leaving the better streets and squares behind, to head for the river and a section of London that few honest people dared to frequent even in the daylight. Sir Christopher was not intimidated. He had seen worse in India and China. Much worse.

The way they took led through a warren of tall, mean tenements and stinking alleys, but he noted they seemed to know exactly where they were going. More than once, when they heard a band of men approaching, they ducked into an alley, or if no alley was handy, a doorway. Sir Christopher followed their example on the other side of the street, and from where he was stationed, he could barely make them out. They had huddled low on the sill, looking for all the world like nothing more than a pile of rags. It was an unusual talent to possess, this ability to disappear so completely, but he could see how invaluable it was in this particular neighborhood. Sometimes they flitted past a low, noisy tavern, still filled with drinkers and revelers even at this hour. Once, he saw the little black boy stoop over a recumbant figure as if to rob it, until the girl tugged him away.

Wilde was beginning to wonder if they would ever reach their destination, when they came to a halt before a house in a somewhat better neighborhood that he recognized. His eyes narrowed, and his mouth grew grim as he saw the two stop to converse. A line of hackneys waited before the house, and the children scurried down an alley beside it to the back. Cautiously and silently, Wilde followed.

When he saw them again, the little black boy was trying to pry a cellar window open. All right, Wilde told himself, enough is enough. He marched forward and grasped the boy by the arm. Out of the corner of his eye, he saw the girl take a knife from her pocket, and he knocked it out of her hand and sent it spinning away in the darkness. Deprived of her weapon, she began to kick and pummel him, while the boy struggled harder than Wilde would have thought possible for one his age and size. What was unusual about the whole thing, almost eerie, was that both of them fought without making a sound.

"Stop!" he commanded. "Miss Simmons will be very disturbed to learn where you have been, now won't she? What on earth do you think you are doing here?"

The two stopped fighting him to stare, their eyes huge in their small faces.

"Ya knows Missus?" the boy asked in a thin, piping voice.

Wilde nodded, but he did not release the child as he kept an eye on his companion. She had moved away from him, but she was not trying to get away.

"Please don't tell her we were here, sir," she begged, her eyes pleading. "She wouldn't like it at all, but—but we had ter come!"

"Here?" Wilde asked, one brow elevated in disbelief.

"Here," she said sullenly.

"Why?" he asked.

He waited, but no more information was forthcoming, and at last he shrugged. "Very well. You won't tell me. We'll see what you have to say to Miss Simmons, shall we? Come along!"

For a moment, he thought they might protest, and he swept his evening cape back so they could see his pistol and dagger. As resignation came into their eyes, he nodded. "Very wise of you, I'm sure," he said dryly. "I'm not only bigger and stronger and armed, I can also outrace you if you should think of trying to escape."

He marched both of them around to the front of the house where the hackneys waited. Bundling the children into one of them, he ordered the driver to take them to Upper Brook Street. The journey was accomplished in complete silence, his two young companions staring straight ahead, looking as if there was nothing anyone could do to drag their secret from them. Sir Christopher was more than annoyed with them, he was furious. Every time he thought of that knife he itched to spank the little girl. Hard.

After he had paid off the cab, he hustled his charges around to the back of Number Seventeen to pound on the door there. He could see a light through a crack in the curtains, so he was not surprised when the blond woman opened the door so promptly to peer through the opening that was all a sturdy metal chain allowed.

Her eyes widened when she saw him standing there, looking so ferocious she took an involuntary step backward. And such was the power of his gaze, it wasn't until George squirmed a little that she even noticed the two children he held firmly by the scruff of their necks.

"Let me in!" Wilde said savagely. Lucie hurried to obey.

Once inside the big kitchen, he released the children. They were quick to scurry away from him to the safety of the other side of the deal table.

"I'm Sir Christopher Wilde," he told Lucie, ignoring them. "You will fetch Miss Simmons to me at once."

As Lucie hesitated, still staring at him open-mouthed, he snarled, "*At once*, do you hear?"

"But it's almost four in the morning, sir," she croaked from a dry throat. "Miss Felicia's fast asleep!"

"Wake her then, for I'll either see her, or I'll take these two imps of Satan to the Watch. Well, which is it to be?"

Lucie wrung her hands. Troubled by another toothache, she had come down to make herself a hot cup of tea, liberally laced with some of Joe's rum. Now she wished she were still tossing in her attic bed.

But she saw she had little choice. This man seemed quite capable of dragging the children off, and taking her along with them, too. And he looked so angry, he might well decide to invade the upper floors in search of Miss Felicia, and that would never do. Sighing, she went up the stairs, wondering where the children had been. Jacqueline was forbidden to leave the house after dark, and to her knowledge had never done so before. As for George, well, Lucie had never had an inkling what went on in his brain, or even where he spent his time when he was not at home.

Below, Christopher Wilde leaned against the big dresser that almost filled one end of the kitchen, never taking his eyes from the children who stared back at him, terror in their eyes. And as he watched, tears began to fall down the boy's pudgy face, although he did not make a sound. Unfortunately for George, Sir Christopher was not a man much moved by childish tears, especially in this instance.

It was so quiet, they all heard Miss Felicia's voice asking questions as she made her way down the flight and Lucie's carpet slippers slapping on the stairs behind her.

When she entered the kitchen, Felicia's gaze went immediately to the big man who leaned so casually at his ease against the dresser. She thought he looked livid, and she felt a quiver of alarm. Then her cheeks turned pink as she saw him inspect her, slowly, from head to toe, and one hand crept to the neck of her dressing gown as if to make sure it was completely closed.

"What has happened, sir?" she asked in as dignified a manner as she could when clad in nothing but her nightrobe and gown, and with her hair loose and her feet bare. "Why do you come here at this hour?"

"I come because earlier, I noticed these two brats sneaking from the house. Curious as to where they might be going, I followed them. And I do assure you, madam, that where they went was no place for children.

"I have no idea of your relationship to them, but since they appear to live here, you must be in charge of them. And I tell you, you have not been doing a very good job caring for them if you allow them to go to the worst part of London at this hour of night. For they went to Seven Dials!"

Felicia tried to look away from his accusing eyes. In his anger they seemed to burn with almost fiery light, and she had the strangest feeling she could easily get singed by that light.

"They would not tell me what they were planning to do there, nor why they had come, and even before I could tax them with it, that one," he said, pointing a stern finger at Jacqueline, "had the temerity to try and attack me with a knife. Fine doings for a child, is it not?

"Furthermore, the house they were attempting to break into is one of London's most infamous brothels. Yes, well you may stare, madam. A brothel!"

"Jacqueline? George?" Felicia whispered, her face now as pale as Mrs. Doherty's dish towels that hung near the fire to dry. "You went to a brothel? But *why*?"

The two children stole a glance at each other and hung their heads.

" 'Cain't tell ya dat, missus," George muttered at last.

"Of course you can tell her," Wilde said brusquely. "And I suggest you do so at once, if you know what's good for you, young lad."

"Don't cry, George," Felicia said, her voice soothing. "It can't be that bad. And I promise you, no one will punish you for it. . . . "

A disgusted snort came from the vicinity of the dresser, but she ignored it.

111

"Come on now, tell Miss Felicia wot ye wuz up ter," Lucie Watts ordered. "Nothin' ter be feared o'."

"We went there to get somethin'," Jacqueline volunteered.

"What?" Felicia asked, still looking confused, as well she might.

"Wal . . . Ah used ta work dere, an' . . ."

"Work there?" Felicia asked, horrified. "In a house of ill repute? Oh, my dear child!"

"Ah was a page dere, an' sometimes Ah wuz in a table," George went on, more at ease now, and not at all loath to hold center stage.

"In a *table*? Whatever do you mean?" Felicia echoed again.

"Sometimes dem ladies, Ah mean wimmens, would pose like, an' den de curtain would go up. It wuz special, it wuz, all dose candles an' sceneries! Dey wore flimsy gowns or wide trowsers and spangly things wit veils on dere faces, but ya could see troo dem all. Ah was dere, too. Ah had a fancy suit ta wear, an' a satin turban, an' Ah held a big feather fan, pretendin' Ah wuz coolin' dem. . . . "

"But why?" Jacqueline demanded, caught up in the tale. "Sounds to me they must have been cold already, if they had so little on. And why were they . . ."

"That will do, Jacqueline," Felicia ordered.

Jacqueline subsided.

"Oh," Lucie said, her voice unsteady. "He means he was in a *tableau*, Miss Felicia. Not a table."

Miss Felicia's face was scarlet now, something she was sure Sir Christopher was noting, and that knowledge did nothing to ease her complexion. She noticed Lucie's face was also bright red, and the maid seemed to be struggling to hold back laughter.

"We had tableaus in the theaters, sometimes,"

Lucie said into the silence. "Not like that, ter be sure! But historical scenes, battles at sea and such."

"Never mind that now," Felicia said in what she hoped was a firm, controlled voice. "I am much more interested in knowing why you two were there tonight, both of you."

Silence fell again, and Sir Christopher pushed himself away from the dresser where he had been leaning all this time. "Perhaps they would find it easier to confess if I were not present, ma'am?" he asked. Felicia heard the hidden laughter deep in his voice, and she stiffened.

"Yas! Ah'll tells ya den, Missus. When—when *he* goes!" George piped up.

"Very well, I shall take my leave. But might I suggest you keep a sharper eye on these two? They might have been robbed, even killed, in that neighborhood. Or *they* might have robbed or killed. After observing them tonight, I have to think the latter more likely. Rapscallions!

"Give you good night, ma'am."

Felicia nodded. She knew she should thank Sir Christopher for bringing the children safely home, but she did not trust her voice. Nor did she care to encounter the amusement she was sure filled his eyes. A moment later, she heard the kitchen door close softly behind him.

No one moved until all sounds of his footsteps faded away. Felicia sat down at the table then and beckoned the children to do so as well. All unbidden, Lucie Watts joined them.

"Well?" Felicia asked, fixing them with a stern eye. "I am waiting."

"We, er, we went ta get a hat fer ya, Missus," George said.

When Felicia just stared at him, he went on, "Ah knows dem wimmens has lots o' hats! Seed dem on 'em all de time! Dey wuz real fancy ones, too! So

113

Ah tells Jackie 'bout dem, an' we went ta swipe a few. Ah heard tell ya *needs* hats, an' we wanted ta surprise ya."

When Felicia still stared at him, frowning, he began to cry again.

She took a deep breath. "I see. That was wrong of you, George. You know you must not steal. But I suppose I should thank you for thinking of me. However, I intend to buy a hat shortly, so there was no need to put yourself, and Jacqueline, too, in danger. You have been very naughty, but I cannot find it in my heart to punish you. However, I must have your promise that you will never, ever, sneak out of this house at night again. And you must promise me never to go to such a place again, even in the daylight. Well? Do I have your promises?"

Both children agreed eagerly, and she sent them up to bed.

Only the sound of the old kitchen clock high on the wall broke the silence for moments after they had disappeared. Then Lucie, who could contain herself no longer, buried her face in her hands and burst into muffled laughter.

Felicia, at first appalled at her reaction, began to see the joke. Stealing hats from a brothel—such fancy hats, too! She wondered what they would have looked like, and if she could ever have worn one if the children had been successful and brought some home? And how would they have explained such a windfall? she wondered. Picturing George standing before her holding out an elaborate satin bonnet crowned with a bird of paradise or some such thing, and trying to explain how he had just happened to find it in the park, or on a bush, or behind a tree, was too much for her, and she joined Lucie, both of them laughing until the tears ran down their cheeks. No doubt if Sir Christopher could have seen them, he would have shook his head in disgust.

Or perhaps not, since that gentleman was even then enjoying a hearty chuckle of his own as he pictured George performing in a "table" at Mrs. Huddlefield's infamous house.

Nine

*T*O HER SURPRISE, her stroll with Sir Christopher, Mr. Ainsworth, and Miss Pierce much later that day was very pleasant. Felicia had steeled herself for an uncomfortable time of it, but nothing at all was said about the children's expedition to Seven Dials in the dead of night. Of course she had not expected Sir Christopher to be so gauche as to refer to it directly, but she had expected some sly innuendos, knowing smiles, and indirect references to either the escapade or the district he had found them in. Perhaps even a lecture on the proper way to raise the young?

Even when they had taken their leave of Mr. Ainsworth and his cousin later and started the walk home, Sir Christopher did not refer to the incident. Felicia wondered why, for surely he must have been intrigued by it. At last she said a little stiffly, "I wonder you do not ask me about the children, sir, now we are alone, inquire why they went to that—that place last night."

He glanced sideways and down at her, and for some reason, the amusement she could see in his eyes annoyed her. "*I* inquire? About something you would not have told me, ma'am?" he asked. "I know that would be a waste of time, and I don't like wasting my time."

"I see," Felicia said shortly, staring straight ahead again.

"Would you have told me if I had asked?" he persisted.

She shook her head, but still she would not look at him.

"Of course you wouldn't! However, I must say I look forward to the time when you feel you can be honest with me," he said, almost as if to himself. "Ah well, I've found sometimes that waiting for something unknown can only enhance the pleasure of it. In this case, I am sure to be vastly amused, so I'll bide my time. Sometimes, I surprise myself. I have never thought myself a patient man."

Felicia refused to be drawn. His tone of voice, so bland, did not fool her. Sir Christopher was taking a great deal of enjoyment already out of her awkward predicament.

"Perhaps you can tell me how the children came to live with you instead," he went on, serious now. "It is most unusual. George is obviously no relation of yours, and as for that other little hellion, somehow I doubt she is kin either."

"No, Jacqueline isn't," Felicia admitted. "I took her in because I found her on the streets alone, eking out a precarious existence there by begging. The streets are no place for a child, sir! George came to me later. I could not resist giving him a home as well, although Mr. Livingston said . . ."

She stopped suddenly, as if she had been too open, and Sir Christopher bent closer. "Who is Mr. Livingston?" he asked mildly.

"My father's valet. I have known him all my life," Felicia told him, glad he made no further reference to the children or her philanthropy in housing them. She did not like to discuss it.

"And that blond woman with the pitiful face that I've seen more than once?"

"That's Lucie. Lucie Watts. Her complexion was ruined by the use of paint. She—she was in the the-

117

ater at one time, first as an actress, then a dresser when she got too old and ugly to perform. But she was down on her luck, reduced to . . . to other things when I asked her to be my maid."

"Is the scarred sailor her husband?"

"Joe? Oh, no. They don't really get along that well. Joe was wounded at Trafalgar, but he had no money when he was beached, as he puts it, for he didn't have the right certificate. His captain and the surgeon signed one for him after he lost his leg, but he forgot to get the signatures of the master and the senior lieutenant of his ship as well, so he had no recourse to a pension. It is too bad, the laws are so stringent, don't you think? I mean, poor Joe! Destitute all for the oversight of two names!"

"Indeed," Wilde said absently.

They had almost reached Number Seventeen, when the Perkins's smart carriage drove up and halted before it. Felicia stopped walking. Sir Christopher stared down at her for a moment, then noting the spoiled beauty who left that carriage, he ceased to wonder at her hesitation.

"I see Miss Perkins continues in residence," he said in a cold voice.

Felicia tried a tentative smile. "As you say, sir. The Season is not forever, and I am sorry for her mother. Besides, where else could they find rooms at this late date?"

"It is unfortunate for you, however," he persisted. "It cannot be pleasant living with a woman who has maligned you in public."

"I do not see her very often, indeed, I have grown adept at avoiding her," Felicia told him, wishing she were not always so honest with the man. A little vexed, she pondered this power he had over her. She did not care for it in the slightest!

"I don't believe I have ever met a true Christian before. I mean one who invariably turns the other cheek. Be careful such goodness does not spread unchecked, ma'am. It would make it so uncomfortable for the rest of us sinners to endure, forever reminding us of our own shortcomings in that regard."

To his surprise, she chuckled. "Oh, have no fear I'm a saint, sir," she said cheerfully, her eyes laughing up into his. "Far from it, in fact! I've a bad temper sometimes, and I do assure you, as many faults as anyone else."

"I am relieved to hear it, ma'am," he said politely as they began to walk again now that Cecily Perkins was safely within doors.

"I understand you are going to the Duchess of Kyle's soiree?" he asked next. "She has honored me with an invitation as well. I look forward to seeing you there."

"Yes, she has been very kind to me and so have her daughters," Felicia told him, sounding a little troubled. He noted the tiny crease between her brows, but he did not question her about it. He knew he would be told nothing to the point. Miss Felicia Simmons was a woman who kept her own counsel about a great many things. What he knew of her situation he had found out in roundabout ways. But he was not discouraged. So much had come to light already, and all unknown to the young lady, too.

As he bowed and thanked her for a pleasant afternoon, his mind was already busy on the list of names he had been given by Bart's great-uncle. Two of the gentlemen on it had been pointed out to him, and they seemed likely prospects. Over middle age now, they appeared not only well-established, but prosperous. The dilemma he faced was somehow to get them to admit that they owed Reginald Simmons money, if they were among the ones who did so indeed. He hoped Lord Bradford would have some suggestions as to how he should go about it.

Briefly, he considered asking Miss Simmons if he could pay her father a visit sometime, so he could question the man himself, but just as quickly he discarded the notion. Simmons was ill. He would not welcome a call from a stranger. Still, he thought as he strolled across the street to his own house, I might be able to manage a word with this Livingston, sometime when I know Miss Simmons is out. The valet might have heard some names when his master was reminiscing, or he might be able to induce him to speak of his debtors. Wilde told himself it was worth thinking about.

Felicia found a note from her godmother waiting for her on the hall table. She took it into the library, hoping it was not an invitation to go shopping for hats.

She had told the children she intended to buy one soon, and she supposed she would have to do so, no matter how upsetting it was to her to spend Livingston's future security for such foolishness. However, she knew she could not wear her old bonnet much longer without occasioning comment. Even today, when her party had stopped to converse with other strollers on occasion, she had had the thought that some of the ladies were staring at her bonnet, perhaps even whispering about it later. It was the only part of her ensembles that was not up to snuff.

Perhaps tomorrow, after my teaching chores, she told herself as she opened the viscountess's note. There must be some reasonably priced hats in London.

The note was an invitation to a dinner in two night's time, just a small affair before a theater party. Felicia sighed. Another invitation. Another stint of sewing for Lucie and Gladys, she thought. But there was also a postscript, heavily underlined. As she read it, she began to frown. Granted, Lady

Bradford was not the most lucid letter-writer she had ever known, but surely this took the prize.

> *Dear* child, I do sincerely hope the Perkins are *still* in residence in Upper Brook Street. It is *imperative* they remain with you! For I have been *very* clever—you will *stare* when you discover how much, for I have solved *all* your problems! I cannot breathe a word of it now. However, dearest, it is the most *delicious scheme*! But one of these days, you will see!

Now, what is that all about? Felicia wondered. Somehow any "delicious scheme" concocted by Marjorie Bradford made her feel supremely uneasy. She wondered if the viscount knew what his wife was up to?

Coming home from teaching the following afternoon, Felicia chanced to meet Lucie Watts. Lucie had been to the market stalls again, but today she had had no luck finding the pale green ribbon she wanted to trim a muslin morning gown.

As the two walked together along Bond Street, Lucie chatted of her errand. Suddenly she stopped short, greatly inconveniencing a portly old gentleman who was walking along behind them. Lucie ignored his indignant "harumph!" as she stared into a window alongside.

"Oh, do look, Miss Felicia, do," she whispered. "Did ye ever see anythin' so 'andsome? An' wouldn't ye jess look a treat in it!"

Felicia's gaze followed her pointing finger. Displayed in the window in solitary splendor was a glorious bonnet. Made of natural-colored straw with a high crown, it was trimmed with a profusion of sky-blue ribbon rosettes and matching veiling. Felicia had to admit it was tempting, but she could tell from the appearance of the shop, its shiny brass knocker and engraved plaque, that the hat would be far above her touch.

"I imagine it's as expensive as it is stunning," she said firmly. "No, Lucie. I'll shop for a hat another day."

To her surprise, Lucie set her mouth stubbornly. "An' woi not now?" she demanded, grasping her mistress's arm as if to prevent her from escaping. "Wouldn't hurt ter look at it, now would it? Try it on-like?"

Felicia stared at her seamed face, those pleading eyes. No, of course it wouldn't hurt, although she was afraid if she tried that wonderful confection on, she wouldn't be able to say no to it. Besides, she was wearing her old muslin and looked dowdy. And Lucie was not the ideal companion to take into one of the better shops. True, she was dressed respectably in a navy gown and shawl, but anyone could see the life she had led. It was written all over her raddled face, crowned as it was by the brassy hair nature had never bestowed on her.

"Do come on," the maid insisted, tugging her arm. "Only take a minute, it will."

Against her better judgment, Felicia allowed herself to be escorted into the shop. When she saw the scornful look the shopkeeper gave them both after a careful inspection, she lost her diffidence and her temper as well.

"Yes?" the woman asked as she rose. Her disdain was obvious as she added, "There was something *you* wanted here?"

"I would like to see the hat in the window," Felicia said calmly, although her chin was tilted at an imperious angle and her blue eyes flashed.

For a moment, the woman seemed doubtful. Her eyes slid over to where Lucie stood, a respectful two paces behind, and she stiffened.

"Well, what are you waiting for, my good

woman?" Lucie demanded. "Bring Miss Simmons the hat at once. We do not have all day."

Felicia's jaw dropped at her grandiose accents. That was Lucie sounding like a duchess? *Lucie*?

Bemused, the shopkeeper went to fetch the hat as Felicia removed her own old bonnet and smoothed her hair. The hat was lowered reverently before it was tilted at a becoming angle.

"It does become you, Miss," the shopkeeper said, her voice grudging.

"Hmm," Felicia said as she studied her reflection in the glass the woman held up. "Yes, I suppose it is attractive in an ingenuous way, wouldn't you say, Miss Watts?"

"I would remind you, Miss, how much you admired that cherry silk we saw earlier," Lucie said, still in those artificial tones. "Then there was the blue with the matching plumes. Stunning, that one, I thought. And I do not think this is the shop the Duchess of Kyle meant when she advised you to investigate it. Somehow it does not seem like her kind of place, does it? You have so often mentioned the duchess's exquisite taste."

"I might have mistook the name," Felicia admitted, entering into the game with a will as she removed the hat and replaced it with her own. "Come, let us be on our way."

The shopkeeper had heard of the Duchess of Kyle, and more importantly, of those five daughters of hers she had to bring out, and she would do anything to gain her custom, even to letting this hat go for a song. "Why not just take it home, Miss? Try it on again?" she begged, smiling for the first time. "It's very reasonable. Only twenty guineas."

"Miss Simmons is not concerned with the cost of it, nor does she walk through the streets carrying bandboxes," Lucie told her grandly. "Nor do I. Send the hat to Seventeen Upper Brook Street, if you

123

insist on it. If Miss Simmons decides to keep it, we will notify you."

When Felicia left the shop, bowed away by a suddenly obsequious shopkeeper, Lucie followed, nose high in the air. Nothing was said until the two were some distance away. Then Felicia, beckoning the maid to walk beside her again, couldn't help saying, "My word, Lucie, you certainly startled me in that shop. Wherever did you learn to speak that way? You sounded as grand as could be!"

Lucie's smile of grim satisfaction changed to an expression of indignation. "Well, o' course I did!" she said. "Ye haven't fergot I wuz in the *theater*, have ye, Miss Felicia? Many the times I've played some Society lady. Oh, I can sound the posh any time I like! It was good fer the gentlemen, too. Made 'em feel ter home, no doubt. As me first protector, Lord B. 'e wuz, sez ter me, Lucie, he sez . . ."

"Please don't tell me that," Felicia said hastily. "I—I understand."

The two walked on together in silence for a moment before she added thoughtfully, "But what I don't understand is why you don't speak that way all the time, since you can."

To her surprise, Lucie chuckled, vastly amused. "S'pose I could, but it's 'ard work, it is. 'Ave ter think too much ter get my mouth around all them fancy words. Then, too, wouldn't seem right coming from this face, now would it? 'Sides, it would make Joe—all the others—nervous. An' imagine 'ow Mr. Livingston would take it. Apt ter think I wuz mockin' 'im, an' that would never do. That fond o' Mr. Livingston, I am."

Felicia said no more, although Lucie's revelations had stunned her. At last she frowned a little and said, "I wish you hadn't told her to send the hat. It was so expensive! And just think of the number of poor children I could feed with the money. . . . "

Lucy tossed her brassy head. "Now jess ye listen ter me, Miss Felicia," she said sternly. "Ye've got ter forget them little waifs fer a bit—'ave a good time yerself. An' it may be that there 'at will pay fer itself many times over. Jess mark my words!"

Felicia did not see any reason it should, but when she asked Lucie to explain, the maid only shook her head and changed the subject.

On the evening appointed for the Bradford theater party, Felicia received a note from Sir Christopher Wilde, asking if he might escort her to Berkeley Square in his carriage. Although, Felicia thought as she read it, it seemed more an order than a request, it was so brusque. She conferred with her father's valet, and he gave it as his considered opinion that she might accept the offer with impunity, as long as Gladys accompanied her.

"An open sporting carriage, during the daylight hours, is perfectly acceptable, Miss," he told her. "But a closed one at night, no, no. Every feeling must be offended."

"It does seem rather a waste of Gladys's time," Felicia began, but Livingston wouldn't listen to her. And when she mentioned it to Gladys, the maid said she had every intention of coming along, and Miss was not to fret about it. Felicia accepted defeat.

That evening, she wore one of the gowns Lady Bradford had given her, a soft violet silk, and, of course, the diamond set. She was sure she looked very grand indeed, with her hair dressed à la Sappho and threaded through with a matching violet ribbon.

To her relief, Sir Christopher made no comment about the presence of her maid, and the drive was spent discussing only innocuous subjects. Gladys was left with the other servants at the door, however, and it was then that Felicia stole a glance at her tall, tanned escort. He was wearing a frown this evening. Perhaps he had had bad news of some sort? she wondered. But she did not question him. She did not feel she knew him well enough for that, and for some reason, she suddenly felt shy with him.

Marjorie Bradford surged forward to greet them both as they entered the drawing room. As she hugged Felicia and exclaimed over her ensemble, Felicia looked around the room. To her relief, only a small group of guests had assembled. When she greeted Lord Bradford, he whispered how splendid she looked wearing the diamonds, and she could not resist kissing him in thanks again. The gentleman colored up for a moment before he patted her hand and told her she was not to make such a to-do about such a little thing.

As he turned to speak to Sir Christopher, Felicia ventured to ask her godmother about that mysterious note she had sent. Lady Bradford winked at her and smiled, but she refused to explain.

"Not *now*, dear child!" she whispered. "You must come and greet the others. But I *promise* to tell you sometime soon. I have quite surprised myself, for I would be the *first* to admit I am not generally so quick witted. Far *from* it, in fact. And the idea occurred to me at the *most* unlikely time! Ah, Sarah, here is my goddaughter, Felicia Simmons. Felicia, Mrs. Jackson and her husband.

"I believe you have already met Viscount Ormsby? Miss Nancy Remington?"

Felicia made her curtsies before she accepted a glass of Madeira from the tray a footman was presenting.

"I do hope you are enjoying the Season, child," Mrs. Jackson said with a coy smile. "And I hear you are as clever as you can hold together as well.

You young misses of today put my generation to shame, indeed you do. But I will say no more, for of course, you do not care to speak of it. I quite understand.

"Horace, my love, don't you think Miss Simmons very like her mother in appearance?"

After Mr. Jackson agreed, Felicia began to talk of Lady Bradford's ball. She had not understood Mrs. Jackson's remarks in the least. *What* didn't she care to speak of? *Why* did the lady think her clever? Out of the corner of her eye, she could see Sir Christopher regarding her seriously, before his attention was claimed by Lord Bradford. The two men were soon deep in a conversation that was held somewhat apart from the rest.

Felicia had been more than a little nervous about this party, as indeed she continued nervous when pitched into any ton doings. For no matter how accepted she seemed to be, she was always waiting for someone to snub her because she rented rooms. But by the time the dessert course was served later, she was having a very good time. Lord Ormsby was attentive and greeted all her remarks with a smile and nod of approval. Miss Remington appeared full of admiration, and the Jacksons continued kind. Only Sir Christopher seemed strangely quiet, preoccupied. She wondered what he was thinking.

After the ladies adjourned to the drawing room again so the gentlemen could enjoy a glass of port, Felicia took a seat beside Miss Remington. "Have you been to London before?" Felicia asked. "I seem to remember you saying your home was in Sussex."

"This is my first Season," the girl confided. "I am having such a marvelous time! Lord Ormsby is my cousin, you see, and he takes me everywhere. And even now there are two gentlemen who . . ."

She paused and blushed, even tittered behind her hand before she said playfully, "But I must mind what I say to *you*, now mustn't I, Miss Simmons? For it would never do, if you were to—but I shall not put you to the blush! I understand only a few people know. You may be sure your secret is safe with me. But do let me tell you how much I admire you. Imagine doing what you are. It quite thrills me!"

Before Felicia could ask what she meant, Lady Bradford rustled over to them to suggest they visit the withdrawing room before everyone must leave for the theater.

Lord Ormsby insisted the younger people go in his carriage, so Sir Christopher dismissed his, and with it, Gladys, her duties as chaperon over. Felicia had not been to the theater since she had been a little girl. She thought it very grand, albeit noisy, hot, and filled with all manner of people from the highest to the lowest estate. As she stared down into the crowded pit, heard the raucous laughter and suggestive conversations that drifted upward, she was glad Lord Bradford had reserved a box for them. Those wooden benches looked very uncomfortable, and she did not like the way the beaux ogled any pretty face.

She forgot the crowds, however, during the performance. How magical it seemed to her, acting. To think only costumes and a few lines could transport the audience to faraway places, wonderful doings, strange mysteries.

At the interval, she turned to Sir Christopher and said impulsively, "My, isn't this grand? I never suspected a play could be so absorbing. No wonder Lucie was enthralled with the life."

"Yes, it seems glamorous, of course, from this side of the footlights," he told her, frowning a little. "But in reality, it is a tawdry existence, and not at all a dependable way to earn your bread. Unless you become famous—one way or the other," he added with a wry twist to his mouth.

Remembering the buxom ingenue, and sure he was recalling her as well, Felicia blushed a little. Then she considered his words, and hiding a smile said as if to herself, "Still, I wonder if I would care for it? I am said to have a clear, true singing voice, and I am sure I could remember lines. It would be quite an experience for me, even a thrill, to win the applause and compliments of the ton."

She had not looked at him as she spoke, but she had sensed that he stiffened. When he made no comment, she turned to him and was surprised to see a little smile hovering on his lips. "Do you think I would care for it, sir?" she asked innocently.

"Are you by any chance teasing me, Miss Simmons?" he asked, bending closer so the others would not hear. "For I don't believe you have the slightest intention of seeking fame and fortune on the stage."

She chuckled, a little breathless at his nearness. "No, of course I don't. And yes, I was teasing you. It seemed to me you were warning me away, and I thought perhaps, knowing as you do the unfortunate things I have been engaged in, you might take me seriously. How disappointing you are not gullible, sir."

"No, I'm any number of things, but I'm not gullible," he told her in his deep baritone.

Felicia did not know whether to be glad or sorry when the houselights dimmed just then and the curtain rose on the second act. But even though the play continued to hold her attention, now she was very conscious of Sir Christopher's broad shoulder so close to hers, the strong tanned hand that held his program, even the unusual ring of heavy gold he wore.

The party broke up after the play, Lord Ormsby once again offering to convey Miss Simmons and Sir Christopher, this time to their homes. On learning they lived right across from each other, he threw up his hands in mock disgust.

"Unfair, Wilde," he mourned. "Most unfair!"

Sir Christopher did not reply to this raillery. Instead, he engaged Nancy Remington in conversation, mentioning people he knew from Sussex and asking if she were acquainted with them.

Lord Ormsby took the opportunity to invite Felicia to drive out with him some afternoon soon. It seemed he had recently acquired a perch phaeton of which he was very proud and a team of horses he was sure Miss Simmons must approve. Felicia managed to parry any definite appointment by saying her time was much bespoke these days, and she was not at all sorry when the carriage pulled up before Number Seventeen. It was true Lord Ormsby was a nice young man, but she was not at all attracted to him. Somehow he seemed like so many other young Society men, not only shallow but callow—superficial even, in his interests and pursuits. But she thanked him prettily for his escort and told Miss Remington how delighted she had been to meet her again, before she allowed Sir Christopher to help her down the step the groom had lowered for her.

The two stood for a moment, watching the carriage drive away. Then Sir Christopher cupped her elbow to help her to the door. When he would have sounded the knocker, she put a deterring hand on his arm. His brows rose as he stared down at her.

"May I ask you something before I go in, sir?" she said, wondering why she felt so breathless.

As he nodded, she went on, "Then I would ask you if you have heard anything odd about me of late."

"Odd?" he asked, frowning over the word. "No, not a thing."

Felicia sighed a little. "I see," she said slowly. "It is just that this evening not only Miss Remington, but Mrs. Jackson as well, said the most incomprehensible things. Something about keeping my 'secret'—how 'clever' I was. And Miss Remington had been about to tell me something concerning her beaux when she suddenly stopped short and claimed she would have to be very careful what she said to *me*. I don't understand it in the slightest, and I thought you might have heard something that would explain it."

"No, I haven't, but I'll inquire if you like. Discreetly, of course," he said.

"As always, you are very kind," she replied, wondering why she did not feel she could look away from him. It was almost as if his gaze held her captive against her will. And still she stared up at his tanned face with its handsome, rugged features. In the flambeau's light, they seemed almost carved from stone, the high cheekbones highlighted, the sweep of sculptured mouth strangely powerful. And his eyes—those mesmerizing silvery eyes!

She sensed him lean toward her then, and as he grasped her arms she held her breath waiting for whatever would come next.

To her great regret, the door opened behind them just then, and the light from the hall candles flooded the stoop, banishing what to her had been a magic spell.

When she turned, she saw both Lucie and Gladys standing there, staring at Sir Christopher with suspicion, and as he released her and stepped back, she did not know whether she wanted to laugh at them or scream in frustration instead.

"Thank you for your escort, sir," she said as she held out her hand to him. "It was a wonderful evening, was it not?"

Ten

W HEN FELICIA LEFT the house the next morning
for an early teaching appointment, Sir Christopher
Wilde watched her go. He noticed she still carried
the old music satchel, its handle repaired neatly
with twine now, and he grimaced a little as she
made her way down the street.

He had not slept well and as a result was short
tempered. Now he ran a hand through his auburn
hair in exasperation. Wouldn't you think the girl
could at least buy a new case? he asked himself.
She can't be that poor!

He saw her stop to speak to three ragged little
boys and watched her point to her house before she
turned and left them. As he continued to watch, the
children scurried up the street and let themselves
into the gate that led to the back door of Number
Seventeen. He had heard from Ted Bowers of the
waifs who visited the Simmons's home so often, and
now, as he had before, he wondered what they were
doing there.

Then he forgot them very quickly as he remembered last evening, and Miss Felicia Simmons. The
color of her gown had turned her eyes an almost
violet blue, and the delicate diamonds she had worn
that had shimmered at her ears and on her breast
were but a poor tribute to her youth and beauty.
And she had been so carefree, too. So happy and
gay.

Remembering how she had teased him at the theater, he smiled to himself. And later, when she had detained him on the doorstep, it had been all he could do not to take her in his arms and kiss her.

Whatever was happening to him? he thought, frowning again. He was not in the market for a wife. He never had been, and he hoped he wouldn't be for many a year. To be sure, women were useful creatures in their own way, but they were of little importance in his scheme of things. He supposed he should be glad her two maids had interrupted them last night, for if they had not, he might well had found himself caught in the parson's mousetrap Bart Whitaker had warned him about. A close escape, that!

He reminded himself he must inquire for any gossip of Miss Simmons today, as she had asked him to do. But now, knowing she was safely off the premises, he determined to call on her father's valet, the Mr. Livingston she had mentioned.

His knock on the door across the way was answered by a strange footman he did not know. Another of Felicia's charity cases? he wondered as the man took his card and went up the stairs, leaving him standing in the hall. Then he frowned as he saw the bouquet on the hall table that must have just been delivered. By straining a little, he could see the card attached to it was addressed to Miss Felicia Simmons. Ha! That idiot Ormsby, no doubt, he thought with derision. He had seen how captivated the man had been by Felicia last evening, had heard him begging her to drive with him. And, he admitted, had been pleased when she would not commit herself to a definite time and place. Still, if Ormsby continued to pursue her . . .

Thus it was when Mr. Livingston came down and invited m'lord to step into the library where they could be private, Sir Christopher wore a ferocious frown. Fortunately, Livingston was not intimidated and merely asked in his well-bred voice how he might be of service.

Recalled to his errand, Wilde began to explain. The valet heard him out without speaking, and if he thought it very singular for a stranger to be inquiring of Mr. Simmons's debtors, he certainly did not mention it. Seen up close for the first time, he found the baronet an imposing figure, and he liked his steady eye, those rugged determined features. A fine figure of a man, Livingston told himself. One I feel I can trust.

None of his thoughts showed as he said at last, "Yes, Mr. Simmons has named names on more than one occasion, sir. There was one gentleman in particular, Claude Garrison, the Marquess of Binchfield. My master has reminisced about him more than once and wondered how the poor man was getting on—hoping he had not run into debt again. And there were some others. . . ."

"Could you give me those names while I write them down so I can investigate?" Wilde asked, his voice betraying his eagerness. He knew the Marquess of Binchfield for a wealthy man with an imposing town house. At last, he thought. I'm getting somewhere positive at last.

Livingston gave him some other names, which Sir Christopher noted on the pad he carried in his pocket.

As he turned away to take his leave, he remembered the strange behavior of the valet which he had noted many times.

"May I ask why you open the windows over here every day at noon?" he began. "You have done so even in stormy weather, for I have observed you more than once. Forgive me for inquiring—it just seems so odd to me."

Livingston bowed a little, his lined old face expressionless. "I do so at my master's request, sir," he said, stiff with dignity. But when he saw the bewilderment in Sir Christopher's eyes and remembered his hopes for this man and Miss Felicia, he relented and went on, "Mr. Simmons likes to hear the church bells chime the noon hour. Most especially, he listens for those of St. Mary-le-Strand, for it was at that church that he and his wife were wed."

Remembering the number of bells coming from all directions, the confusion of sound, Sir Christopher said, "But surely he cannot pick out those particular bells from all the others. It would be impossible!"

"As you say, sir," Livingston agreed. "However, he *believes* he can, and it makes him happy. He loved Mrs. Simmons dearly, and that love has not died to this day."

Sir Christopher thanked him and went away abstracted. Reginald Simmons must be ill, for such behavior was not normal, he thought. And he wondered, not for the first time, what manner of man Felicia's father might be. He did not appear to be a strong man, nor one who faced life's problems bravely and squarely, for surely the kind of love his valet had described pointed to an almost feminine weakness. He himself could not imagine loving a woman that way, mourning her still three years after her death. No wonder Simmons had never pressed his debtors for repayment of his loans to them. It would not be in character for him to do so, so unmanly and sentimental as he appeared to be.

Mentally, Sir Christopher shook his head and put the ineffectual Reginald Simmons from his mind. He was pledged to Bart Whitaker this afternoon for an appointment at Gentleman Jackson's Rooms. Perhaps he should ask Bart if he had heard anything odd about Miss Simmons lately? Anything the least bizarre? He had not seen the man for some time. To his disgust, Bart appeared to be dancing attendance on Cecily Perkins these days. He would have thought he had better taste, to say nothing of the acumen to avoid being taken in by that conniving, vicious little shrew! But, he told himself, as he had learned himself this morning, where women were concerned, most men could not be trusted to maintain good sense. Fortunately for him, he was not among their number.

Wilde spent that evening at home before a small fire, reading and relaxing. As he did so, he told himself how much more enjoyable such evenings were than dressing up and prancing about doing the pretty in Society, and once again, he wondered why he stayed in London. His business was all but finished; he had no reason to remain. Except, he reminded himself, this business of Felicia Simmons. His book slipped unheeded to the floor as he studied the fire before him. Among the flames, he seemed to see her face, those dancing blue eyes as she laughed or teased him. And in the quiet crackle of the wood, he imagined he could hear faint echoes of her delightful laughter.

I am acting like a fool, he told himself coldly. What I feel for Miss Simmons is no more than I would feel for any other human being who was being oppressed. Still he wondered what the ladies had meant at the theater party the other evening. Bart had had no information for him, for he had not heard even a hint of gossip. What could it be?

The next morning he called on Lord Bradford at eleven. As he sent in his card, he hoped he had not come too early. He had grown accustomed to the late rising of the ton by this time, although he himself deplored it. Used to taking the early four to eight watch when at sea, and at all other times coming awake with the sun, he found he could not change his routines even here in town.

The Bradford butler returned, saying m'lord would be pleased to receive him, as he led him to the viscount's library. Sir Christopher saw m'lord was already at work at his desk, although the man rose courteously to greet his guest and offer him coffee or ale.

"Neither, sir," Wilde said as the viscount waved him to a seat. "I'm here because I've discovered the names of some men who might be Reginald Simmons's debtors. But I must confess I'm at a loss as to how to go about discovering if any of them are the ones we seek. I am so much younger than they, and a stranger. Surely they would consider it impertinent if I should ask such a personal question. Likely to have me thrown out of their houses if I were to attempt it!"

He grinned then, a grin Lord Bradford thought improved his rugged good looks a hundredfold.

"And as willing as I am to help Miss Simmons, I must admit I've no liking for being tossed out into a number of streets on my backside."

"I don't believe I know a single butler in London who would dare attempt it, sir," Lord Bradford said dryly. "Unless, of course, he had the help of several large footmen.

"But I see your dilemma. Fortunately I have come up with another scheme. And any inquiry of mine, coming as it does from the husband of Felicia's godmother, could not be considered impertinent."

"No, you're right," Wilde said, leaning back at his ease now. "You relieve my mind, sir. But I would like to be there when you question them, if that is possible."

Lord Bradford nodded, his austere face expressionless, although his mind was busy at work. Did

Wilde have a clue as to how involved he was becoming with Felicia Simmons? Did he even suspect he was falling in love with the girl? Somehow the viscount was positive he did not, and he hoped *he* would be there when the scales dropped at last from the eyes of this arrogant, oh-so-sure of himself young man.

"Certainly," he said. "That can be arranged. You see, I had it in mind to invite them all here some afternoon soon. And when they are thus assembled, I shall explain the situation, and then we'll see."

"But surely you don't expect them to confess, in front of their friends and peers?" Sir Christopher asked, his voice disbelieving.

Lord Bradford snorted. "Of course they won't, but allow me to keep what I plan to do a secret for now, sir.

"Those additional names you mentioned," he said into the little silence that fell between them, "if I might see them?"

Wilde handed over the list, and Lord Bradford read it carefully. "Hmm, Garrison, eh? I wonder he did not occur to me. He and Reginald Simmons were thick as thieves at one time. And Dalton, Lord Geer, even Holland. Yes, any one or all of them could be guilty, to their infinite shame. I've a few more names I've thought of to add as well.

"Shall we say the day after tomorrow at three in the afternoon? I'll word my invitation in a way that will intrigue them and ensure their attendance, since I don't have any intention of repeating this performance."

He grimaced as he rose. "Nasty business, my boy," he said as Sir Christopher bowed. "Hopefully, it will have a satisfactory conclusion. And if it does, Felicia will owe you a great debt of gratitude."

He saw Wilde's frown, the way he waved a deprecatory hand as if to deny any such thing, and he kept his face carefully impassive as he said his good-byes. Only when the library door closed behind his visitor did he permit himself a small smile of satisfaction as he returned to his desk and the multitude of paperwork he had set himself to deal with before summoning his secretary.

That same morning, Felicia had been surprised to find herself awakened quite early by Lucie Watts. The maid came in, set down her tray of chocolate and biscuits by the bedside before she bustled about opening the draperies and the bed curtains.

"Best ye wake up, Miss Felicia," she said briskly. "There's trouble."

"Oh, no," Felicia moaned as she rubbed her eyes and stretched. She had had a good night's sleep, except when she had heard the Perkins come in quite late. The girl's high, loud voice had even penetrated the upper floors, and sleepily, Felicia wondered what had upset her this time. She seemed to be having an argument with her mother in the hallway, and Felicia had hoped the noise of that argument would not wake her father. She had been relieved, even though she winced, when the drawing room doors slammed shut behind the ladies and peace reigned once again.

"What trouble, Lucie?" she asked as she pushed herself up on her pillows. "Is it my father? Any of the others?"

"Oh, it's naught ter do with us, Miss," Lucie told her from the depths of the armoir where she was searching for a clean chemise. "It's that Miss Perkins, o' course. Melvin came down first thing ter tell us she wants ter see ye, as soon as yer dressed.

"Well, sez I ter him, an' 'oo does she think she is ter be givin' orders ter Miss Felicia? An' wot's it all about anyway, sez I. Melvin didn't know. Only said there'd been a helluva to-do—beggin' yer pardon—when she came home last night. Tantrums and carryings-on like ye wouldn't believe. Ha! I, fer one, would believe anythin' o' *that* one!"

"Oh, dear," Felicia said as she sipped her chocolate. Relieved that her father had not been taken ill again, nor either of the children, she found she had little interest in what might have upset Cecily Perkins. Still, she told herself as she pushed back the covers at last and went to the dressing room, best I find out.

To give herself courage, she had Lucie lay out one of her prettiest morning gowns, a white muslin sprigged all over with pale blue forget-me-nots, and she tied up her curls with a matching blue ribbon. Finally ready, she took a deep breath to steady herself as she went softly down the stairs.

Her knock on the drawing room doors was answered promptly by the footman, Melvin, whose grimaces and rapidly blinking eyes seemed to portend an uncomfortable time of it for her.

Stepping past him, Felicia saw Mrs. Perkins sitting bolt upright in a chair near the fireplace, looking not only distressed, but haughty as well. To Felicia's surprise, the lady was dressed for the street, for she was still wearing her hat and gloves. Then she forgot her as a furious Cecily Perkins rushed toward her, fists clenched.

Felicia opened her mouth to ask how she might be of assistance only to be forestalled by Miss Perkins who stopped dead and pointed an accusing finger at her. *"So,"* she screamed, "so, you actually *dared* to come here and face me after all, did you? I cannot credit your audacity, madam!"

"But you did ask to see me, did you not?" Felicia asked, looking from one to the other in complete confusion. "Naturally I came."

"And you think you have been very clever, don't you?" Cecily Perkins rushed on. Felicia thought the girl looked far less beautiful this morning than she ever had. She still wore her dressing gown, her hair was in wild tangles, and her face was red and distorted. A little unnerved, Felicia clasped her hands tightly before her, lest they begin to tremble. Something was wrong indeed. Very wrong.

"Well, you have outwitted yourself this time, you terrible creature," the girl went on. "But you will find out what your cleverness will bring when you find yourself standing in a court of law, accused of your crime!"

"I—I don't understand. . . ."

"Be quiet! I have written my father this morning. He will know how to go about the matter. No doubt he will speak to his solicitors as soon as he receives my message. And then we shall see how you like being prosecuted for your infamy, your—your dastardly behavior, you—you *she-devil!*"

A small choked protest came from behind her, but Miss Perkins was beyond heeding her mother's strictures on what was nice and what was not just now.

"Yes, I call you she-devil! Would I knew a worse word, for if I did, I would use that instead! And it is no more than you deserve, after what you have tried to do to me! But you won't get away with it, no, indeed! And far from making *me* appear a figure of fun, you will find yourself languishing in jail!"

"Miss Perkins, you must explain," Felicia said as firmly as she could. "I have done nothing to you, or to your mother that I can recall, that would call down such censure on my head. In fact I don't have the vaguest idea what you are talking about. But calling me names, accusing and threatening me, will not serve us here.

"Come now. Just what am I supposed to have done?"

Miss Perkins sneered and tossed her head. "You

know very well, you sly thing! So innocent you look in your pretty gown of virginal white, so pure! But you are as black and as guilty as the worst murderer! And to think you would try to ruin *my* reputation through your deceit. . . ."

"I have done nothing to your reputation," Felicia interrupted. Her head was beginning to ache from Miss Perkins's wild, screaming accusations. Turning to the girl's mother, she begged, "Won't you tell me what it is that I am supposed to have done, ma'am? Since your daughter seems incapable of doing so?"

Cecily Perkins snorted and wheeled away to pace the length of the drawing room, her dressing gown swirling about her in her rapid progress. For a moment, there was blessed silence at last as Mrs. Perkins stared at her landlady in distaste.

"It is as Cecily says," she began in a constricted voice. "And never would I have thought it of you, Miss! You seemed such a refined, lovely young woman. But to even take us as lodgers with such a terrible scheme in mind puts me out of all charity with you. I quite agree with my daughter. You are a despicable person!"

"But you still have not told me what I am supposed to have done," Felicia wailed. "And how can I defend myself against your charges if I don't even know what they are?"

"We have it on very good authority that you are writing a novel," Mrs. Perkins began, clutching her handkerchief to her face and avoiding Felicia's eye as if in meeting it, she might be contaminated. "A novel! No doubt one of those ghastly, lurid romances that no woman of refinement would read.

"And we heard that you invited us to rent these rooms so you might observe my daughter and her behavior, with the eye to using that as the basis for one of the more horrid characters in your book."

"I see you do not defend yourself now, do you, girl?" Cecily Perkins interrupted as she came closer again, although Felicia was so dumbfounded she could not have spoken to save her soul.

"Did you think we would never find out? Never know?

"And of course that is why you stole my maid away from me, so you could question her about my habits, my beaux, my background and engagements; force her to speak of the most intimate details of my life; tell you little lies about me. Oooh, you horrid, contemptible, monstrous *thing*!"

Felicia did not even try to point out that far from stealing Gladys away, it had been Miss Perkins herself who had turned her maid off. Gladys was not the issue here, and besides, Miss Perkins was far from being able to think logically just now.

"And did you think to keep this despicable, depraved business from us until we chanced to read your novel sometime in the future?" the girl rushed on, panting now in her fury. "Perhaps you planned to publish under a pseudonym, or say the work was by 'A Lady of Quality' to escape prosecution for defamation of character? Lady of quality, indeed!

"But no matter how you disguised me, no matter how you changed the circumstances, *I* would have known!" she cried. "*I* am unique!"

Yes, you are that, Felicia thought silently, although her brain was working feverishly. But where had the ladies received such information? Who could have started the rumor that she, of all people, was a writer?

The Lady Majorie Bradford's merry face came to mind, and it was all she could do not to groan aloud. Of course! This had to have been her godmother's "delicious scheme" to explain away Felicia's renting rooms. She might have guessed, and knowing the viscountess as she did, she berated herself for not insisting earlier on an explanation of what the lady had in mind, so she could have put a stop to it. And when she thought that Mrs. Jackson, Miss Remington, and heaven knew how many others had heard the story by now, she wanted to sink.

"We are leaving here today," Cecily Perkins cried, and Felicia forced herself to concentrate on the matter at hand. She would deal with Lady Bradford later.

"Yes, we are moving across the street to the Kentons' establishment. My mother has just returned from engaging rooms there. Mr. Whitaker told me of them last night. Fortunately, the man who rented them has been called to the country and had to give them up.

"I had hoped never to set eyes on you again, but I see now it would be better to keep you under my eye. And when the officials come to take you away to prison, I shall be there to cheer, just see if I'm not!"

"I do not intend to remain here and be maligned a moment longer," Felicia said in as controlled a voice as she could manage. "But before I go, I will tell you you have been misinformed. I'm not a novelist. I even have trouble writing an interesting letter."

Then, crossing her fingers in the folds of her skirt, she added, "I have no idea who started such a preposterous story, nor why they did so, but I assure you, on my honor, not a word of it is true.

"However, I quite agree to your leaving. Give you good-day."

She turned then and left the room, Miss Perkins still sputtering behind her. As she closed the door, she heard the girl screaming for her new maid and the footman, and as she went up the stairs, Felicia shook her head in dismay.

Yet in spite of how unnerved she felt after the distasteful interview just concluded, still at the same time she was angry—very angry—at Lady Bradford. How could she *do* such a thing to me? she asked herself as she reached her room and rang for Lucie. How *could* she?

Eleven

FELICIA WAS STANDING on the steps of the Bradford town house a short thirty minutes later. She would have gone there immediately, except she knew the viscountess was probably still in bed, so she had delayed to write a short note, begging an interview on a matter of great importance.

Lucie had been big with questions, but Felicia, a strange light burning in her eyes, had refused to answer any of them. Gladys, who accompanied her to Berkeley Square, knew better than to ask, although she kept darting little glances of concern her way.

The butler who admitted the pair looked astounded at the time of the morning call and said rather dolefully that he was not at all sure Lady Bradford was ready to receive guests.

"Please be so good as to see she has this note at once," Felicia said crisply. "It is urgent."

"Certainly, Miss Simmons," he said as he beckoned a footman to take the note upstairs. "Should you care for some coffee while you wait? I fear m'lady may be some time. . . ."

Felicia forced herself to smile and nod as he led her to a small salon to wait to be summoned. Almost an hour passed before the butler returned to tell her that Lady Bradford would see her now. He took her up to the viscountess's bedchamber himself.

"*Darling* Felicia!" Marjorie Bradford cried from the depths of her huge four poster. "Whatever can be the matter that you come here at *dawn*? Oh, how my heart *palpitated* when I read your note! You must not, *positively* you must not *startle* me like that ever again!"

Felicia eyed her godmother truculently. That lady reclined among a number of lace-trimmed pillows, and the tray that was set before her showed she had been breakfasting in bed. Her morning's correspondence was also in evidence, spread around her on the satin counterpane. As well, the lady's hair had been arranged, and the discreet cosmetics she was never seen without had been applied to her face. All done while I cooled my heels below, Felicia thought, her anger rising again. Thank heavens this was not a matter where minutes could have made a difference.

"How *charming* you look in that bonnet! Is it new?" the viscountess asked, waving her goddaughter to a chair nearby. She looked a little nervous now, for Felicia had not even smiled at her, never mind offered to kiss her. "It is *most* becoming!"

"I did not come here to show off my bonnet, ma'am," Felicia said in a voice that quivered with rage.

Lady Bradford laughed gaily. "Of *course* you did not, dearest, but one must *never* treat a compliment lightly, you know.

"Now, I see you are upset about something. *Do* sit down and tell me what is troubling you. I am sure it is only a very *little* thing and we can soon put it right. Oh, it is not bad news of your father, I pray?"

"No, not my father," Felicia told her. "But something serious. I have just had a most unpleasant interview with my lodgers, ma'am. They are moving out today, and they threatened me with the law, no less! It seems they have heard some gossip about me."

She glanced sharply at Lady Bradford and saw her lower her eyes and blush a little, and at this evidence of her guilt, it was all she could do not to rush to the lady and shake her as hard as she could.

"You started that rumor that I was a novelist, didn't you, ma'am?" she asked bluntly. "And that the only reason I had rented rooms to the Perkins ladies was in order to use them as characters in a book? Well, didn't you?"

For a moment, she thought the viscountess would try and deny it, but then Marjorie Bradford's chin came up. "Indeed I *did*, and a *very* clever thing to do it was, if I *do* say so myself. Besides paying that ill-mannered little snip *back* for distressing you the night of my ball.

"*Really*, Felicia, I do not see *why* you are so perturbed. For only consider how such a rumor solves *all* your problems! No one can sneer at you *now* for renting rooms. No, for indeed you *had* to do it to gain knowledge of provincial gentry entering Society for the first time, in order to use it in your book."

As Felicia opened her mouth to speak, Lady Bradford raised an imperious hand. "No, *no*, let me finish, dear one. And I will not hear a *single* word of thanks! It was the *least* I could do for you.

"You see I happened to overhear two ladies discussing Mrs. Larimore's newest novel at a party I attended a little while ago. It was in the lady's withdrawing room and I was behind the screen. Well, I told you the idea came to me in the *most* peculiar place, didn't I?

"It seems this Mrs. Larimore has become quite famous in certain circles. And the ladies were discussing the amount of—I believe they called it *re-*

search that was necessary to write a book. And, my sweet, it was *then* that I had the thought that such an occupation would be just *perfect* for you!

"And that was why I *told* you it was imperative the Perkins stay in residence. Well, it is too *bad* they are going, but surely you would have had enough time to study them by now anyway, don't you think? It's not as if you were planning to make Miss Perkins the *heroine* of the piece. Certainly not!"

Firmly repressing the urge to point out she had never intended making her anything, Felicia said, "You didn't consider that calling me a novelist might make me seem a trifle, er, eccentric, ma'am?"

Lady Bradford appeared to consider this seriously for a moment, for she tipped her head to one side, and her eyes grew vacant with thought. At last she shook that head and said, "No, I don't *believe* so. And better eccentric than poor and needy, you know. Besides, the English not only tolerate eccentricity, they secretly *admire* it. Look at Lady Hester Stanhope! Why, only last year she sailed for the Middle East with just a female companion and a doctor. I heard she went to Jerusalem first, then crossed the desert with some Bedouin tribesmen. I can't imagine *why*, can you? I should think such a journey *most* unpleasant myself. Camels, you know. All that sand.

"Then there is Mary Wollstonecraft. She wrote a *number* of things, even took a lover, some horrid American soldier of all people, and she lived abroad doing *heaven* knows what! And consider all those novels Maria Edgeworth penned! I quite *adored Castle Rackrent*, didn't you? And . . ."

"But I am not a novelist," Felicia interrupted, since her godmother's list of eccentrics seemed endless.

"Of course you aren't, dear girl, but who's to know *that*?"

"What will happen when time goes by and no novel ever appears? Did you think of that, ma'am?"

Marjorie Bradford's eyes widened. "Oh, everyone will have forgotten *all* about it by then!" she said merrily. "And after all, I am sure it must take *forever* to write a book. So *tedious*, don't you think? Page after page after *page*!

"If anyone should be so *gauche* as to inquire for it, you must simply say you have decided to rewrite it, or you're having trouble with parts of it, or—or *something*! You're so *clever*, I'm sure you can think of *something* plausible.

"There now. Stop *fretting*, child! It will *all* work out."

Felicia fumed in silence for a moment until Lady Bradford asked innocently, "What *did* the Perkins say to you, dear? Surely it was *Cecily* who put you in such a *taking*! I have always liked Leila Perkins, but I'm afraid her daughter is not at all well-bred. But then, Leila *would* marry that bluff, hearty countryman. And he a nobody, too. Or as good as. I tried to warn her, but . . ."

"They insulted me extremely. In fact, Miss Perkins called me a she-devil, among other distasteful things, and she has written to her father to see about having me prosecuted—sent to jail."

"Of course you are not going to jail! Montmorency will see to *that*! Besides, without the book, where is the evidence?

"I wonder they did not just go home? It would be so much *better* if they had."

"Instead of which, I am sure to come upon them for the rest of the Season," Felicia said bitterly. "How pleasant it will be to receive the cut direct! And if I know Cecily Perkins, she will keep this story, and the scandal of it, alive."

"Then she will be a *remarkably* foolish girl, and when I call on Leila I shall tell her so," the viscountess said as she threw back her covers and slid from bed. "Just help me with my robe, will you, dear? Thank you.

"For if she continues to *bemoan* you using her as a model for one of the characters in your book, people will begin to wonder why she would *object* to it so much. Wonder what there could *be* about her that she does not wish made public? I must *remember* to point that out to her mother.

"Now, darling, *do* run away and stop worrying! I assure you nothing *bad* will come of this, nothing at all. My little schemes are *never* harmful, you know. But I *must* dress! I am promised to m'lady Roberts for a luncheon and an afternoon of silver loo, and just *look* at the time!"

Felicia rose, and seeing the scented cheek Lady Bradford was presenting, relented long enough to give her godmother a kiss in parting. As she went down the stairs, she shook her head, even smiled a little now. No, the lady had meant no harm. In fact, she had been trying to help. Still, she herself could not take such a cheerful view of the situation. She would have to see how she was treated by the ton at her next engagement. Mentally reviewing her calendar, she saw that would be at the Duchess of Kyle's party only two days from now. And perhaps while she was there, she might have a chance to talk to the duchess herself? She had admired the woman's wry humor and good sense, her no-nonsense attitude. Maybe she will know what I should do about this rumor Lady Bradford started, Felicia told herself as she beckoned to Gladys and the butler hastened to open the door for her.

If there is anything I can do, she added gloomily as she went out into the soft, misty day. It looked like it would rain soon. Well, that would suit her current mood perfectly. For as much as Felicia admitted she was delighted to see the last of her lodgers, the Perkins's going meant that the little ease she had found for herself and her family would be no more. True, she had the rent for June in hand, but what was she going to do when that was gone?

And to add to her worries, several of her pupils were going out of town for the summer, so her income from teaching would be a great deal less until the autumn.

She supposed she would have to try and find new lodgers, no matter how distasteful such a course would be after the disaster her last ones had been. She decided she would do so only as a last resort, and in defense she told herself that it would be difficult to get the quality to come now that the Season was winding down. And if the Prince Regent decided to leave London early, to go to his Pavilion in Brighton, the Season of 1811 would be only a memory.

Whatever was she to do?

When she arrived home, she discovered Melvin and the Perkins's new maid carrying the ladies' belongings across Upper Brook Street. Melvin looked stern and upset as he did so, for he had grown attached to the occupants of Number Seventeen and would be sorry to leave them, especially Gladys who came from his home village. The new maid, no doubt filled with stories of Felicia's infamy, shied away from her and would not meet her eye.

Felicia ignored her as she went upstairs to remove her beautiful—and, alas! expensive—new bonnet.

Livingston knocked on her door almost at once. When Felicia saw him she wondered at his happy smile, and she became angry. Very well, she knew Livingston had never approved the lodgers, but it was really too bad of him to be so openly gleeful at the news of their departure. But she had misjudged the man. He was only happy because his master was in such spirits today.

"Quite his old self he is, Miss, so rational," he told her, beaming. "I knew you would want to see him as soon as you came in."

Felicia smiled. "That is good news!" she exclaimed. "I'll go to him at once."

When she entered her father's room, she found him seated by the window, watching all the activity in the street with a great deal of interest. She said a small prayer that he would not notice the servants going in and out of his own house and inquire who they might be. But his words of greeting drove the Perkins from her mind immediately.

"Mary, my love!" he cried, holding out his arms. "Do come here quickly and see this enormous carriage."

"It's Felicia, Da," she said as she came forward, trying hard to smile at him. Perhaps Livingston had been mistaken? Or perhaps her father had slipped back into the mist he lived in so often now?

She watched his lined white face fall for a moment, saw the way he raised a trembling hand to his brow.

"Of course," he said, his voice no longer ebullient. "Forgive me, child. It was just that, for a moment, you looked so like your dear mother that I was confused.

"But how lovely you are! I like that gown," he added valiantly as he patted the seat beside him.

Gratefully, Felicia sat down and took his hand in hers to squeeze it. "Why, thank you, kind sir," she said, smiling easily now. "It is new."

"I am glad to see you buying some pretty clothes. And Livingston tells me that Lady Bradford has been taking you about. I am delighted to hear it. You have lived confined with me for too long. I know I should have insisted you join Society much earlier."

"Oh, Da, I did not mind," Felicia said, even as she resolved not to tell him a single thing about their financial difficulties.

"And do you have beaux?" he asked, a twinkle in his eye. "I am sure you do, you are so attractive, so gracious."

Felicia tried not to blush. Still, she wondered why Sir Christopher Wilde came immediately to her mind. *He* was not her beau! Even the thought of it was ludicrous when he only gave her orders and didn't seem to have the least bit of interest in her as a woman.

"There have been a few," she said tentatively, for she did not want to disappoint her father.

"With any other young woman, I would be concerned not to be able to see them and judge for myself what manner of men they might be. But I do not worry about you, my child. You have so much good sense.

"All I ask is that you choose wisely. As I know from my own experience, a happy marriage is a truly wonderful thing. I would not have you settle for anything less than your mother and I shared, 'Licia."

"I promise you I won't, when the time comes for it, Da," she made herself say. Her heart was aching a little just hearing his old pet name for her. He had not called her " 'Licia" for such a long time.

Reginald Simmons insisted she give him the names of her beaux, and Felicia sacrificed Lord Ormsby to the cause, as well as Duke Ainsworth. And then, as if it were an afterthought, she mentioned Sir Christopher Wilde as well.

"Yes, I know their families, if not intimately, at least by name and reputation," he said, sounding relieved. "Lord Ormsby would be what the world considers a good catch, but 'ware hurry!"

The two sat together for a long time, and for this visit at least, little of that time was wasted discussing the past. Instead, Reginald Simmons wanted to hear all about the Season, the balls and receptions, the political news of the day, and the new prince regent. Felicia saw he grew serious when she mentioned the king's illness, and she was quick to change the subject. She knew the regent was not universally admired, that there were those who scorned his wild way of living and heavy expenditures, and she could see her father was among their number. What he had done with his own fortune was one thing. What the regent did with the wealth of the nation was quite another.

She would have been happy to sit with her father for hours, but all too soon he wearied and fell into a doze. Quietly, she kissed his cheek before she went to summon Livingston. And as she did so, she told herself that no matter how sad she had been feeling earlier, and no matter what happened in the future, seeing her beloved Da alert and happy again more than made up for it.

The afternoon of the Duchess of Kyle's party, Lady Bradford insisted that Felicia call on her at two-thirty. She would not give any reason for the summons, but obediently, Felicia walked once more to Berkeley Square, attended by the faithful Gladys. As she did so, she hoped the visit would not take too long. She wanted to have her hair washed, and she knew Gladys had an elaborate hairdo in mind for the evening that would take some time to achieve.

The viscountess received her in her private blue salon at the back of the house and ordered tea served. Then she plied Felicia with so many questions, her goddaughter's head was spinning. First, of the Perkins again, then of her beaux. Felicia was glad to tell the lady of her father's recent signs of recovery, although she had had to add that he was ill today with one of his sick headaches and had returned to the shadows of the past.

"I am sorry to hear it," Lady Bradford said, glancing at the clock as she had more than once. "Poor, *poor* man!

"But *tell* me, my dear, what think you of Wilde?"

"Sir Christopher?" Felicia asked, putting down her cup in amazement. "Why do you ask about him, ma'am?"

Lady Bradford chuckled and shook a playful finger at her. "Now, my dear, there is no need to be *shy* with me," she said. "I want to know if you *like* him, of course!"

Felicia frowned a little. "I must say he has been very kind to me, yes," she began slowly. Then she added a little tartly, "And yet at the same time, he does seem to enjoy giving me orders."

"*All* men do," the viscountess agreed as she took another macaroon. "But one does not have to do more than *pretend* to agree with them. Montmorency is *forever* telling me things, for my own good, you understand, and I have learned to smile and nod before I do *exactly* as I please. Well, *most* of the time," she added, as if determined to be truthful.

"But Sir Christopher is not my husband," Felicia pointed out, feeling a little breathless as she did so. "And he is not a relative. What right does he have to tell me this and that? Treat me like a mindless little girl?"

"Perhaps he would *like* to be a relative? A very *special* one?" Lady Bradford suggested.

Felicia laughed. "I doubt that, ma'am," she said. "From what I can see, that gentleman has little use for women."

"Oh, pooh! As if *that* has anything to say to the matter!" Lady Bradford exclaimed. "No man does until he falls in *love*. But when that happens, my dear, *how* the situation changes!"

"Somehow I doubt Sir Christopher is the type to succumb to that finer passion. I do not know why he has been so kind, so attentive, but I do know that love does not enter into it. And that you may wager on, ma'am."

Lady Bradford smiled and pressed her to take another cake.

All the while the two ladies had been discussing love in general, and Sir Christopher Wilde in particular, that gentleman had been leaning against the mantel a few rooms away. Lord Bradford was with him, as well as a number of other men who looked as if they would rather be anywhere but in their present location. They had all come promptly to the meeting called, full of smiles and compliments for their host, but after only a few minutes, most of them were frowning and looking uncomfortable.

"I am sure you feel the family's misfortunes as deeply as I do," Lord Bradford was saying now. "That is why I asked you to come today. For I know you were all well acquainted with Reginald Simmons at one time. And it occurred to me that perhaps you might know whom he lent money to in the past. Money, that unfortunately, has not been repaid."

Sir Christopher studied each middle-aged face as unobtrusively as he could. Some of the guests were looking around at one another, some staring down into their wine glasses as if they could find the names the viscount sought there. Only one man appeared completely at his ease.

Claude Garrison, Lord Binchfield, wore an air of

deep concern and, from what Wilde could see, not a trace of guilt on his fat, florid face.

"It is, as you say, m'lord, most unfortunate," he said now into the silence that fell. "And it is true Reggie and I were close friends. If you want the truth of it, I was half in love with his wife. But then, most of London was, as I'm sure all the gentlemen here will agree. Such a lovely woman, Mary Bradford!

"It is too bad she has passed away and a tragedy that Reggie has failed so since her death. I did try to keep up with him, you know, but he refused to see me whenever I called. After a while I stopped calling and writing to him. But perhaps I should try again? Poor man!"

For some reason, Christopher Wilde was angry at these sensible, caring words. And yet why should that be so? he asked himself as he sipped his wine. M'lord spoke noble sentiments, and yet . . . Perhaps it was because those sentiments were said so smoothly? In so concerned a voice, one that was rich with pity and love? Because somehow they rang false?

"And you cannot think of anyone who might still owe him money? Or any of you other gentlemen?" Lord Bradford persisted, looking at each one in turn.

"Monty, Monty!" Lord Binchfield said, laughing. "How can you expect such a thing? To be sure, Reggie loaned a great many people money, but he never talked of his generosity, you know. How would any of us know who the guilty party might be? Not the sort of thing a man would brag about, even to his cronies, for it is dastardly business."

"Quite," Lord Holland agreed. "Reggie lent me money years ago, money that I was quick to repay as soon as I was able. But I don't have any proof of that, and I'd be amazed if Reggie did either. He was not a stickler that way. A man's word was his bond."

Just then a knock sounded on the door, and Lady Bradford ran in, dressed for a drive in a stunning cherry silk gown and matching bonnet. At the door behind her, Felicia hesitated when she saw the gentlemen assembled, feeling shy with so many older men.

"Oh, I *do* beg your pardon, Montmorency!" the viscountess exclaimed. "I had no idea you were entertaining guests, or I would not have *intruded*. I just wanted to tell you I am taking my goddaughter home now before I drive in the park."

"Of course," Lord Bradford said. Turning to Felicia, he added, "Do come in and make your curtsy, my dear. These gentlemen all knew your parents at one time. Sirs, Miss Felicia Simmons."

Reluctantly, Felicia joined the group, giving the assembled guests a shy smile as she obeyed. Lord Bradford introduced her to one and all, but it wasn't until he reached Lord Binchfield that her eyes lit up.

"My dear sir," she said warmly. "Why, I have not seen you this age!"

"You remember me then, Felicia?" he asked, although to Sir Christopher's watchful eye, the man seemed a little unnerved to be singled out by her.

"As if I could ever forget you when you were so kind to me!" she said. "That beautiful doll you brought me when I was a little girl. I have her still, you know. Oh, no, indeed, I could never forget my 'Uncle Binchy.' "

M'lord took her hand and patted it, but Sir Christopher thought his smile uncomfortable, even embarrassed, and he wondered at it. Surely just the use of a nickname would not make the man appear so conscious. Would it?

"Felicia, we *must* be on our way," Lady Bradford

said with another flashing smile for her husband's guests. "Give you good-day, sirs."

Moments later she whisked Felicia from the room and shut the door firmly behind her. Sir Christopher caught Lord Bradford's eye for a moment and was not surprised when the viscount nodded a little. How clever to confront them all with Felicia, he thought, admiring the man's acumen. For not for a moment did he think the interruption just then a coincidence.

And if Felicia's lovely face and winsome ways don't do the trick, he told himself, I don't know what will!

Twelve

LORD AND LADY Bradford took Felicia up in their carriage to the Duchess of Kyle's soiree. Felicia told herself she was grateful to them, even as she wondered why she felt a pang of regret that Sir Christopher Wilde was not to perform that service.

The viscountess was in raptures about her god-daughter's appearance in the gold brocade gown and the diamonds the viscount had given her. And she declared she had never seen her hair dressed so well.

"You will have every other girl there *green* with jealousy, my dear," she said, patting her hand. "Isn't that *so*, Montmorency?"

The viscount was not required to do more than nod his head, for Marjorie Bradford was off once again, this time demanding to know Felicia's maid's name.

"It's Gladys Johns, but she is not my maid, ma'am," Felicia told her with a little frown. "She was Cecily Perkins's until she got turned off for helping me once. I do so worry about Gladys! She is supposed to be looking for a new position, but no matter how I tax her with it and beg her to stop spending so much time taking care of me, she refuses to consider it. But—but I don't need a fancy maid, or at least I won't when the Season is over."

Lady Bradford opened her mouth, caught her husband's eye, and just as quickly closed it.

"Perhaps not, but you certainly need her now," that gentleman said. "Aah, we are here. How delightful there won't be a crush this evening. I've about had my fill of those."

Felicia was also delighted when she saw the duchess had only invited three dozen guests to the party, and Cecily Perkins was not one of them. Still, she felt shivery and breathless as she waited to be snubbed by someone, or tittered about behind raised hands for her outré behavior. To her surprise, nothing of the sort happened. Instead, Lord Ormsby hurried to her side as soon as she left the reception line, to claim the first, as well as the supper, dance, before he took her to where his mother was seated with the chaperones to introduce her. Lady Ormsby was not an outgoing woman, nor had she any degree of personal warmth. She looked suspiciously at this new young lady her Charles was pursuing, but there seemed to be nothing more than that in her manner, no matter how hard Felicia tried to find it.

She went in to dinner on Marmaduke Ainsworth's arm. Sir Christopher took Miss Pierce who was looking as terrified as she always did in the presence of the tall, tanned, forceful man. They were seated some distance from Felicia, and a large flower arrangement, some tall candles, hid them from her view, to her infinite regret. Only because, she assured herself as she laughed at something Mr. Ainsworth was telling her, if I could see Drusilla, it might make it easier for her. She hoped Sir Christopher was doing his best to make the girl comfortable.

Duke Ainsworth was full of gossip of the ton, the play he had seen the evening before, and a coming concert of sacred music he hoped she would attend with him and his cousin. And when she turned to her other side, Mr. Whitaker had a friendly smile for her as he inquired how she was going on.

"Very well, thank you," she said a little stiffly, for she had not forgotten how friendly Bartholomew Whitaker had become with Miss Perkins, nor how it had been he who had told her of the vacant rooms across Upper Brook Street. "The ton is nowhere near as intimidating as I had supposed," she made herself add, afraid she had been too curt.

"Would that 'Silla thought as you do," Duke Ainsworth said in a gloomy voice. "Still as frightened as a mouse facing a large, hungry cat."

"And, I've noticed, especially around Chris Wilde," Whitaker remarked as he stirred his soup.

"That's easily explained," the girl's fond cousin said more cheerfully. "Think she's fallin' in love with him. Seen how she colors up when he notices her. Won't come to anything, though. Wilde's not for her. Maybe not for anyone."

Bart Whitaker laughed, and Felicia made herself smile pleasantly before she changed the subject to ask Mr. Ainsworth more about the concert.

When the guests returned to the largest drawing room after a delicious dinner of three courses, each with several removes and accompanied by an assortment of wines, an orchestra was already playing.

Lady Sylvia was led forward by her father the duke, and the guests clapped as they began to dance. In a short time the other young people took to the floor in prearranged couples. The older ladies retired to chairs and settees at the sides of the room, while the older gentlemen present beat a hasty retreat to the salon set aside for card playing.

Felicia began to enjoy herself. Lord Ormsby's obvious admiration was balm to her spirits, but even as she laughed at his flirting, smiled at him and conversed, she told herself she must find a moment to speak to the duchess. Ask her advice about how she best handle Lady Bradford and her mad starts.

She was sitting a little apart from the others some time later when Sir Christopher came to take the seat beside her. Without so much as a by-your-leave, either, she thought indignantly. He might have at least asked!

"I've heard the talk about you, Miss Simmons," he said abruptly. "Is it true you're a novelist?"

Although others this evening had alluded to her imaginary profession, no one had been as blatant as Wilde, which did not surprise Felicia in the slightest. For when had the man ever been subtle, she thought in exasperation.

But as she looked up at him, saw the twinkle lurking deep in his gray eyes, she had to smile. "Of course I'm not," she said. "It was all a scheme of my godmother's to explain away my lodgers. She thinks she has been very clever, and all my remonstrations to her had no effect at all."

She sighed. "I do love the lady, but sometimes I wish I could shake her. Hard," she added, looking fierce.

To her surprise, Chris Wilde began to chuckle, then laugh out loud. When he had control of himself at last, he shook his head. "Forgive me, but it was such a mad thing to do. However, I might have known that particular lady was behind it. Her mind seems to work differently than other people's.

"But tell me, was that what you meant the other evening when you asked me to listen for any gossip about you?"

Felicia nodded. "Yes, for at that time I had no idea the rumor was going around. You can imagine my horror when Cecily Perkins accused me of it."

He leaned closer. "Come now, you can't stop

there! It would be most unkind, for somehow I have the feeling Miss Perkins was not a bit pleased at being immortalized that way."

"Pleased? She was incensed! The things she called me! And she threatened me, too, with jail for slandering her. Of course, as Lady Bradford was quick to point out, that wouldn't come to anything since there will never be a book."

"But what a shame," he said, chuckling again. "I think Miss Perkins would make a splendid, er . . ."

"Heroine? Are you mad?" Felicia demanded.

"No, villainess, of course! Are you quite, quite sure you would not care to take quill to paper, ma'am? Think of the enjoyment we would all derive from such a story."

"Certainly not. Even if I could write, and I can't, for I understand Newgate is most unpleasant. I'm not a bit tempted to find out for myself.

"It is a shame she only moved across the street," she went on, a little pensive now. "We're sure to encounter each other, and I'd rather not see her."

"Cut her then. After all, she insulted you, didn't she?" he said carelessly. "Yes, I was disturbed myself to learn she and her mother had taken over the Kentons' ground floor. I don't want to see her either."

He did not add how angry he had been at Bart for arranging it, nor how amazed Bart had been at his lecture. "But I only did it to keep the lady under our eyes," he had said. "No telling what she'll get up to next to try and hurt Miss Simmons. That's why I've been dancing attendance on her, you know, for your sake. Thought you'd thank me for it, my boy, indeed I did. And instead, you ring a peal over me!"

Lost in remembering, Chris Wilde was startled when Felicia rose suddenly.

"Please excuse me, sir," she said. "I must have a word with the duchess."

She was gone before he had a chance to bow, and he frowned at her abrupt leave-taking. Was she trying to distance herself from him? Was she afraid people might think they were spending too much time together?

He had seen Ormsby flirting with her, even introducing her to his mother, and that distinction had not pleased him. In his eyes the man, although heir to an earldom, was a mindless fop. He was certainly not worthy of Felicia Simmons, and Wilde hoped the girl was not being taken in by his blond good looks, his title, and his wealth. Perhaps he could do something to make sure of it?

As Felicia curtsied to the duchess, she hoped they would not be interrupted. "Ma'am? If I might beg your advice?"

The duchess smiled her wintry little smile and nodded to the seat next to her on the sofa. Gratefully, Felicia sank into it.

"No doubt you've heard the gossip about me, ma'am," she began without preamble. "I have discovered it was the result of a story invented by my godmother."

"Of course it was," her grace said dryly. "Just the sort of thing Marjorie would do, all in the guise of assisting you, of course."

"Yes, but what am I to do about it? Say? And what can I do to keep her from whatever mad scheme she thinks of next?"

The duchess leaned over and patted her knee. "Nothing, unfortunately. Once Marjorie comes up with a plan. . . ! I suggest you just ignore her. Eventually, whatever gossip she causes will die down.

"When I heard the rumor, I did think of taking Marjorie to task myself, but I've learned over the years that that does no good at all. She is so

166

sure she is being helpful, you see. And yet some people's, and most certainly Marjorie's, acts of kindness often make their beneficiary feel more the victim.

"But there now. Here is your next partner coming. Don't worry, Miss Simmons. Monty can be trusted to keep his wife from any truly outrageous starts. And I do assure you that although the ton cherishes gossip, there is something they love even more."

As Felicia rose and curtsied, looking a question, her grace added, "The newest piece of gossip, of course. Fortunately, some is always coming along."

Felicia was a little bemused as Mr. Whitaker led her into the set that was forming. Pray the duchess was right, she thought.

Lord Ormsby was quick to bow to her for the supper dance much later. By that time, a great many of the older ladies had adjourned to the card room or the dining room, and since the duchess had been called away to deal with some crisis in the kitchen, the soiree was in danger of becoming a romp.

Felicia could not like the way Lord Ormsby's right hand pressed her waist, as if he were intent on drawing her closer to him than convention decreed. Nor did she care for the way his other hand clutched hers, his thumb caressing her glove. She struggled, trying to keep her distance, and he smiled down at her, well aware that his physical strength made it impossible for her to do so. But when he danced her into an adjoining salon and shut the door behind them, she began to fight him in earnest. As she fought, he put both arms around her and pulled her close.

"Stop it! Let me go!" she cried.

"No, I can't," he said simply, his eyes glowing as they devoured her. Felicia began to suspect m'lord

167

had made too many trips to the punch bowl, and when he giggled a little, she was sure of it.

"I won't, either," he continued. "And what would you say if I told you I was going to keep you here until I had your promise to go driving with me tomorrow?"

"I would say it would be a ridiculous waste of both our time," she snapped, more annoyed than afraid of him. "Eventually, my godmother and her husband will come in search of me to take me home, and if they should be so careless as to forget me, I imagine one of the servants will be here as soon as the party is over anyway.

"Oh, do let me go, you ridiculous man! I shan't ever go driving with you or anywhere else if you persist in this idiocy!"

To her dismay, although he released her, it was only to kneel at her feet and clasp her around the knees. Tottering a little, she grabbed a chair back to steady herself, and where before she had prayed someone would come in, now she prayed just as fervently that they would not.

"Miss Simmons, no, Felicia, you must listen to me!" Lord Ormsby said. "I am very attracted to you. I am sure it could be much more than attraction, but how am I to find out if you will not let me see you alone? Please, dear, *dear* Felicia . . ."

"You will release dear, *dear* Felicia this instant," a cold harsh voice said from the doorway behind them.

Felicia gasped in dismay. Forgetting she was hobbled at the knees by Lord Ormsby's grasp, she tried to turn, overbalanced, and fell to the floor. As she did so, her hapless captor went down as well, taking her full weight as he did so.

"Oh, for heaven's sake!" she said, much flustered as she tried to untangle herself and rise. As she pushed herself up, she heard a sharp groan, and she realized she had used Lord Ormsby's stomach to aid her. She prayed he would not be sick because of it.

It seemed an age before she was free of him, and she scrambled to her feet as quickly as she could. And when she turned to Sir Christopher she saw him regarding her with eyes that resembled pieces of gray slate, his face as immobile as any statue's.

But not a benevolent statue. A furious one.

Felicia was frightened, and she admitted it, for she was worried that Sir Christopher might do the murder he looked so capable of at that moment. And although she had no love for Lord Ormsby, she did not want him to die.

"Thank you for coming in when you did, sir," she made herself say as she moved to his side and took hold of his arm. It was like grasping marble. "I'm afraid Lord Ormsby has had a bit too much champagne. I beg you will not do anything we would all regret because of that."

When he did not speak, she turned to the other man in the room. He had risen now, holding his stomach in both hands and gaping at them. "Do run along now, sir," she said as forcefully as she could. "Yes, yes, I am sure you are very contrite, but I am not in the mood for apologies. Sir Christopher will take me back to the drawing room. And may I suggest you take yourself home?"

Lord Ormsby's mouth opened and shut a few times, as if he were trying to think of something dignified to say. But whether it was the fright in Felicia's eyes, the desire to kill in Sir Christopher's, or just his own inarticulateness, he couldn't speak at all. There was nothing left for him to do but give them a shaky bow before he staggered bent-over to the door.

Felicia did not draw a deep breath until that door

closed behind him. Then she wondered that Chris Wilde had been mute since his one order when he had first come in. Releasing his arm, she moved away from him a little as if to inspect herself in the large mirror over the fireplace. She was sure she looked a perfect fright after the tumble she had taken, but she was not concerned with that. No, for even as apprehensive as she was feeling, she was too aware of the man behind her, so stern and unforgiving. So silent.

Just as she was about to demand he speak, he said, "I suggest you tidy yourself, Miss Simmons. We cannot remain here for long. People will notice your absence from the festivities—mine as well. And even if you don't care about your reputation, believe me, I do."

Felicia ignored this provocative statement as she smoothed her hair and straightened her skirts. She really wanted to ask him what there had been about the incident that bothered him so much. After all, she had not been caught in a passionate embrace, and Lord Ormsby had been only tipsy, not dangerous. Nothing had happened. Nothing at all.

Besides, what business is it of his anyway? she asked herself indignantly. He is not a relative of mine, nor my guardian! Turning to mention this, she found he had moved closer, and she gasped in spite of herself. His face was still harsh and disapproving as he offered his arm and she was forced to take it.

Again he did not speak as they entered the hall by another door, nor did he until he had seated her beside Lady Bradford. As he bowed to the lady, he begged to be excused.

After he went away, the viscountess leaned close to Felicia, her eyes wide. "What is the *matter* with Sir Christopher?" she asked in a stage whisper. "I have *never* seen a man look so dangerous!"

"Please ma'am, I cannot tell you now," Felicia whispered back. Or ever, she reminded herself. For if she explained the predicament, her godmother might well come to her rescue, and then heaven help her, for no one else could.

"Oh, my *dear*! You haven't been *quarreling* with Sir Christopher, have you? What*ever* about? But perhaps it was only a *little* brangle? One that can soon be mended? *Do* let me advise you."

"Thank you, but there is nothing to be done. And I doubt this can be mended," Felicia said, wondering why she felt so much like weeping.

To her surprise, Lady Bradford had no comment to that remark, although she appeared preoccupied for the rest of the evening.

Later, Felicia discovered that not only Lord Ormsby but Chris Wilde had left the soiree, and it seemed to her it dragged on endlessly from that time. She was delighted when the Bradford carriage returned her to Upper Brook Street, and she hurried inside, determined not to spare a single glance at his windows to see if he were home.

To her surprise, when Felicia left the house the following morning, dressed in her gray muslin and severe bonnet and carrying her music case, she discovered Chris Wilde in the doorway opposite, waiting for her. She hurried away, but he caught up with her easily.

"No, you'll not avoid this meeting, my girl," he said, still in the same cold voice he had used last evening. "I've a great deal to say to you that I could not say last night, and I will be heard."

"I don't have to listen to you," Felicia told him, avoiding his eye.

"Yes, you do," he said as he took her arm and matched his strides to hers. "You must tell me first, ma'am, how you could be so upset at the gossip there was about your renting rooms or writing a

171

novel, and yet make such a cake of yourself at the party. It might well be all over London by now, you know, how you flirted with Lord Ormsby to the point that he lost control of himself and you had to be rescued from a folly of your own making.

"But stay! Perhaps he was proposing to you? He was on his knees, as I recall. In that case, maybe you are angry that I interrupted?"

"He was not proposing! He was only bosky from the champagne and trying to get me to agree to a drive."

"How disappointing for you. Still, you should be ashamed of yourself, ma'am. I never thought you so careless and bold.

"And why didn't you call out for help, if he was coercing you against your will? Tell me that, if you can."

"I couldn't. It would have caused an awful scene," Felicia said quickly. "Besides, Lord Ormsby is not a dangerous man, nor did he mean me harm. But no doubt you base your suppositions on the way women have reacted to *your* attentions, sir?"

Before he could reply, she hurried on, "And how dare you say such things to me? Accuse me this way? What I do is no business of yours! Let me go at once! I don't want to hear another word from you—ever!"

"And if I don't you will make a scene now, this time in the open on Park Lane where not only the ton but the common folk can be edified by your behavior?" he demanded. "Perhaps you were right, ma'am. Perhaps you were destined for a life in the theater, since you seem to revel so in public displays."

"I hate you!" Felicia gasped. "You are the most impossible man I have ever met! And I wish I hadn't! Leave me alone. I don't want to have another thing to do with you. Go away!"

He stopped then, and since he did not release her arm, Felicia was forced to stop as well. Out of the corner of her eye, she saw they were indeed being observed by such a disparate group as a chimney sweep and his climbing boy, a party of gentlemen on horseback just coming from the park, two farmers delivering milk, and three ladies whose carriage, directly opposite, had been stopped by traffic.

"I wish I could have you alone for a moment," Sir Christopher said, his gray eyes as cold as they had been last evening. Irrelevantly, Felicia wondered that she still had the feeling she could be singed by their light, if she stared at them too long.

"I'd teach you a lesson then," he went on, looking as if he were aching to do just that. "For it is obvious, when all is said and done, that your manners are not any better than those of Miss Perkins."

Felicia gasped at the insult, her face white with shock. Wanting to rip up at him as she did, it was all she could do to say in an even, only slightly unsteady voice, "This conversation is pointless, sir, and I wish to end it. I have an appointment, and I am late. I may seem as crudely mannered as Miss Perkins, but your detaining me against my will makes you no better than Lord Ormsby."

To her great relief and surprise, he released her at once.

"Ah, no, I didn't mean a word of it! You must know I didn't!" he muttered, throwing out his hands and looking harassed.

Startled by the tortured look in his eyes, Felicia took a step backward. She had never seen a man who looked more confused and unhappy.

"I couldn't help myself, not after seeing you last evening with Ormsby kneeling at your feet. . . . I wanted to kill him then and there for daring to touch you. . . . I wanted to take you in my arms and kiss you—protect you from such as he. . . . I wanted . . . Miss Simmons—no, Felicia! Will you marry me?"

Thirteen

THE TWO STOOD staring at each other, looking identically stunned, and, in the case of Chris Wilde, appalled. *Dear Lord, what have I done?* he asked himself feverishly. *Proposed to Miss Simmons? Proposed? Me? Who doesn't even want a wife? Have I gone mad?*

"Have you gone mad?" Felicia managed to say, inadvertently echoing his own chaotic thought. "You don't propose to someone on a busy street, someone, moreover, whom you have just been reviling! Besides, if I had to be forced to walk with you against my will, why ever did you think I would want to marry you? Well, I don't, and I won't! So there!"

Instead of being relieved at this vehement refusal that safely ensured his continued bachelorhood, Chris Wilde felt a stab of regret. Still, he did not dare to say anything, for he had no idea what might emerge from his treacherous mouth, all unbidden and unplanned.

"I do not think I have ever been so insulted," Felicia continued, oblivious to the housemaid who knelt, mouth agape on the steps of the nearest mansion, her scrub brush forgotten. The chimney sweep had paused to lean against a convenient lamppost, his boy huddled at his feet, and a footman running an errand for his master stopped dead in his tracks to listen.

"You ask me to marry you just like that, when

you have never shown the least indication that you cared for me that way?" Felicia went on, her voice rising a little. "Who do you think you are, sir? Perhaps *you* have been drinking? I can think of nothing else to explain such a mad suggestion. And I'll thank you to say no more on the subject, or I'll treat you to a scene you'll live to regret. And believe me, nothing in this world could make me consider marriage with such an arrogant, unfeeling dictator! Nothing, do you hear me?"

Glancing around for the first time, Chris Wilde saw that several people could hear her as well as he could himself, and his rugged face reddened. Stepping back, he muttered, "I—I beg your pardon. Give you good-day, ma'am."

Felicia watched him turn and almost run back the way they had come.

Alone on the field of battle, she was recalled to reality when the maid exclaimed, "Well, now I've seen everything, I 'ave! The quality! Sumpin else, ain't they?"

Felicia put up her chin and tried to look indifferent as she marched away. But as she did so, she wondered why such disparate feelings as anger and depression warred in her breast. Oh, she did not wonder at the anger, it was the depression that surprised her, and how with every step she took, that emotion seemed to be getting the upper hand.

But why should that be? she asked herself as she turned the corner. She was free of that impossible man at last, wasn't she? Why couldn't she just say good riddance to him and have done with it?

When she arrived home that afternoon, Felicia found two bouquets waiting for her on the hall table. The enormous one composed of various spring blooms, and accompanied by an abject apology, was from Lord Ormsby. The other, of deep pink roses, was from Sir Christopher Wilde.

She read Lord Ormsby's missive first, and paid it scant heed, for her eyes kept straying to the other letter. She could see it was sealed with red wax that bore the unusual dragon imprint she had noticed before on Sir Christopher's signet ring. For a moment she was tempted to return the flowers and note unopened, but her curiosity got the better of her.

Breaking the seal, she spread open the sheet of hot pressed paper with hands that trembled a little. What would he say? What *could* he say to excuse himself, she wondered.

The note began innocently enough, an apology for embarrassing her that morning. But then Felicia stiffened as she read on. So, he was "delighted she had not taken him seriously," was he? And he "didn't know what had got into him"? Well! As if she had not been insulted enough! she told herself as she called down to the kitchen to ask one of the maids to put the flowers in water. She would place Lord Ormsby's offering in the drawing room. Sir Christopher's roses could grace her father's room. She certainly didn't want to see them again.

For the following few days, Felicia tried to go about her life with a steadfast heart, if not a happy one. She saw to the household, went to her teaching appointments, and spent more time with Jacqueline and George, whose own lessons she felt she had neglected. Jacqueline blossomed under her attention, although George did not seem to care for lessons—of any kind. Mrs. Doherty had spoken to him harshly for stealing cookies from the crock, Joe had threatened to take a stick to him for skimping on his chores, and Lucie had scolded him for coming in late one night. George listened to them all, and sometimes he managed to shed an easy tear, but he continued to go his own way.

Felicia did not seem to notice anything. Some

days when her father was brighter, she was happier, but inevitably, when he sank back into apathy, her sour mood returned.

She had written to excuse herself from attending the concert of sacred music with Mr. Ainsworth and his cousin, unwilling to meet Sir Christopher whom she feared might be included, and she also refused all of Lord Ormsby's invitations to drive or stroll. She wondered, though, if she were feeling blue-deviled because she had retired a little from Society. Surely she had not become spoiled by the life in such a short time, had she?

At last she decided that she must write to Chris Wilde and at least thank him for all his kindness to her, for it went very much against the grain to dismiss him so arrogantly.

For he had been kind on many occasions, she told herself as she pared her quill. It was only right that she tell him so, no matter he thought her as ill mannered as Cecily Perkins! She would show him she was not by being as cool and gracious as she knew how to be.

As she was finishing the letter later, Livingston came in with some coffee for her, and she asked him to deliver it across the street.

The old valet agreed, a little frown on his face as he watched her fold and seal it. He knew something was amiss, but what it could be, neither he nor Lucie nor Gladys had any idea. He was sorry for it. Sir Christopher Wilde had seemed such an excellent candidate for Miss Felicia's hand.

The next morning, Felicia was surprised to receive a visit from her father's man of business.

"Do sit down, Mr. Frawley," she said as she indicated a chair in the library. "I do hope there is nothing wrong?"

Mr. Frawley beamed at her as he adjusted his coattails and sat. He was a short, fat man with only a fringe of lank brown hair left, but more importantly, he was a competent one who had been more than kind to her in her troubles.

"Far from it, Miss Simmons, as I am happy to be able to tell you," he began, smiling even more broadly now.

Felicia was relieved, although she wondered at his air of suppressed excitement, the way he almost bounced in his seat. And she wondered as well, why he did not get right to the point. He was like a little boy, hiding a wonderful secret till the very last minute.

"I am so glad to hear it," she said encouragingly.

"And you will be in alt when you discover what I have to tell you," he said, winking at her and then coughing behind his hand as if he felt he might have offended with such familiarity.

After he had mopped his brow with his handkerchief, restored that handkerchief to his pocket and settled back in his chair, Mr. Frawley got down to the matter at hand at last.

"I trust your father is in reasonable spirits, miss?" he asked. "Not, er, wandering about in his mind?"

"No, today he is very well," Felicia told him.

"Good! For now, perhaps, you will be able to tell him the marvelous news I bring, while he can understand it. You see, I have been greatly surprised to receive communications from three gentlemen, telling me of debts they owed your father that have never been repaid. Think of it, Miss Simmons! *Three* gentlemen in the same week! A miracle, don't you think?"

"I do indeed," Felicia said calmly, although her heart was beating faster in anticipation.

"All of them asked to remain anonymous," the agent went on. "Of course you can understand that wish, for these debts are many years old, and it would not place them in a very good light if news of their default came to be common knowledge."

Felicia told herself she didn't care if she never knew their names, as she leaned forward and asked, "How much money did they owe my father, sir?"

Mr. Frawley drew a sheaf of paper from the case he carried. "The first gentleman, eight hundred pounds. The second, fifteen hundred. And the third—ah, the third!—was in debt to the tune of five thousand."

"But—but that's seven thousand three hundred pounds," Felicia whispered through suddenly dry lips. "It cannot be!"

"I do assure you that it is, miss," the agent said quickly. "And then, as I pointed out to them, there is the matter of interest. . . ."

"But you must not tax them for that," Felicia was quick to say. "I am sure my father would never ask such a thing of his friends!"

"Now, now, Miss Simmons, you just leave such matters to me," Mr. Frawley said, his voice soothing. "I do assure you the gentlemen were all agreeable. For they know well the interest would be much higher with a regular money lender. Furthermore, they would not have had all these carefree years. Instead, they might have found themselves having to flee the country to avoid being thrown in prison for debt."

"But it was a loan to friends, and you don't charge your friends interest," Felicia protested.

Mr. Frawley got up and came over to take up her hands and pat them. "The deed is done, Miss Simmons. I did not come to see you until the debt and the interest had been paid. You see, I knew, good lass that you are, you would never agree to that interest. But, and if you'll forgive the pun, I have your best interests at heart, and it was easy for me to do it.

"There now," he said briskly as he went back to his chair. "I suggest you forget all about this business. Plan instead how you intend to spend such largesse. Some new furnishings, perhaps? New gowns? A carriage and team?"

"Nothing like that," Felicia said quickly, both hands to her hot cheeks. "I would not waste the money on such foolishness, sir. There is my father's future security to consider, my household's as well, and then there are the waifs. . . ."

"Indeed," Mr. Frawley said absently as he restored his papers to the case. "I applaud you for your foresightedness. But safely invested, this money will still provide enough for you to command some of the elegancies of life you have had to do without these past years.

"I've opened an account for you at Wilson and Barnes, bankers in the city. You may draw on it for your needs. I know you intend to be careful with it, but I do wish you'd buy something frivolous for yourself. I've a daughter your age, you know, and I understand how dear such things are to females. And you have economized for so long!"

Felicia rose as he did, to take his leave. "I do thank you so much, sir," she said with a warm smile, although she had no intention of wasting a ha'penny of this windfall. "I am truly grateful to you for taking such good care of us all."

"And you'll tell your father?" he asked as they walked to the hall.

Felicia shook her head, frowning now. "No, I can't. He doesn't know that things got to such a pass, you see, and I would not trouble him with them now, even though those worries are over. He would fret so!"

After Mr. Frawley had left, Felicia went to the drawing room in a daze. Once there, she looked around the old-fashioned, yet still elegant room. To think of it! All that money! Now she could not only repay Livingston, she could even give him more. And she need never take lodgers again. The drawing room was hers to do with as she wished, to fill with her own belongings, to receive guests in. Why, she could ask Drusilla and her aunt—any others she liked to tea soon, even invite Lord and Lady Bradford to call. It was truly a miracle, and she closed her eyes for a moment and said a fervent prayer of thanks for her good fortune.

Across the way, with a grim look of satisfaction on his face, Chris Wilde watched Mr. Frawley leave Felicia's house. Ted Bowers, who was clearing the breakfast dishes away, studied him with a frown on his own face.

The guv was in bad spirits these days, although he had no idea why. And, he wondered as he lifted his tray, why m'lord remained in London, since the place depressed him so. Bowers knew his business was completed; why didn't they go down to Devon? Some hard work and exercise would do the man more good than moping about here. Besides, he thought he had caught sight of a most unwelcome face only the day before, watching this address from a vantage point a few houses beyond. It'd be a good thing if he could get the guv out of town, if he had seen who he thought he had. However, the man had hurried away before he could be sure, and he resolved to say nothing until he was sure of his identity. Perhaps he had only been imagining that narrow, ferretlike face, those shifty eyes? For India was a long way from here, and it was highly improbable that either Samuel King or his henchman could be in London.

Chris Wilde did not hear the door close behind Bowers. He had gone to his desk to take Felicia's letter out again, to reread it. As he did so, he wondered why he bothered, when he had it to heart. But perhaps it was so he could look at the handwriting, imagine her penning those words of thanks? Yet even though she had also apologized for her rude words to him, there was never a doubt in his mind that she had written a dismissal. She did not care to see him again. She had, in effect, said good-bye.

The clock struck the hour then, and he rose and stretched. He had been summoned by Lord Bradford, and he did not want to be late for their appointment. As he went to get his hat and gloves and cane, he wondered what m'lord wanted to see him about? Had he some news of Mr. Simmons's debtors, perhaps? Good news? How satisfying that would be!

At that very moment, Marjorie Bradford was sweeping into her husband's library, and he dismissed his secretary when he saw she wanted to speak to him on a private matter.

"Now, Marjorie, tell me at once what is troubling you," he said as he put his arm around her still slim waist and hugged her to him. "For Christopher Wilde is coming soon."

"I know. He's who I wanted to see you about," Lady Bradford said. "For here's Felicia as *silent* as silent could be, no matter how I beg her to reveal what has happened between them. But not a *word* escapes her lips! I must say, Montmorency, I don't understand her at *all*! Why, if it were *me*, I'd have told me at once, and *begged* for my help!"

Lord Bradford smiled a little at that tangled sentence. "Of course you would have, my love, and I've no doubt half of London beside. But Felicia is different than you are. That is why I asked Wilde to come today. I hope to find out from him what has happened. I was so sure he was in love with the girl, and I didn't think she was exactly indifferent to him either, did you?"

"No, I didn't," his wife said as she tidied a pile of books before she went to the window to stare out into the mews behind the house. "Indeed, I was already planning the most *delightful* wedding for the two of them, and Felicia's *gown*, and I even thought they might like to go to our plantation in Jamaica for their honeymoon, if, that is, Felicia is *not* troubled by seasickness!"

"Nor Sir Christopher either," Lord Bradford said, a twinkle in his eye. "Very well, my dear, leave this to me for now. I'll do my best to ferret out the cause of their coolness, but it might take a bit of doing. Chris Wilde is just as reticent as Felicia ever thought of being, and he is a man who, once his mind is made up, is difficult to shift. Run along now, pet. I'll see you at luncheon later. By the way, is it tonight we are pledged to the Ormsbys?"

Lady Bradford nodded before she held up her face for his kiss. "You remind me, Montmorency, that young Ormsby was very taken with Felicia. I wonder if . . ."

She moved toward the door then, her head tilted to one side as she considered the possibilities. Her husband watched her go, a fond smile playing over his austere face. How Marjorie hated a mystery! he thought. But then, most women did. And he admitted that in this instance, he himself was just as curious as any woman could ever be.

When his guest had been admitted, Lord Bradford indicated two leather chairs that flanked the fireplace before he poured them both a glass of burgundy.

"Can it be you have heard from some of Reginald Simmons's debtors, sir?" Wilde asked. "Perhaps even from the Marquess of Binchfield? For some reason, I'm sure he's one of the guilty ones."

The viscount shook his head. "Nary a word, I'm afraid. And I had such hopes my little theatrical turn with Felicia would work wonders. It seems I was wrong. I would not have thought the nobility capable of such hardheartedness."

"But since they did not repay their debt originally, why would they do so now?" Wilde asked, a cynical twist to his mouth. "If any names ever got out, they would be ruined, for who would receive them?

"However, I myself did happen to see Frawley, Mr. Simmons's man of business leaving the house only a short time ago. Perhaps he had some good news for Miss Simmons? News that we, of course, could not know?"

Lord Bradford's stern face brightened. "Pray you are right, sir! And certainly, it would be easier to admit your debt to an agent, rather than to either one of us. I didn't think of that."

There was a little silence, and Chris Wilde looked at his host with a question in his eyes.

"Er, I have it from Marjorie that Felicia has stopped accepting invitations. My wife is disturbed by this, but the girl won't tell her why she does so. Would you, perhaps, know anything of the matter, sir?"

Chris Wilde sipped his wine to give himself time to think. M'lord's question was perilously close to prying, and he could not like it. Besides, he had no intention of ever revealing to anyone—except to those people who had happened to overhear his proposal of marriage that fateful morning—what an idiot he had made of himself. He had too much pride for that.

Now he forced a shrug. "I'm afraid I do not. But then, it's not likely that I would know, is it? Miss Simmons and I are scarcely on such terms that she would reveal her intimate thoughts to me. As a

185

matter of fact, I haven't seen her lately. Perhaps she is ill? Or her father is?"

Lord Bradford shook his head. "No, she's not ill, and as far as I know, neither is Simmons. Well, there was no harm in asking, I suppose, although Marjorie will be disappointed you cannot clear up this little mystery. She does love Felicia so, and she hates to see the girl unhappy."

Firmly repressing the urge to ask just how unhappy Miss Simmons was, and about what, the baronet changed the subject, to compliment m'lord on the quality of the wine.

Walking back to Upper Brook Street a short time later, Chris Wilde wondered he could have been in such control of himself and his statements to Lord Bradford when he had been so out of control only a few days ago.

Why had he done such a mad thing as propose to the girl? he asked himself for perhaps the hundredth time. Was it because he was in love with her? But he didn't believe in love. Oh, of course he had desired women, felt passion, but he had never loved a one of them and certainly had never thought of spending the rest of his life with one. Definitely not!

But if what he was feeling—so moody and preoccupied, so uneasy and unhappy—didn't indicate love, what did it mean?

Perhaps it was just because he had always hated having his will crossed? What a lowering thought!

But that couldn't be it, not when he thought of her so often, wondering about her, even worrying. He could conjure up her lovely face with its warm smile and sparkling eyes, hear the sound of her delightful laughter, in a moment. Was she to haunt him forever?

Perhaps he had better go away, he told himself as he nodded to Mr. Kenton and took the stairs to his rooms two at a time. Go home to Wildewold, throw himself into the improvements he had started in the manor house and around the estate. But as he opened his door and threw his hat, cane, and gloves on a table, he knew he would not do that. Not yet, at any rate.

"Thought I heard you come in," Ted Bowers said behind him. "Got bad news, guv."

"What is it?" Wilde asked, his gray eyes narrowing. Not Felicia, he thought. Pray it did not concern Felicia!

"Happened to see Bob Yates outside the house after you left," Bowers told him, watching him carefully. He was astounded when Chris Wilde grinned at him in relief.

"Did you hear me, guv? Yates was there, two houses away, as plain as the nose on your face, and not in Bombay where we left him. And you do remember Yates, don't you?"

"Of course I do," Wilde told him as he went to stare out the window.

"He's not there now," Bowers said, his ugly face showing his concern.

"And where Yates is, we can be sure to find Samuel King, now can't we?" Wilde asked idly.

"Aye, that we can," Bowers agreed grimly. "I thought I spotted the little weasel yesterday, but I wasn't sure. But today, I saw him plain."

He hesitated for a moment before he added, "Want me to see to him? Discourage him—like from hanging about? Do more than that?"

"No, I'll take care of this myself," Chris Wilde said as he walked to his desk and drew his pistols from the drawer there. He checked them, although he knew he would find them primed and loaded. Bowers would have made sure of that. He always did.

His man shrugged. "Let me know if I can help. I've a score to settle with ferret-face myself.

"And guv?" he said as he went to the door. "You remember how dangerous Yates and King are. Especially now. You have a care for yourself."

Fourteen

LADY BRADFORD WAS disappointed but not discouraged when her husband admitted his failure to learn anything from Chris Wilde about why her goddaughter was suddenly so retiring.

"*I* shall find out, Montmorency," she told him as they sat together after luncheon. "Just *see* if I don't!"

She looked so stern and determined, her husband was tempted to laugh; instead, he asked her how she intended to accomplish such a thing.

"*Something* will occur to me. It always does! Perhaps I shall ask Felicia to drive out with me to Hampstead Wells some pleasant day soon. It will make a nice *change* for her, getting out of London proper. And I could ask a few other guests. . . ."

"Including Sir Christopher Wilde?"

"How *well* you know me, Montmorency! Of *course* I shall include him, but there will have to be others as well. After all, one does not like to be considered *blatant*, now does one?

"But then I can *observe* them together. You see, I am *sure* they've had a falling-out, although what it could be *about* when they are both being so *tiresomely* reticent, I have no idea!

"Now let me see. Lady Sylvia, the Duchess of Kyle's daughter and one of her brothers, do you think? Maybe the Earl of Castleton, Miss Remington? Perhaps Marmaduke Ainsworth and that wispy cousin of his? Felicia has taken the girl up, tried to befriend her. Not that anything will come of it. I'd wager anything you like *that* one will return to the country unwed. Such a *shy* little thing she is!

"But I digress, and there is *no* need for you to tell me that I *always* do.

"You must come as well, so there will be ten of us. Unless, that is, you prefer that I ask General Gates *instead*?"

Since the general was an old and most persistent beau of his wife's, Lord Bradford was quick to agree to make one of the party, and the viscountess went away to pen her invitations.

Her goddaughter was easier to persuade than she had thought she might be. But this was because both Lucie and Gladys Johns had spent a great deal of time convincing Felicia that she was being very silly to forego all the treats of the Season, especially now that she had more than enough money to hand.

Felicia had told the others of the repaid debts immediately, promising to return Mr. Livingston's money and pay the others their wages as well. The council of war that met around the big deal table that evening had been all smiles at her news, and each and every one of them was determined that Miss Felicia must be persuaded to rejoin Society.

"I'm sure the reason she's been mopin' ter home has ter do with that Sir Christopher," Lucie declared. "Wish she'd tell me about it. I'm sure I could give 'er some good advice about men in general, an' that one in partic'lar!"

Mr. Livingston had hid a shudder. Pray Miss Felicia never took Lucie Watts's advice, he told himself. That way would lead to sure social ruin for a young unmarried lady of good family.

What Felicia would not admit, even to herself,

was her hope that Chris Wilde would be one of the party. It seemed such a long time since she had seen him. Of course, if he were there, she would be ladylike yet distant, she assured herself as she went to her armoir to choose the gown she would wear. The jonquil gingham? Or perhaps the pretty white muslin with the forget-me-nots and her new bonnet? And she would carry a parasol to match, she decided, and wear new kid slippers.

The day appointed for the excursion dawned sunny, to Lady Bradford's relief. She had arranged for the servants to go ahead with a luncheon and given them instructions to set up the picnic far from any of the lower orders, who, along with the nobility, flocked to the place. Lady Bradford would be the first to agree it was diverting to dance alongside a hearty tradesman and his wife, or listen to the music with footmen and maids enjoying a rare day off, but too close intimacy with such as they was not to be thought of.

Felicia rode in the Bradford carriage. Her heart had jumped when she spotted Sir Christopher's carriage at the start. She waved gaily to Drusilla Pierce, who was traveling with the baronet in company of her cousin. She barely noticed the other guests, although by now she knew them all well.

Once Hampstead Wells was reached, Felicia was quick to accept Viscount Creed's arm, to stroll with him and his sister, Lady Sylvia, down the Well Walk, and she made an effort to appear gay and carefree as she did so.

But when the dancing began, she admitted to herself that she was very nervous. In such a small party, Sir Christopher was sure to ask her to dance, and what would she do when he came to her side?

She was to find out in short order, for he bowed before her almost immediately.

"Yes, *do* dance, Felicia," her godmother urged.

"Such *fun*, is it not? Oh, do look over there, Montmorency! Have you ever *seen* such a large woman? And what a *quiz* of a hat!"

Obediently, Felicia rose and took the hand Chris Wilde was holding out to her, hoping she at least looked cool and collected.

"You are enjoying the party?" he asked after a moment.

"Of course. What a delightful spot this is," Felicia said. "I understand there is also bowling on the Heath?"

"And gambling," he said, staring down at her in his arms. His gray eyes seemed to pierce all her defenses; Felicia did not care for it in the slightest, and she concentrated on staring at his left lapel and refusing to meet his eye.

"I must thank you for your letter," he said after a little silence. Felicia wondered that his voice could be so stiff and lifeless. Was he uncomfortable, too?

She shook her head as if she wanted no thanks, but he went on, "No, it was kind of you. But you refined too much on the little I have been able to do for you, ma'am. And, as I have told you before, it was my pleasure."

"Thank you," Felicia managed to get out, even as she wondered if the dance would ever be over.

"You're looking very lovely today," he said next, and startled, her eyes met his for a brief moment. What she saw shining in them made her lower her own eyes at once. She could feel his hand at her waist through the thin muslin of her gown, smell the lotion he used, and she was beginning to feel dizzy.

"I have missed seeing you these past few days," he went on. "I trust you did not stay away from any parties because you thought it would be uncomfortable to meet me again? I promise you, ma'am, I would do nothing to put you to the blush. And although I agree there is bound to be some slight awkwardness between us, because of the ridiculous proposition I made to you, I pray you will disregard it.''

(Ridiculous, was it? Well, she guessed she knew how to take *that* remark!)

"Allow me to relieve your mind, sir. I have quite forgot the incident," she said stiffly. "It was of no great importance, after all."

(Wasn't it, indeed? Ha! A man doesn't propose every day of the week, you know!)

"I am relieved to hear you say so, ma'am."

(Relieved, are you? Think you've had quite the lucky escape, do you? Oh, how I detest you, you arrogant, conceited, *impossible* man!)

"And I am relieved you are being so gracious about it. I don't believe most men would take a lady's refusal of their hand so calmly."

(Calm, am I? I'd like to "calm" you, my girl! In fact, I'd give a great deal to have you alone for a bit. You'd find out how *calm* I would be then!)

"It was an unfortunate mistake. Perhaps we should stop discussing it, ma'am? Forget it?"

Her hand itching to slap him, Felicia changed the subject. Chris Wilde followed her lead, but he continued to stare down at her until she was sure she was going to miss her step.

When the dance was finally, and mercifully, over, the two were even more estranged than before, although no one would have guessed from Felicia's curtsy and polite smile, nor Sir Christopher's elegant bow, his words of thanks for the honor.

"I could just *scream* at her, Montmorency, *really* I could!" Lady Bradford hissed as she gathered her belongings prior to shepherding her party to the picnic site. "That horrid little *smirk* she gave him! And she barely *looked* at him while they were dancing. It is too bad, and it put me *all* out of charity with her!"

"I agree it appears that something very serious has occurred between them," her husband agreed, as he picked up a handkerchief she had dropped. "But what's to be done now?"

Lady Bradford looked militant. "Never fear, my dear, I'll see those two reconciled if it's the *last* thing I do!"

The viscount shook his head a little, but knowing his wife as he did, he knew there was nothing he could do to stop her. He only hoped that whatever scheme she came up with now would not be too bizarre. As he accepted a glass of wine from one of his footmen, he reminded himself he must keep a close watch on Marjorie.

It was late afternoon before the carriages returned to town. There had been no more private contact between Sir Christopher and Felicia, something that seemed to puzzle Duke Ainsworth. He had suggested that Miss Simmons might like to ride back in their carriage with his cousin Drusilla, but Wilde had not extended the invitation to her. Instead, Felicia went home the way she had come, with the Bradfords, which, in the viscountess's mind, made her appear very much the unsought-after spinster.

Christopher Wilde and Felicia Simmons met often in the following days, in the park or at parties, and invariably they behaved as if they were mere acquaintances. Even when Lady Bradford had a musicale and persuaded Felicia to play for the guests and later accompany Sir Christopher when he sang for them, that did not dispel the icy aura that surrounded them. And they had performed so well together! their hostess thought. How could Felicia not have melted at his beautiful deep voice, the soulful words he sang? She did not understand the girl at all!

Yet she could not help noticing how often her

goddaughter looked at the young man when he was not aware of it, and how often he himself stared at her from where he stood brooding against the wall, or in a doorway, and she refused to be discouraged.

When a number of rumors began to circulate about Chris Wilde, Bartholomew Whitaker was one of the first to hear them. It seemed that suddenly everyone was talking about his vast wealth, wealth it was said had been acquired by dishonest dealings abroad. There were other rumors as well, of concubines and harems—even young boys.

When Bart taxed his friend with these rumors, he wondered at the grim look that came over Wilde's handsome rugged face. "You look disturbed, old chap," he said as the two trotted in the park early one morning. "But why should that be? This is only talk; there have been no accusations made."

"No, and there won't be any, because the talk is far from the mark," Wilde said tersely.

"You mean you're not as rich as Golden Ball and you didn't keep a harem of beautiful slave girls? How disappointing! I was just about to ask you what it was like having them continually at your beck and call."

"Sorry to disappoint you. There was no harem. As for my wealth, yes, that part is true at least. I acquired the money when I began to trade with China. But I came by it legitimately, no matter what Samuel King claims."

"King? Is he behind these rumors? I don't believe I know the man."

"He's been abroad for years. He's a very unpleasant character who lived on the fringes of society even in India. And, as I know personally, he is not an honest man. I cut him out of some profitable deals, and I managed to outrace his ships enough times to almost ruin him. No doubt these rumors he's putting about are his way of getting revenge for that."

"Er, is he apt to be dangerous?" Whitaker asked.

"Yes, he's dangerous all right," Wilde admitted in a hard flat voice. "Only because he will not fight fair—challenge me—bring this out in the open. He is more given to sneaking around behind a man's back, hoping for the chance to stab him there without any peril to himself."

"Sounds like an out-and-outer to me. Look out for yourself. In fact, I suggest you carry a pistol when you go abroad," Whitaker said as they reached the Brook Gate.

"I go armed at all times," Chris Wilde said, patting his waist. "Not only pistols, a dagger as well. One learns in the Orient you would not have a long life else. Life there is cheap. Killings are common."

He saw Bart was looking perturbed, and he made himself smile. "Don't worry, my old friend," he said as they walked their mounts across Park Lane to Upper Brook Street. "I've a deal too much experience to be taken in by any of King's tricks. Why, even now I can tell you everyone who is on the street this morning, which ones are strangers, and, in most cases, their occupations. I've learned to be observant, so don't think King will catch me off guard."

He did not mention that he intended to call on Samuel King that same day. Ted Bowers had followed King's man to a house some distance away. Like the company King kept, the house was on the fringe of the better world, and Wilde had not been at all surprised when he had heard of it.

He knew King's habits. The man never left his lodgings until afternoon, for he preferred the dark hours after midnight for handling any business he might have.

Accordingly, he went to the mean street Bowers had told him about a short time later. The maid who answered his knock on the front door of Number Thirty was only too willing to let him announce himself after a guinea changed hands.

He took the stairs two at a time, then strode to the back as he had been directed.

Yates answered his knock, his eyes narrowing when he saw who the visitor was. But when he tried to slam the door in his face, Chris Wilde put his shoulder to it and sent him sprawling backward. Yates's thin face was pale with fury, and as he reached into his pocket, Wilde drew his pistol and aimed it.

"Just take it out slowly, Bobby, if you know what's good for you," he ordered. Yates took one look at Wilde's stern face and did as he was told.

"Ah, Chris Wilde!" a smooth voice said from an interior doorway. "Somehow I was sure you'd find me—even call. But must you come to reminisce at such an ungodly hour?"

"The light of day still bothering you, Sam?" Chris Wilde asked as he took Yates's pistol and pocketed it. "The knife as well, Bobby," he said, dividing his attention between the little man on the floor and the larger, no less deadly one in the doorway.

Yates gave a muttered curse as he rose and put his dagger on a center table. Wilde motioned him back, to stand against the wall.

"Yes, right there where I can see you. And keep your hands in sight. By the way, Ted Bowers asked to be remembered to you. Says he's got a score to settle with you. I'd be careful if I were you. Bowers is, er, frightening sometimes, don't you think? He even frightens me."

"I must say I take offense at being ignored," the man known as Samuel King said as he strolled in to take a seat near the fireplace. "I think most gentlemen would consider it insulting."

"You're hardly a gentleman, but let that go," Chris Wilde told him, eyeing the silk dressing gown worn over soiled breeches, the heavy-lidded eyes and the dark stubble of his unshaven beard. Samuel King yawned in his face. He was a man in his forties, tall and still slim, and he was used to being considered a handsome man. He was not handsome now.

"And knowing you as I do, I've nothing to fear from you," Wilde went on. "For when did you ever soil your hands in such a way? You've always left it to Yates and others to do your dirty work, now haven't you?"

King waved a careless hand. "What did you come for, Wilde?" he asked, abandoning his disinterested air. "I hardly think it was to exchange pleasantries."

"How right you are. If it were up to me, I'd not have a thing to do with you. But I've a quarrel to pick. I've heard rumors going around about me. Rumors that only started when you arrived back in England. I don't care for those rumors, and, as you know well, none of them are true."

King shrugged, his long mouth twisting a little. Chris Wilde turned the pistol toward him. He could see Bob Yates clearly out of the corner of his eye, and he was not concerned the man would try to rush him.

As Sam King stared at the hand holding that pistol, he stiffened. "Still wearing the mandarin's ring, I see," he sneered. "The ring that should have been mine!"

"To the winner goes the spoils, you know that, Sam. I reached Canton first. You were a distant second. If the mandarin chose to do business with me, that was his right. But perhaps his earlier dealings with you had convinced him he could do better elsewhere? I guaranteed the quality of my goods. They were not second-rate or short-weighted. The ring was given to me as a sign of trust.

"But we are straying from the mark.

"Now, about these rumors. They must stop."

"Must they indeed?" King asked as he poured himself a glass of wine.

"If you do not see to it, I'll have the law on you."

"And how will you convince the law that it was I who started the rumors? Surely there are others returned lately from India who could have done so."

"I know of no one who hates me as you do," Wilde told him. "I'm sure I could find some proof of your infamy. You have always tended, in your arrogance, to leave a wide trail. And if by chance, a lawsuit would not work, you might meet with an unfortunate accident."

King pretended amazement as he crossed one leg over the other and leaned back in his chair. "Hardly your style, is it, Wilde? Accidents?"

Now it was Chris Wilde's turn to shrug. "It hasn't been in the past. But I believe vermin must be stamped out, one way or the other."

For a moment, he thought King would forget the pistol and go for his throat, he looked so furious at the insult. He knew how the man prided himself as a gentleman, although the supposition was ridiculous.

Backing up to the door, he said, "I'd suggest you get on with it at once. I'll give you a week."

There was silence in the shabby, undistinguished room as he looked from one to the other. Then he opened the door and backed through it, closing it softly behind him. He stood listening for a moment, his ear to the wood, but from the curses he heard, the conversation that began, he did not think they would try and pursue him. Not now, at any rate.

Chris Wilde hailed a hackney cab a little distance away and rode back to Upper Brook Street deep in thought. Would it work? Somehow he doubted it, but he had had to try. And since he didn't think he had much of a chance getting evidence against Samuel King, no matter what he had said to the man, he was afraid it would have to be settled personally. And although he had killed men before, that had been in situations where his life was at stake. Pirates once, in the Gulf of Tonkin, and a pair of thugs in a Madras alley. He had never dueled. He thought such things ridiculous, even childish. If a man insulted him, he would fight him with his fists until he apologized. Pistols for two, or foils some dreary dawn, seemed the height of theatrics.

As he stepped from the cab before the Kentons' house, Wilde saw Felicia Simmons just coming home from one of her teaching appointments. Their eyes met for a moment, and she was quick to look away, her head held high as she marched up her steps and let herself into her house. Wilde's face assumed a dark, displeased expression.

This seemed to have no effect on Miss Cecily Perkins whom he met in the hall. She and her mother were just leaving their rooms, and she smiled at him warmly. Truly, Miss Perkins was a vision this afternoon. She wore a rose carriage gown that fit her voluptuous figure perfectly, and her black curls were crowned by a white chip straw bonnet that tilted intriguingly over one eye.

"Sir Christopher, well met!" she exclaimed, holding out her hand to him. When he did not take it, only bowed coldly, she blushed a little and went on, "I am so glad to see you, sir. I have been meaning to ask you to call, for I am so anxious to hear all about India. So many people have told me of your adventures, I quite long to hear them for myself.

Do say you will honor my mother and I soon? Come to tea, perhaps?"

Chris Wilde longed to say something cutting, to pay the chit back for the way she had treated Felicia, but one look at her mother's gentle, distressed face, stayed his tongue.

"That won't be possible, ma'am," he only said instead. "I am much engaged these days. Give you good morning. Mrs. Perkins? Your servant."

He brushed past them then, leaving Cecily in a rage. She had heard the rumors of his vast wealth, and she had decided that since she could not seem to interest the Earl of Castleton in matrimony, which object she had been busily pursuing all Season, she would be happy to settle for a wealthy baronet instead who could keep her in jewels and luxuries. She had also heard about his harem, but she put little importance on that. So what if he had had a number of foreign women? Most men had their mistresses, the number of them meant nothing. And since she had no intention of ruining her figure with endless childbirths, she hoped her husband would acquire one almost immediately. In fact, the sooner, the better.

Well! she thought now as she swept from the house, her skirts swishing, and her mother making soothing little noises behind her which she did not even hear. She knew Sir Christopher had been very attentive to her former landlady, seen the flowers he had sent the girl when she herself had been in residence, noticed how he always sought her side at any party. But to think he would refuse *her* invitation, extended in her most dulcet tones when she looked so beautiful and melting, quite confounded her. How could he prefer that insipid little blonde to *me*? she asked herself as she stepped up into the carriage, fuming. How *could* he?

But no doubt the devious Miss Simmons had been

poisoning his mind with untruthful stories about her. Of course! That must be it. But Miss Felicia Simmons would pay for her infamy. And since her father had written and told her that without evidence there was no way to prosecute the author, she would have to find another way. For she was determined that somehow, some way, Miss Simmons would pay. On that Cecily Perkins was adamant.

Chris Wilde had no engagements that evening. He had been invited to a number of parties, but he had refused them all, for he was not in the mood for gaiety. Not because of the false stories going around town about him. He knew he could have ignored the rumors easily. No, it was his estrangement from Felicia that was making him moody.

He ate his dinner alone, then tried to read. But tonight the printed page could not hold his interest, and his thoughts returned to Felicia time and time again. He went over their meetings, the first one kneeling over her broken music case—how he had rescued her at the Bradford ball—their drives and walks—even the scene at the Duchess of Kyle's when he had found Ormsby kneeling at her feet— their confrontation the next day, and all its awful consequences.

At last, tired of telling himself he would think of her no more, and then in the next minute finding himself doing just that, he went to fetch his hat and gloves. Bowers had told him he was playing cards with Mr. Kenton this evening, so except for the servants, he was alone. But it was only ten thirty. Plenty of time for a look-in at Whites. He was sure to find someone there who wanted a hand of picquet, and the game would take his mind off Felicia Simmons.

He made sure he had his pistol, and before he stepped from the front door, he carefully checked the street in both directions. He could see no one. The street was quiet. For a moment, his eyes strayed to the lighted, discreetly draped windows opposite. Was she there? Was she, perhaps, thinking of him? he wondered.

A hackney cab was approaching, and he stepped down to the street and raised his hand to it. But the cab did not slow down. It must already have a fare. No matter. He would walk. It wasn't far.

He noticed the hackney had stopped two doors away, and curious, he watched to see who would emerge. Then, feeling a little uneasy for no reason he could understand, he ran toward the safety of the dark shadows across the street.

The shot that rang out shattered the tranquil silence that prevailed in Upper Brook Street this warm evening in June.

Chris Wilde gasped as he was hit, the ball entering his right shoulder. And as he spun around, trying to reach his pistol, he saw the hackney speed away.

Damned fool! he cursed himself, grasping his shoulder and already feeling the blood dripping down his arm. Duped like a greenhorn because he had let down his guard for a moment!

Must get home, get Bowers, he told himself as he tried to force his legs to take him there. But the cobbles of the street seemed to be moving in waves as he stared at them, his head was reeling, and it felt as if his shoulder were on fire.

He made a great effort once more, for he knew the hackney might return so the marksman—no, Yates—could complete the killing. But even as desperate as he was to reach safety, he only succeeded in falling to the pavement, and as his shoulder was jarred, he fainted from the pain.

Fifteen

SEVERAL CURTAINS WERE twitched aside after the gunfire, but only two doors were thrown open, one at Number Seventeen, the other at Eighteen.

Felicia Simmons had been reading in the drawing room when she heard the shot. Jumping up, her hand to her heart, she ran to the front window just in time to see the hackney disappear around the corner to South Audley Street. What had happened? she asked herself, bewildered. Surely she had heard a shot?

She could see little, for it was dark in front of her house. Still, she did not hesitate, for she suspected someone was in trouble. Running to the front door, she opened it wide. The lights from the hall candles streamed out over the pavement, and she cried out when she saw Sir Christopher lying there. He was not moving, and she had to grasp the doorjamb for a moment to steady herself.

"Don't let him be dead," she whispered as she ran down the steps to kneel at his side. "Please, don't let him be dead!"

As she knelt, the door across the way opened, and Ted Bowers appeared, pistol in hand. Cursing, he hurried to his master's aid.

"He is breathing still," Felicia told him, not even looking up at the man who had come to help.

"Here, missus, let me have a look," Bowers growled. Noticing the fear in her eyes as she turned her head to him at last, he added, "I'm Ted Bowers. Sir Christopher's man."

Obediently, Felicia moved back a little, although she did not let go of Wilde's limp hand. Expertly, Bowers investigated. Felicia gasped as his hand was withdrawn, covered with blood.

"Aye, he's been shot, but I don't think it's fatal," the ugly man said tersely. "Took the ball in his shoulder, he did. But he's losing a lot of blood. Best I get him up to his bed. . . ."

"No!" Felicia cried. "Bring him in here. I've a room on the ground floor. It will be quicker and less painful for him."

When Bowers nodded, she let go of Sir Christopher's hand and gasped again, for her own was stained with blood now, too. Telling herself this was no time for hysterics, she ran back up the steps and into the hall. To her relief, Livingston was standing there, his lined old face concerned.

"We must send someone for the doctor at once," she told him. "Sir Christopher Wilde has been shot!"

She ran past him to the basement stairs and called down, "Gladys! Lucie! Tell Mrs. Doherty to start heating water, and then you both come up here and help me. We must prepare a bed for Sir Christopher, and we'll need a lot of clean sheets for his wound. And Joe? Please run for the doctor! As quickly as you can!"

The household went into immediate action. Livingston went before Felicia to turn down the bed in Cecily Perkins's former room. Gladys and Lucie bustled in with a pile of old sheets which they set about tearing into strips, and Joe stumped out the door, his scarred face set in a frown.

He met Ted Bowers carrying a still unconscious Chris Wilde, but when he paused to ask if the man needed help, he was curtly refused.

As Bowers carried his master inside, both George's and Jacqueline's eyes widened from where they watched at the back of the hall.

"In here," Felicia said as she held the door wide so Bowers could maneuver through it without jarring the injured man.

He laid him down on the bed and said a little breathlessly, for Chris Wilde was a big, well-muscled man, "I'll need scissors to get this coat off."

Lucie hurried forward with a pair.

"I'll also need a thick cloth pad to try and stop the bleeding," he added.

"Is it—is it bad?" Felicia asked, her blue eyes huge in her drawn face.

"Can't tell yet," Bowers told her, busy with the scissors. He was glad Sir Christopher remained unconscious as he cut the coat away. As he removed the cravat and ripped the bloody shirt open, he heard the lady gasp in horror, and he admitted she had reason. It was a gory sight.

The bullet had entered fairly high, however. He did not think any vital spot had been hit, and he himself sighed in relief. Gently, for such a big man, he turned his master a little, his frown returning when he discovered no exit wound. So, the bullet was still lodged inside, was it? Digging it out would be painful for the guv.

"I'll just bind this up," he said, more to himself than Felicia and the maids. "Nothing I can do till the doctor arrives."

A short time later, bandages crisscrossed Wilde's broad chest. Felicia watched anxiously, praying the bleeding would stop.

As she did so, Mr. Livingston came in, bearing one of her father's nightshirts. "Now then, you must leave, Miss Felicia," he ordered. "We've got to undress Sir Christopher, make him more comfortable."

He did not wait to see if he were obeyed, but instead bent to take off the unconscious man's evening shoes and stockings. Reluctantly, Felicia did as she was told.

She was not allowed back in the room until after the doctor had come, dug the bullet out, left a number of instructions, and gone away again. During that time, she sat by herself in the drawing room, her hands tightly clasped as she prayed hard for Chris Wilde's safety. Gladys, taking one look at her pale, strained face, went to fetch her a cup of hot tea, and Lucie insisted on adding a generous tot of Joe's rum to it.

Once, Felicia thought she heard an agonized groan, and knowing vaguely the pain he must be suffering, prayed even harder. "Please don't let him die, dear Lord," she whispered. "I couldn't bear it if he did!"

It seemed hours before Mr. Livingston came to fetch her at last.

"He—he is all right?" she asked as she leapt to her feet.

The old valet smiled a little. "The doctor says he should have a complete recovery, barring complications, of course. But with careful nursing . . ."

"I'll see to that," Felicia told him, her eyes shining.

As she entered his room again, Felicia could barely restrain another gasp. Chris Wilde was covered with blankets, and he was so still and pale under his fading tan that for a moment she was sure he had died. She hurried to his side to bend over him and take his hand to hold it gently. To her relief, his skin was warm, and now she was closer, she could see by the rise and fall of his chest that he did indeed breathe.

She closed her eyes for a moment to say a prayer of thanks, and when she opened them, she saw he was awake, staring up at her as if he could not credit what he saw. Suddenly, Felicia felt closer to those hypnotizing gray eyes than was comfortable, but she could not look away. And she was aware they were alone together.

"Felicia?" he asked, his deep baritone weak. "What are you doing here?"

"It's my house," she told him, trying to ease her hand from his. He did not let her go.

"But why aren't I in my own rooms?" he asked, sounding confused.

"I'll explain everything tomorrow," she promised him. "You must rest now. Are you comfortable?"

A ghost of a smile curved his lips. "I wouldn't really call it comfortable, but at least I'm not in the pain I was a little while ago. But I feel as weak as a kitten."

"Then you must sleep," she said, this time succeeding in pulling her hand away. "Rest well, and don't worry."

His eyes closed again, and she couldn't resist reaching out to softly smooth his hair back from his brow. As he smiled a little, she flushed and hurried away.

While she had been with Sir Christopher, Livingston had realized that he must send for Lady Bradford. True, there were all the servants in residence, and Miss Felicia's father upstairs, but he, poor man, was no more than a sop to propriety. Accordingly he sent Joe around to the Bradford town house with a note for the lady explaining the situation. Since the Bradfords were out at a party that evening, it was well after two before Marjorie Bradford arrived with her maid and a hastily packed portmanteau.

"My dear Felicia!" she exclaimed as she came into the drawing room. "What has *happened*? Your man—and sometime soon you must tell me where you *got* such a singular servant—said Sir Christopher had been shot. Can it be *true*?"

Wearily, Felicia told her everything she knew, and her godmother sat bemused throughout the telling. "My *word*," she said when Felicia fell silent at last. "I wonder who could have *done* such a *dastardly* thing? But how fortunate *you* were here, and so could *aid* the dear boy! Now, my dear, you are *not* to worry! Young men recover from wounds quickly, and Sir Christopher is as strong as an *ox*. And *I* will be here to protect your reputation.

"But where did you *put* him? Is he upstairs?"

"No, down here in one of the bedchambers I fixed for the Perkins," Felicia said, feeling light-headed with exhaustion. "I intend to sleep across the hall in the other, in case I am needed."

Lady Bradford looked shocked. "Most certainly *not*!" she said. "I shall sleep there, while you go up to your own bed, for it wouldn't do at all to . . ."

Her voice died away as Ted Bowers entered the room and bowed. "Begging your pardon, missus, but do you have a pallet I could use tonight?" he asked.

Felicia promised to see to it, and he went away.

"*Another* ugly man!" Lady Bradford exclaimed. "Where do you *get* them?"

"He is Christopher's man," Felicia told her, not noticing the way her godmother's lips curved for a moment at her inadvertent dropping of his title.

"Did Sir Christopher have *any* idea who shot him and why? I do not know what things are *coming* to, when a gentleman, and in a *respectable* neighborhood, too, can be attacked this way! The thugs of London are becoming *much* too brazen. Something must be *done* about them! I shall speak to Montmorency."

Felicia did not see what that gentleman could do about the situation, but she did not say so. Instead, she said, "He was in no condition for questioning. Perhaps tomorrow . . ."

"Yes, no doubt you're right. *Now*, my love, we must get some sleep. And *don't* worry. I'll have my maid keep watch over Sir Christopher, and if there is *any* change in his condition, we'll wake you *at once.*"

Felicia did not have the strength to argue about being sent to bed like a small child, and she had to hang on to the banister as she went upstairs.

When Ted Bowers saw that Lady Bradford's maid was a competent, motherly sort of woman, he went down to the big kitchen for a cup of tea. There he found the other occupants of the house, with the exception of Mr. Livingston, and he nodded to them all as he took a seat at the table.

"Wot's this all about, then?" Joe Griffen growled.

Bowers nodded his thanks to Mrs. Doherty as she handed him a cup of tea. "I've a good notion, but I'll have to wait till the guv's himself, to ask him if he saw anyone," Bowers told him. "But there's a man who's hated him for years, a Samuel King. He's back in London now. My guess is, he's the culprit, or his man, Bob Yates. I expect they've gone to ground now that the attempt failed. But I'll find them, and when I do . . ."

Gladys looked frightened, and even Lucie seemed a little uneasy at his menacing tones, his grim, ugly face. Over by the fire, Mrs. Doherty crossed herself.

Bowers told them more then, of his life in India with Chris Wilde, the things they had done, and the adventures they had shared. Once, during the telling, George whispered to Jacqueline behind his hand, and she nodded.

As Bowers paused to sip his tea, George piped up, "Ah kin help ya find dem peoples, mistah. Ain't nuffin Ah don't know 'bout Lunnon!"

Ted Bowers eyed the little black boy with misgivings. This was not something a child should be involved in, not even one who claimed to know the city's seamy underside.

"We'll see," he said shortly.

"Time we all got to bed," Joe Griffen said as he rose. "You brats take yerselves off. The excitement's over."

"I want to thank you all for what you did for the guv," Bowers said earnestly. "You, an' your missus, too. It was good o' you to take the trouble, for a stranger."

Joe waved a careless hand as he shepherded the others to the stairs.

Bowers and Lady Bradford's maid alternated watching over the bedside that night, but even so, it seemed a long time till dawn.

Early the next morning, Felicia knocked softly on the door. She was dressed in an old morning gown, her curls tied back carelessly with a ribbon. Her gaze went first to the quiet figure lying in the bed. How big he looked there, she thought. Yet somehow, vulnerable as well.

"He is all right?" she whispered to Bowers, who in the light of day and still unshaven, was a ferocious sight.

He nodded, "If you're going to be here for a minute, missus, I'll just step down to the kitchen. I'll bring back some broth for the guv when I return. It's almost time for his next dose of laudanum."

As he went away, he saw Felicia bend over the bed, and the expression on her face made him whistle soundlessly. So, that was the way of things, was it? He wondered if the guv felt as she did, and for her sake, he hoped so.

Chris Wilde began to move restlessly a few minutes later, muttering under his breath now the pain had returned.

"Please, Christopher, you must lie still," Felicia

told him, afraid his tossing would open the wound again.

His left hand came up then to grasp her shoulder, startling her with its strength. "So," he said slowly, his face only inches from hers, "you were real last night, were you? I thought I must have died and gone to heaven. But you are here still. With me."

"Of course I am since Bowers carried you into my house," she said, only a little breathless. "Is the pain bad?" she added, trying to change a subject that she felt was strewn with pitfalls. "Bowers will be here soon to give you your laudanum."

"Never mind that now," Wilde said curtly. Felicia stiffened.

"It was good of you ma'am, to come to my aid," he went on. "And good of you to take me in. I trust I did not ruin any of your carpets by dripping blood all over them?"

"As if that mattered," Felicia scoffed, wondering why he did not let her go, or she herself, insist on him doing so.

"Felicia?" he whispered, trying to raise himself.

"No, no, you must lie still, sir!" she cried. "Your wound . . ."

He sighed then but subsided on the pillows, letting her go in the process. She tried to tell herself she was relieved.

"Damn my wound," he said grimly. "Where's Bowers then?"

"Right here, guv," a familiar voice said behind them. Felicia turned to see the ugly manservant bearing a tray containing a mug of broth, the medicine, and a pile of clean bandages.

Eyeing those bandages, Wilde grimaced. "Best you leave me now, ma'am," he told Felicia. "I gather I'm to have my wound dressed, and I wouldn't want my language to put you to the blush."

212

"Of course," Felicia said, nodding to Bowers as he arranged his tray. "I'll come back later to sit by you."

She was to follow the pattern several times that day. By late afternoon, Sir Christopher was demanding food, a glass of wine, and cursing his man for denying him sustenance. Lady Bradford covered her ears at his language, but Felicia only smiled, for surely it meant he was in no danger anymore.

Lady Bradford had an engagement that evening. She had fretted all day about canceling it, but Felicia would not hear of it. "I do beg you will not be so silly, ma'am," she said briskly. "You have seen Sir Christopher. You know he is in no condition to take advantage of me, even if he cared to, and I do assure you, he does not. The servants are within call as well. Do go to your party. I'll be fine."

Not at all reluctant, Lady Bradford went home to prepare, although she promised her goddaughter she would be sure to return early.

Felicia had arranged with Bowers to feed Sir Christopher his Spartan supper herself, and, tucking a napkin under his chin, she sat down on the bed beside him with the bowl.

"I hate gruel," he said, looking mutinous.

"No, you don't," she replied cheerfully. "You just want something else. Perhaps tomorrow, if there is no fever."

"I'll be going home tomorrow," he told her, eyeing the spoon she held out with distaste. "There's no need to put you to more trouble, ma'am. My own servants can care for me."

Felicia laughed and spooned the gruel into his mouth. "You only say that because you think that once out of my sight, you will be able to bamboozle Bowers into serving you a large sirloin and some ale, isn't that true? No, don't answer. Swallow."

"I'll be up tomorrow, just see if I'm not," he said

when he had disposed of the spoonful. "And I must say you have become just as tyrannical as you once claimed I could be. 'Do this'—'don't do that'—'swallow.' Quite a new come-out for you, is it not? But I'll not be ordered about, nor will a simple wound keep me tied to a bed for much longer."

Felicia had no comment. His face was getting flushed, and she did not want him to get excited. Instead, she held out another spoonful and waited patiently for him to open his mouth. Seeing the adamant look in her blue eyes, Sir Christopher capitulated.

True to her word, Lady Bradford returned so early from her party that she was able to appear in the drawing room the following morning only a little past ten. She found Felicia there, waiting for the doctor to finish his examination of the patient.

For a while, the two chatted of the party and some gossip Lady Bradford had heard. Eventually, however, the viscountess went to stare out into the street.

"How *peaceful* it looks now," she murmured. "And yet to think only the night before last, Sir Christopher was *shot* here! I have spoken to Montmorency; he was as shocked as I. Perhaps, as he told me, it *is* time we had a police force. The Runners, the watchmen, seem impotent.

"But perhaps what happened was only *fate* taking a hand?" she added coyly, peeking over her shoulder.

"Fate, ma'am? What had fate to do with it?" Felicia asked, busy selecting another length of gold embroidery thread.

"Why, that Sir Christopher was set upon at *your very door*!" the lady said, her eyes wide. She came to sit beside Felicia then, taking her hands and spilling her threads. "*Dear* child! Let me be honest

214

with you. It was my *fondest* wish that you and Sir Christopher form an attachment. I was *so* distraught when you had that little brangle, and there seemed to be *nothing* I could do about it, since you wouldn't *confide* in me. But, well, *now* we see that fate played a part after all, don't you agree?"

Felicia stared at her, a terrible suspicion forming in her mind. But no, she told herself, that couldn't be! Surely not even Marjorie Bradford with her wild, madcap schemes would have arranged to have Sir Christopher shot! Would she? No, no! How could she even think such a thing of the lady?

Still, it *had* been only a minor wound. And if you wanted to kill someone, surely you would have employed a better marksman. But perhaps he was only supposed to get a flesh wound? Perhaps the assailant had been an expert after all?

"And he is such a *wonderful* young man, too," Lady Bradford went on. Felicia forced herself to concentrate. "So *kind*, all unbeknownst to you, of course. I have been *quite* affected by his concern."

"You will have to explain. I don't understand, ma'am," Felicia said, her voice stiff.

The viscountess smiled, and for a moment she looked conscious. Then she gave her merry laugh and shook her head. "I don't suppose it will do any *harm* to tell you, dearest, not *now*, for I have seen how he looks at you; how you look at *him* as well. Perhaps it is time you learn of everything he has *done* for you."

When Felicia only stared at her, she went on, "You see, it was *he* who called our attention to your plight in the *first* place, told us of the roomers, your teaching music, how *hard* you were trying to keep your father comfortable. And he told us of those unpaid debts. *He*, who discovered the names of the men you saw in the drawing room that afternoon so Montmorency could shame them into paying.

215

And *three* of them actually did, didn't they? I was *so glad* to hear of it!

"But wasn't Sir Christopher *selfless*? *Noble?* I am sure if you had any doubts of his worth *before*, those doubts have flown away now!"

Felicia rose abruptly to her feet to walk away down the length of the room. Perplexed, Marjorie Bradford watched her stiff back where she stood there motionless.

"So, he took it upon himself to interfere in my life?" Felicia asked as she turned to face her godmother again.

Lady Bradford gasped, Felicia looked so pale, distraught. "Dear child, what do you *mean*? He has been *everything* that is good, and . . ."

"Why?" Felicia interrupted. "Why would he do that? And who gave him the right to appoint himself my savior? It seems to me he should be censured for taking so much on himself, not commended, ma'am. I do not understand his motives, but although I suppose I must be obliged to him, I find I dislike taking charity."

"Oh dear, you are not *pleased*!" Lady Bradford moaned. "And here I thought you would be *delighted* to learn how much he cares for you!"

"Cares for me? He cares for nothing but getting his own way!" Felicia snapped. "Well, I'll not have it! The money shall be repaid. . . ."

"*Why?* It was *owed* to your father," the viscountess pointed out. "You are not thinking clearly, my dear. And certainly you must not mention it at *all* to the chivalrous gentleman who arranged the payments, only accepting his hand with *delight* when he proposes."

"He has already asked me, and I refused him!" Felicia told her, stung to honesty.

"You never *did* so! Oh, *foolish* girl, I . . ."

A knock on the door just then brought an abrupt

ending to the conversation, and Felicia was forced to admit the doctor who had some new instructions for her regarding the patient. She tried to concentrate on what he was saying, but in truth, she barely heard him.

So, it had been Christopher Wilde all along, had it? She did not understand why he would do such a thing, but she doubted very much that, as Lady Bradford had claimed, he had done so out of a sense of chivalry, or a secret yearning to make her his bride. Why, just remembering the things he had said to her made that only too clear. "Didn't know what had got into him," "an unfortunate mistake," "a ridiculous proposition," he had said. And those were the words of a man in love?

When the doctor took his leave a short time later, Felicia refused to resume her conversation with her distraught godmother. Instead, she excused herself in a dead little voice and fled to her room.

Sixteen

FELICIA REMAINED SECLUDED there for some time. Eventually she forced herself to rejoin her godmother after luncheon, although she refused to reopen the one subject that lady was most interested in pursuing. At last, the viscountess was forced to leave for a fitting at her modiste's.

And Felicia refused to go to Sir Christopher's room, not even when Bowers came to tell her his master was inquiring for her. Seated in the library behind her father's massive desk, a pile of papers spread out before her, she told the ugly manservant that he must tell Sir Christopher she was very busy.

She knew both Duke Ainsworth and Bartholomew Whitaker had come to see him, the latter gentleman remaining for some time, so she knew Chris Wilde could not possibly be pining for lack of company. No doubt he had only wished to give her another order, which he probably felt he had every right to do, having as good as bought her, she told herself bitterly.

But perhaps there is such a thing as fate, for only an hour later, a distraught Lucie Watts came to find her.

"Do come quick, Miss Felicia!" she said, wringing her hands. "There's them Bow Street Runners in the kitchen, aquestionin' us all!"

"The Runners are here?" Felicia asked in amazement. "Has it to do with Sir Christopher's getting shot?"

"Don't think so," Lucie said as the two went to the kitchen stairs. "Never mentioned that, they didn't."

When Felicia entered the kitchen she found all her household, with the exception of Mr. Livingston, assembled there, Ted Bowers as well. For a moment, staring at everyone's frightened faces, she wished Lady Bradford was beside her to lend her consequence.

"I am Felicia Simmons," she made herself say to the two men who stood near the door, both looking very stern. "I understand you are from Bow Street? How may I help you?"

"Well, mum, that's the problem," the taller of the pair said as he scratched his head. "In the execution of our dooties, we're forced ter question ye. We've 'ad a report about this 'ouse, an' the people 'ere, an' we mean ter investigate."

"A report?" Felicia said, raising her brows. The front door knocker sounded then, and she nodded to Ted Bowers. For some reason the man looked uneasy to her. Perhaps it would be better if he were not here? He was not, after all, an intimate of the house.

"Now, you must be plain with me, sirs," she said, giving the Runners a level glance as Bowers left the room.

"Our report sez that there's nefarious doin's goin' on 'ere," the second runner said as he elbowed his way past his taller colleague, as if determined not to be left out of the questioning. "Very nefarious doin's they be, too."

He paused, but when Felicia only looked at him, perplexed, he coughed and continued, "About them children, mum."

Felicia looked at George and Jacqueline. They sat

close together at the big deal table, looking identically guilty. *Now* what had they been up to? she asked herself silently.

"The only children here are the ones you see before you," she said. "Do you mean this concerns them?"

"Wot's yer name?" the tall Runner asked, pointing a bony finger at George. "Seems ter me I've seen this young nipper afore, Alf, 'aven't ye? Fact is, I'd swear ter it."

"Ah'm George," the boy said, his dark eyes round.

"George *who*?" the Runner asked, bending closer.

"Ah'm—Ah'm George Simmons," the boy said at last. He stole a glance at Felicia then, as if he were afraid to see condemnation on her face for his boldness. She smiled at him, and he beamed.

The Runners looked from the little black boy to Felicia, and then at each other. Were they being mocked?

Everyone heard footsteps on the stairs then, and Felicia turned toward the sound.

"But Cecily dearest, I really don't think we should invade Miss Simmons's kitchen...." she heard Mrs. Perkins's gentle voice saying, and she stiffened.

When the girl stepped into the room, her face wore a look of complete satisfaction. Behind her, her mother looked distressed.

"So, the Runners have come, as I expected," she said. "And, as you can see, I have come as well, to witness your downfall, you vile creature!"

"An' wot right has ye ter come pushing yer way in 'ere?" Lucie demanded as she got to her feet and leaned her fists on the table.

"Every right, for I summoned these men today," Miss Perkins said as she smoothed her gloves. "And

I intend to remain here so I can watch them take your mistress to jail."

"For what reason?" Felicia asked, holding her head high, although she was beginning to tremble inside.

"Accordin' ter the report we got, mum, ye've been runnin' a child thieves' ring from this 'ouse," the shorter Runner said as he consulted his notebook.

"Wot?" Lucie gasped, while Joe Griffen snorted, Mrs. Doherty shook her head, and Gladys turned pale.

"All them nippers wot come ter the back so often," the other officer elaborated. "It's been remarked up an' down the street."

Felicia suddenly wished she could sink down onto a bench, her knees were so weak.

Before she could speak up and deny the charge, she heard more footsteps coming down the stairs. Livingston? she wondered. She had thought him with her father.

To her astonishment, Sir Christopher Wilde entered the room, followed closely by his manservant. He was dressed in breeches and a white shirt. Felicia noted he kept his right hand braced on his hip, no doubt for support.

His ferocious frown swept around the crowd assembled, lingering for a moment on Cecily Perkins's flushed, triumphant face. Then he moved closer to Felicia to put his good left arm around her waist.

"I understand from Bowers there is some problem, Felicia?" he asked, his voice caressing. "You should have called me. But what are all these people doing here?"

"These Bow Street Runners have come to question me," she said, wondering how Sir Christopher managed to appear so cool. And so healthy. You would never know from looking at him, or listening to his unconcerned voice, that he had been wounded only a short time ago.

"Indeed? But why are these other, er, persons here?"

As he went on, Mrs. Perkins raised a handkerchief to her face. "Unless it is because the young woman is so inquisitive? Yes, I am sure that must be it! She has been jealous of you since the beginning, my dear."

"Jealous? Of *her*?" Cecily Perkins said scornfully. "You must be jesting, sir! Jealous of my *landlady*, a woman *writer*, a—a *child exploiter*?"

" 'Ere now, that's enough o' that," the taller Runner interrupted. Turning to Wilde, he asked, "An' who might you be? Sir?"

"I am Sir Christopher Wilde. Miss Simmons is my betrothed," the baronet told him, his hand tightening on Felicia's waist when he felt her start.

In the awed silence that followed this admission, he added, "I have been staying here for the past two nights to consult with her father about the marriage settlements. Since he is so ill, I can only see him for short periods of time. The lady's godmother, Viscountess Bradford is also staying, although I recall she mentioned she had some errands this afternoon. Isn't that so, dearest?"

Not waiting for Felicia's reply, one which she was quite incapable of giving anyway, he went on, "What is the nature of these ridiculous charges that have been brought?"

"That this 'ere Miss Simmons is guilty o' runnin' a child thieves' ring from the 'ouse," the shorter Runner said truculently. His lower lip protruded as he stared at Sir Christopher. Bert might be influenced by a few titles, but he, Alf Davis, was made of sterner stuff.

To his amazement, Sir Christopher began to laugh, long and helplessly. When m'lord could speak again, he said, "Now I've heard everything! And have you, love? The things I have to learn about you!"

Felicia stared up into his gray eyes. The light in them made her swallow. Hard.

"Of course I haven't!" she said. "It is nonsensical."

"Well, then, an' wot about them nippers wot come ter the back door so reg'lar-like?" the taller Runner asked.

Mrs. Doherty decided to take a hand then. Advancing on the Runners, she planted herself before them, arms akimbo. Both men eyed the large iron ladle she clutched with misgiving.

"Those waifs come here 'cause they know how kind a lady Miss Felicia is," the cook said stoutly. "She's a saint, if iver I seen one! Gives out that many mugs o' hot soup, slices of bread and cheese to the little ones to keep them from starving, she does. Every day, too. Many's the time she's gone without herself so the waifs could be fed. Child thieves' ring . . . bah!"

"It appears to be a stalemate," Sir Christopher remarked. "For you have only Miss Simmons's word and her servants' against this other, er, person's.

"Unless, of course, you can question the—nippers, I believe you called them? Yes, that's what you should do. And if you don't stop bothering the lady, I shall be forced to take steps.

"But surely even you can see how it was, can't you? This other, er, person, did this out of spite. She has no evidence, none at all. How could she, against such a kind, good-hearted lady? If I were you, I'd charge that one with giving false information."

The Runners put their notebooks away, looking identically chagrined.

To everyone's surprise, Mrs. Perkins spoke up

then in quite the firmest voice Felicia had ever heard her employ. "I must apologize for my daughter to you all, but most especially to you, Miss Simmons. Although what Cecily tried to do is unforgivable."

"Mother!" Cecily Perkins gasped.

"Yes, I am your mother, although I am ashamed to admit it. And for the first time I am going to assert my authority as such. You will come away with me right now, and we will return to the country tomorrow morning. For you did not deserve a Season in London since you could not behave as a lady, and you'll not have another one. And don't think you can persuade your father otherwise. I've a great deal to say to that man myself; things he should have heard years ago."

Grasping her stunned daughter's arm, she turned her about and herded her to the stairs. "And you'll not wrap *me* around your little finger, miss, so don't think you can! Now, just you march up these stairs, and don't let me hear a single word or it will go harder for you. Furthermore, from now on . . ."

No one said anything until her voice died away. Moments later, the sound of the front door closing behind them told everyone that the ladies Perkins had left the premises.

"Sorry ter 'ave bothered ye, missus," one of the Runners said. "Sir."

The baronet had nothing to say now, and Felicia wished the law officers would be quick to leave, too. She did not have to look into Ted Bowers's concerned face to know his master was in pain, for she could feel him leaning on her even as he tried not to.

The door had no sooner closed behind the Runners than Bowers was at Chris Wilde's side to take his weight from Felicia's shoulder.

"All's well, guv," he said gruffly as he put Wilde's left arm around his neck. "Lean on me, now."

Sir Christopher's face was very white, and he had no eyes for anyone but Felicia as he said, "Beg you forgive my boldness, ma'am. It was all I could think of to do to . . ."

Felicia's hand went to her mouth as he slumped unconscious in his manservant's arms.

The next hour was a horrid reminder of the evening that Chris Wilde had been shot. The wound that had begun to heal had opened again with his exertions, and he lost a lot more blood. Lucie and Gladys tore up more bandages, Ted Bowers wore a ferocious frown, and even Joe was pressed into service carrying ewers of hot water up the stairs and taking basins and stained bandages down them.

Felicia was told she would only be very much in the way, and she wandered into the drawing room, deep in thought. If only he had not left his bed, dressed and climbed down those stairs! she told herself. Why had he done it?

But she knew why. He had done it to repay her for taking him in after he had been shot. Yes, that must be it, for Sir Christopher Wilde was so high-rumped he probably could not bear to be beholden to anyone, and most certainly not to a woman!

She tried not to remember how she had felt when he had said they were to wed, that fierce stabbing elation that threatened to overpower her. She must have been daft, she told herself coldly.

When Bowers came to see her, she was sitting before the window, holding a book she was not reading.

"Begging your pardon, Miss Felicia, but the guv would like to see you now," the man said.

"He is conscious then? The bleeding has stopped?"

As Bowers nodded, she went on, "But I don't understand how you could have allowed him to do such a mad thing, Bowers. You must have known it would make his wound worse!"

To her surprise, the manservant chuckled a little. "Aye, that I did, Miss, but there's no one who can stop the guv when he gets a notion in his head. And when Mr. Whitaker told him this afternoon what that Miss Perkins was planning, and he discovered the Runners were in the kitchen worrying you, there was no holding him."

"I don't think it would be wise for me to see him now," Felicia said, trying for a calm, reasonable tone. "Surely he needs his rest. Tell him I'll come tomorrow, when he is feeling better."

Instead of bowing and going to relay the message, Ted Bowers frowned and stared down at his feet. "I know this is out of place for me to say, Miss, but I feel I must," he said. "And I hope you'll forgive me the liberty."

He waited for her nod before he continued, "You see, I'm that sure the guv's in love with you. I saw his face, how frantic it was as he tried to hurry into his clothes. I've never seen him look that way before, not even when we were attacked by pirates in the Gulf of Tonkin.

"An' I thought as how you might love him, too. He's such a good man, so honest and true. I'm privileged just to have known him.

"I tell you, Miss, he's not had an easy life. He as good as ran away from home at seventeen to escape a tyrannical father, slaved in India's miserable climate for years for the Company, until he was able, by working hard and making good investments, to buy a ship of his own and begin trading. The Company didn't like that, and they tried to stop him, but he persevered."

As he paused to take a deep breath, Felicia said,

"Yes, I've seen many instances of his determination and his love of giving orders."

Bowers caught the condemnation in her voice, and he hastened to say, "He's that way because he's had to be, Miss. A soft man wouldn't have lasted a week in India or China. And since he's never been much for the ladies up to now—begging your pardon—he doesn't know any other way to act around them. But he'll learn. The guv's smart, he is! You've only to tell him when you don't like a thing, and he won't do it again. Honest!"

"Still, I don't think I should see him now," Felicia said, feeling a little uneasy. The Sir Christopher that his servant painted was a different man from the one she knew.

"I beg you to reconsider, Miss. I know the guv. He'll not rest easy till you do."

"And if I don't go to him, you wouldn't put it past him to get up and come in search of me? Well, neither would I!"

As Bowers grinned, she rose. "Very well. I'll come. But later you must give him a large dose of laudanum to make him sleep, or we'll have him laid up for weeks."

Bowers left her at the door of Sir Christopher's room. She paused there only long enough to take several deep breaths to steady herself.

Chris Wilde lay propped up on a number of pillows, his chest crisscrossed with strips of cloth that held a thick bandage against his shoulder. Trying not to look at that broad, bare, masculine chest, Felicia said, "You wanted to see me, sir?"

She paused by the foot of the bed, and he said, "Come nearer."

As she raised her brows, he added, "Please?"

Taking a few steps closer, Felicia said, "It was foolhardy of you to get up, but I must thank you,

227

sir. I doubt I could have handled either the Runners or Miss Perkins with such aplomb."

"Implying, of course, that I, on the other hand, have often dealt successfully with vixens and the officers of the law. Should I thank you for the compliment, ma'am?"

Felicia stared at his smiling face, suspicious of the happiness she heard in his voice, the light she saw blazing in his eyes. Why was he so euphoric? she wondered. What was he up to now?

"I hope you are feeling better, sir?" she said, but he waved her question away.

"No, we've no time now to waste on platitudes," he said. "Listen! When I announced a little while ago that we were betrothed, it was as if a blindfold had been removed, and I could see at last how much I wanted it to be true!

"No, don't interrupt! Let me finish, please.

"You see, I never thought I could ever love any woman. I never have before. In fact, I thought men who loved them—completely, exclusively—were weaklings, half feminine themselves. But suddenly I discovered that love doesn't make you weak, it makes you strong. And I found out something even more important: that I loved you more than life itself.

"Felicia, my darling, I know my last proposal was a disaster, but surely it is different now, isn't it? Tell me you love me, too! Tell me you will marry me!"

Felicia pressed her trembling knees against the side of the bed, afraid she might fall else. "I shouldn't," she said, half to herself. "Since I have known you, you have done nothing but order me about and scold me. And yet now you want me to believe you have changed? How can that be? No one changes like that.

"And I learned from my godmother how you took

228

it upon yourself to find my father's debtors and shame three of them into repaying what they owed. I do not like being beholden to anyone. No, I don't think a marriage between us a wise course."

He would have spoken then, but she raised her hand. "Now *I* have not finished. Listen!

"I talked to my father not long ago when he was well enough for it, and he begged me not to give my hand to any man with whom I could not share the love he and my mother had had. But I'd resolved on that course anyway, for I grew up in the glow they radiated, their happiness. And I don't think, no, I'm sure, that you and I could ever . . ."

Quickly, Chris Wilde reached out with his good hand and pulled her down on the bed beside him. Before Felicia could even think of protesting, he had wrapped his good arm around her and was kissing her. She tried to tell herself she could not push him away for fear of hurting him, so instead, she let her arms creep around his waist. How good he felt, she thought. She had not known a man's skin could feel so smooth, like satin. And his kiss was a revelation. It intoxicated her as it went on and on, warm and deep and consuming—right.

When he raised his head at last, he put his hard cheek against hers. *"Don't* you think we could be happy, my love?" he asked, his deep voice unsteady. *"Don't* you?"

Felicia made a little movement, and reluctantly, he let her go. But he saw she only wanted to put her head back so she could judge by his expression if their kiss had affected him as much as it had her. The look on his face made her feel warm all over, and the light in his gray eyes that had often threatened her self-possession before, now burned deep into her heart and soul as it claimed her forever as his own.

She placed both hands on either side of his face,

reveling in the love she saw so clearly, before she said, "Oh, yes. I know we can be happy, Christopher. Now."

It was a long time before they spoke of other things, but at last she asked him how he had been shot. "You have never told me, you know," she said as she lay cuddled close to him. "Did you recognize your assailant?"

"I didn't see him for it was too dark, but I know who it was," he said.

She sat up then and put both hands on his chest. "Christopher, listen! You seem so sure, but it occurred to me, from some things my godmother said, that she might have hired someone to do it, and on my doorstep, too, so I'd have to take you in. You know her, and she's made no secret of the fact that she wanted us to wed. Isn't it possible? . . . Why ever are you laughing?"

"I can't help it," he gasped, holding his wounded shoulder. "No, no, love! Not even the madcap viscountess would do anything so insane! Besides, I'm sure she doesn't even know any assailants, do you? I must stop laughing. It hurts!"

He took a deep breath and went on, more seriously now, "No, Bowers found the man. He and his master are even now on a ship taking them far from England. They'll not trouble us again."

He paused for a moment, then added, "You know, even after all this, you still haven't said you would marry me. But before you speak, let me tell you why it would be such an excellent idea. Beside the fact that I love you so much, that is.

"You see, sweet, I'm a very wealthy man. And since you're so interested in London's waifs, just think of the good you could do with that money. Build orphanages and schools, feed the hungry . . ."

"Do you think to bribe me with your gold, sir?"

she asked, head tilted to one side as she regarded him.

"I'll do whatever I have to to get you," he told her and meant every word.

"Well, the money is very nice, but I wouldn't marry for it, any more than I'd marry out of gratitude. And I have every reason to be grateful to you."

"So?" he prompted, one brow quirked.

"So yes, of course I'll marry you. But for love alone."

When Lord and Lady Bradford arrived to take tea with Felicia, she reluctantly gave Chris Wilde one last kiss before she went to tell them the wonderful news.

As the door closed behind her, he settled back on his pillows, a little smile on his lips.

He decided they would be wed at St. Mary-le-Strand, long enough before noon so that when the bells rang out in celebration, Reginald Simmons would be able to hear them clearly for once.

As he yawned, he also decided there was no need to tell Felicia that Bowers had not only found Sam King and Bob Yates, he had beaten them both senseless before he had had them carried like sacks of meal aboard a ship sailing for Australia. Neither did he think it at all necessary to let on that it had been George and Jacqueline who had located them for Bowers, gone to ground in rooms above a tavern in Seven Dials.

And most certainly not a word would ever pass his lips that none of her father's debtors had ever come forward to pay the monies they owed; that it had been he himself who had concocted the story that they had with Mr. Frawley so she wouldn't know he had provided the money, yet still have enough for an easier life.

231

After all, he told himself just before he fell into a contented sleep, one didn't want one's bride fretting about such dull stuff, now did one?

Afterword

BY THE FOLLOWING spring, a great many changes had taken place in everyone's lives. Sir Christopher and Lady Wilde, attended by Ted Bowers and Gladys Johns, divided their time between their estate, Wildewold, in Devon, and the house at Number Seventeen Upper Brook Street in London. There, Felicia could not only see to the charitable work she undertook so eagerly, but also to her beloved father, who was now comfortably cared for by the faithful Livingston, a new cook, two sturdy footmen, and several maids. Granted a generous pension, Mrs. Doherty had retired happily to Ireland.

Lucie Watts and Joe Griffen had surprised everyone by announcing their plans to wed as well, and they were delighted to accept the baronet's money that enabled them to buy an inn at Dover. Joe had confessed he missed the sea, and Lucie was content with her new role as the innkeeper's good wife.

Jacqueline and George had been the first two children in the orphanage and school Felicia and her bridegroom founded. But although Jacqueline thrived there as long as she could see Felicia on occasion, George did not. At last, Sir Christopher arranged for George to board with an impresario and his wife and help out at the man's theater. No doubt he did so because he remembered the boy's delight in performing in Mrs. Huddlefield's "tables."

TUESDAY'S CHILD